Geoff Tristram has been a pro
over thirty years, working for a
Penguin Books, Embassy Wor
Carillion, Past Times, Winsor &
Pursuit and the television show
name but a few.

He has created artwork featuring celebrities such as Jonathan
Ross, Jeremy Clarkson, Sir Ian Botham, David Vine, Alan
Shearer, Ian Hislop and Gary Lineker, not to mention virtually
every famous snooker player that ever lifted a cue. You may
have even noticed him at the World Championships on TV,
interviewing them as he drew their caricatures!

He has also designed many book covers, album sleeves for
charts bands such as UB40, The Maisonettes and City Boy,
(remember Heartache Avenue and '5705'?) and postage stamps,
notably 'Charles and Diana - The Royal Wedding', 'Miss
World', 'Lake Placid Winter Olympics' and 'Spain 1982 World
Cup Football' editions.

More recently, his series of incredibly detailed 'Cat
Conundrum' puzzle paintings have enthralled and exasperated
thousands of dedicated puzzle-solvers all over the world.

Geoff's younger brother, David, is a well-known and extremely
successful comedy playwright, so it was no real surprise when
Geoff eventually turned his hand to comedy writing, hence this,
the eighth full-length novel to feature the chaotic and accident-
prone artist, David Day. He has also written two novels featuring
a new hero, Adam Eve, a chaotic, accident-prone comedy writer,
just to show how versatile he is.

Geoff's only unfulfilled dream now is to see one of his books
made into a comedy film while he's still just about young enough
to enjoy the proceeds, so he would greatly appreciate it if you
could bombard the BBC with letters on his behalf.

i

Which came first - the chicken or the egg?

Did Geoff Tristram set this story in Pizza Express in order to wring some money out of us for an advertisement, or did we offer him a few quid to include us in the storyline?

Happily, the reality is that neither scenario is true.

Quite simply, Geoff has been a Pizza Express fan for twenty years or more, and always seeks our restaurants out, wherever he is in the country.

He loves Italy, as anyone who has read one of his books will know, and our pizzas are authentically Italian. That's why, if he can't make it to Florence, he comes to Pizza Express Stourbridge instead, so it was only fitting that he chose to set his story there.
At least, that's the line he spun us when he came cap in hand for money!

Pizza Express Stourbridge
Telephone 01384 379358
That Dan Brown comes in on a Wednesday as well!

For Laura

Get well soon. You are breaking a lot of hearts.

David's
Michelangelo
Geoff Tristram

**DRAWING
ROOM**

First published in 2010 by The Drawing Room Press

Printed and bound by 4edge Limited, UK

ISBN 978-0-9551428-9-5

Cover illustration by Geoff Tristram

Contact the author on gt@geofftristram.co.uk

You will recall that I said 'Stealing the Ashes' was to be the last ever David Day book. Well, I lied. I had fully intended this to be the case, but I didn't figure on waking up at 3:37 a.m. one Wednesday morning with a corker of an idea charging around in my head demanding to be let out. What could I do, just ignore it? It would have driven me crazy. I must admit that initially, I'd seen it being the third Adam Eve story, but when I realized that it needed the artistic theme, it had to be David. Then the title came to me and that settled it. So here we are again. After just two months of frantic typing – yes, two months - my books might be rubbish but I'm quick – here is the very final, absolutely last ever, no more in the pipeline David Day story, and I've loved every obsessed minute of it. Writing this epic has got me off mowing the lawn, walking the dog, food shopping in Waitrose and a host of other boring domestic chores, so I will remember it with great fondness. On a slightly more serious note, can I thank you all for the lovely comments about my books. I tried to create a cosy, believable little world of my own when I began writing them. I wanted my characters to pop in and out of each other's stories, and for all the time-lines and facts to match up, so that readers could dissolve into a nicer, safer place than the one we actually inhabit. They may just be daft Ealing comedies in essence, but I think there's a surprisingly sentimental feel about them, something quite believable too, in a strange kind of way, and also quite moral. That said, it has to be the comedy that takes priority at the end of the day, and David's Michelangelo won't disappoint you there. As usual, I laughed like a drain while I was writing it, to the point where my family thought I was deranged and needed locking in a secure unit with padded walls. The trouble is, you see, I actually see it all as clear as anything when I write, like it's a film showing in my head. If the truth were known, I've tried to create my own little paradise; somewhere I can escape to when the real world gets me down and I'm feeling old and sorry for myself. I hope it has the same effect for you too.

Geoff Tristram.

Michelangelo's David (Detail)

CHAPTER 1

Laz sees the light

Laz Homer burst through the front door of Pizza Express Stourbridge with such gusto that nearby diners looked to be in fear of their lives. Outlaws entering Wild West saloon bars in search of the Marshall they suspected of shooting their Pa seldom made as much of a scene. Had any bar room girls been passing at the time, Laz would probably have lassoed them. A mobile phone glued to his right ear, he was concluding a somewhat terse conversation with a man from Bulgaria who apparently manufactured leather chairs, albeit at his own pace. Had Laz spoken slightly louder, he probably wouldn't have needed his phone.

Spotting the Eastern European waitress busy processing a customer's bill, Laz all but snapped his fingers with his free left hand and flashed her a gesture that, in his mind at least, indicated that he needed a large glass of Shiraz, and he needed it now.

The Eastern European waitress - or Gabria Revnik, as we will call her for the sake of brevity - did what Eastern European waitresses do best. She ignored him.

Having now, as far as he was concerned, organized his beverage, Laz turned his attention to finding his friend. He impatiently scanned the bustling restaurant and eventually picked out the slightly embarrassed-looking individual sitting alone over in the far right corner. Barging past families celebrating their children's birthdays and couples who, until this human

1

whirlwind blew in, had been dreamily gazing into each other's eyes, Laz made a beeline for him, finally wrapping up his business call about missed deadlines with a few very loud and very choice expletives.

Meanwhile, in the dimly-lit far right corner, that mild-mannered scatterbrain, the world-renowned artist turned art restorer and Son of the Black Country, David Day, looked on aghast at the mayhem that his oldest friend was causing. He mouthed something about opposites attracting, offered a silent prayer to the ceiling tiles, took a fortifying gulp of his Montepulciano D'Abruzzo, and smiled sweetly at the rhinoceros that was charging in his direction.

"Dave!" bellowed Laz, offering his hand to be shaked, "how are you doin', you old bugger?"

The family to his left fixed him with a disdainful stare. Luckily, their party-frocked and tomato-stained daughter, Jessica, who had turned three that very day, was not familiar with such base language and continued to colour in her picture, her innocence intact.

Laz grinned his Cheshire cat grin and pulled out a chair with that awful, grating squeal often made by fingernails on blackboards.

"I just bought a church!" he announced proudly.

Jessica's parents looked askance, when they should surely have been encouraged that this was at least a step in the right direction. David goggled at his old friend incredulously.

"Where's my bloody wine?" Laz demanded, scanning the room impatiently. "It's taking her long enough!"

"Laz, you only arrived eight seconds ago," David explained calmly. "She'll be over in a sec. She's busy. What do you mean; you've just bought a church?"

Laz helped himself to the rest of David's wine, took a deep breath, and explained himself.

"This is why I needed to see you tonight," continued Laz, spearing David's last olive and swallowing it, without so much as a 'by your leave'. "I've bought this old chapel place that's been disused for ages, and is surplus to God's requirements. It's not one of those boring old Victorian Methodist things that are all over the place round here; it's a really old one, lots of Italian-style twiddles and stuff. I'm going to refurb it and turn it into a swanky Italian restaurant. It's not in town, it's out in the country near Tutton on Stour – fabulous spot - and I want you to help me with a few ideas and artwork and so on. What do you think?"

"Interesting!" replied David. "I wonder if the local Christians ever buy up old restaurants and turn them into churches."

"Funny! Come on, what do you think?"

"Well, you don't know anything about the restaurant trade for a start. You're a very successful pub and restaurant refurbisher, I admit, but that's different to actually running a restaurant yourself, if that's what you're suggesting. Look at what happened with Aeroplane Food."

Laz's face clouded over. "That was a brilliant idea, in fairness. It was the travellers that buggered that up!"

"I know it was a brilliant idea. It was mine!"

"Half yours," Laz reminded him. "I was the chap who knew a chap at RAF Cosford who had a knackered old passenger jet for sale."

"Yes," replied David, "but you didn't know what to do with it did you? Setting up a posh restaurant inside a grounded plane was a stroke of genius, you must admit. And I think my name was inspired, even though I say so myself."

Gabria arrived at the table, smiled sweetly at David, who was a regular customer, and scowled at Laz.

3

"You ready to order?"

"I've only just got here," Laz informed her. "I haven't even looked at the menu yet! Can we have two minutes? I need a drink though. That wine was okay, I'll have a bottle of that."

Gabria stropped off and left them to it. Laz continued to let off steam.

"Everything about that project was expensive. I had to buy the field nearby to park it in for starters, then landscape it and create all the parking places. Then there was the small matter of how you get a frigging great passenger jet into a field a mile down the lane. The entire thing had to be repainted as well. Do you realize how much paint it takes to cover a whole aeroplane, Dave? I was the difference between profit and loss at Stourbridge B&Q that year, I'm telling you. The dining tables and chairs cost an arm and a leg, and I don't even want to talk about fitting the kitchens into the hold below. Then there was the first class area next to the cockpit, which we did out as a lounge where you could study the menu and have a pre-dinner drink. We bought air hostess uniforms for all the waitresses; we dressed the restaurant manager as the captain; I tell you what, it would have been cheaper to just build a bloody mansion in Belgravia. The menu was a work of art, I admit, but boy, the chap who designed it charged like a wounded buffalo…"

"I was very reasonable," interjected David, wounded.

"…and all that's without the cost of head-hunting top class chefs from some of the swankiest restaurants in Brum. I knew we'd have to be in it for the long term to turn a profit, but you have to admit, it got off to a fantastic start and pulled in the punters. Everybody who'd heard about the place wanted to eat there. We were turning away more people than we were feeding most nights."

"Pity you turned away Johnny O'Driscoll really."

Laz turned ashen at the memory. He scanned the horizon in search of Gabria and his fortifying drink, which he now needed more than ever. She caught his glance and strolled over as slowly as she could with the bottle and two glasses.

"Are you ready to order now?" she asked him, sulkily.

"Yes please," interjected David, who was starving as usual.

"I'm gonna need a few more minutes," snapped Laz. "It's his fault, keeping me talking."

Gabria sighed audibly and walked away again. Laz poured a stiff one, swallowed it in one gulp, and poured another.

"I wasn't to know who Johnny O'Driscoll was, was I? He was drunk and abusive to the waitresses, which I couldn't allow, so I had to insist that he and his low-life mates left."

"Quite the right decision," agreed David, "if a little expensive. I'm amazed that even a big gang of travellers like that could completely strip the metal off a passenger jet in one night. It was like a swarm of locusts had descended, but ones that eat metal instead of crops. The poor old plane looked like some kind of giant dinosaur carcass the next day."

Laz sank into his chair and sank his red wine. He groaned as if he were about to keel over and die at any second. Little Jessica lifted her head from her colouring book and asked her mother if the fat old man on the next table was poorly. This did nothing whatsoever to raise Laz's spirits.

Gabria arrived at the table once more with her notepad and a look that seemed to suggest that if Laz didn't order this time, he could try the McDonald's over the road.

"One 'La Reine' with extra oregano and a 'Sloppy Guiseppe' please, Gabby," said David, with a quiet authority. Gabria smiled at him and wandered off again.

5

"Why did you just order for me, you cheeky sod?" asked Laz indignantly.

"Because every time you come here you ask for exactly the same thing, after perusing the bloody menu for an hour and three quarters, that's why, and because if I don't eat in the next five minutes, I will die. So anyway, to cut a long story short, and some would argue it's already far too late for that, why on earth are you taking on another restaurant after the trauma of the last one?"

Laz pursed his lips and pondered for a while. "I dunno. I think I just fell in love with this old church, for starters. It's in an idyllic location, the place isn't too big; it's quite intimate in fact - more like a country chapel than a proper big church, and I think I've learnt a lot since Aeroplane Food. I want to turn this into an authentic Italian that serves *proper* pizzas in the daytime, just like this place does, but mainly fine Italian cuisine at night - not that Anglicized crap that a lot of them do nowadays - you know, lasagne, cannelloni, spaghetti Bolognese, tiramisu, blah blah. I want to hire real Italian chefs from Italy who know how it *should* be done. Every Italian restaurant I've been to around here is staffed by Eastern Europeans, Indians, Greeks, Iranians - anything but Italians, and if they *do* have a real Eye-Tie, he's usually become Anglicized and serves huge tasteless stodgy portions of Anglo-Italian shite. There's even an Italian restaurant near here owned by a Welsh bloke. What the frigging hell do bloody Welsh folks know about pasta, for God's sake?"

Jessica's parents flushed bright red, and reached for their coats.

"Okay, okay, I get the point," agreed David, placing his finger to his lips in a vain attempt to stem his friend's colourful language. "I've worked in Italy on and off for years, as you know, and I've never once eaten at a so-called posh Italian restaurant in England that even got close to getting it right. That's why I prefer to come here. We'd have eight courses in

Arona some nights, and I still wouldn't be as bloated as I am when I eat two in those phoney English Italian places."

"Exactly," smiled Laz, "and that's precisely the kind of quality that Leonardo's will be offering."

"Is that what you want to call it then?" asked David.

"Yes. And I'll tell you why," said Laz, leaning forward in conspiratorial fashion. "The reason I asked you to come tonight is because I've got a business proposition for you. I want you to create the look for my new venture."

"Oh yeah?"

"Yeah! I want you to recreate the Sistine Chapel ceiling in Tutton on Stour.

The mouthful of red wine David had just taken in now re-emerged dramatically, spraying the front of Laz's best suit.

"WHAT?" asked David incredulously, as soon as he was able.

"The Sistine Chapel ceiling. Well, not the exact same one, obviously. For a start, my church is tiny compared to the Sistine Chapel, so you'd have to do a sort of scaled-down version.

Gabria returned bearing two pizzas, placed them down in front of the two men and turned sharply on her heels again before she became tempted to smack Laz forcibly in the mouth with the giant pepperpot.

"There are a couple of potential pitfalls with your idea," explained David, hacking a trivial pursuit segment out of his pizza.

"Which are?"

"Numero uno, do you know how long it would take me to paint a Sistine Chapel-style scene on a ceiling, and therefore how much it would cost you?"

"Fair point."

"And numero due, the Sistine Chapel ceiling was painted by Michelangelo, you ignorant turd!"

CHAPTER 2

Painting by Numbers again!

Having slept on Laz's outrageous proposition, surprisingly, David awoke with a new-found spirit of compromise and reconciliation. This was largely because he'd had a brainwave at three-thirty-seven in the morning – he was sure of this because he was inches away from the red neon glow of his radio alarm clock at the time – and he wanted to relate his brilliant, money-saving scheme to Laz right away. So fired up by his idea was he, that he momentarily forgot all about Laz's legendary dislike of early mornings, and promptly rang him at nine. The response was typical, and if little Jessica thought the middle-aged, pony-tailed bohemian opposite her at Pizza Express was coming up with some unusual and hitherto unknown phrases, this was nothing to the expressions he was giving an airing to now. Sailors in Valetta's seediest brothels would have blushed. However, to his credit, once the mists of sleep had rolled away, the first strong coffee had been swallowed and the first fag sucked to extinction, reason was restored to its throne and Laz realized that his friend was only guilty of enthusiasm, and for Laz's new project at that. In hindsight, it now seemed rather churlish to have called David what he did, just because he was an obsessive anally-retentive insomniac cretin.

"Thank God you have a genius, and a forgiving one at that, as a best friend," David began, once he'd allowed Laz to vent his spleen and subsequently 'apologize', "or I might have told you just where to shove your ornate renaissance ceiling, and it would have been up your bloody poop-chute without the aid of KY Jelly, just in case you were wondering. Instead, however, you artistic Philistine – Leonardo indeed! – I have come up with a cost-saving solution for you, so that Michelangelo's might even get off the ground. Now bloody well grovel at my feet if you'd like to hear it."

Laz came as close to grovelling as he'd ever done, which was nowhere near, and instead said something along the lines of "Shut up whingeing and get on with it."

"Right," said David, "see if you can follow this. As you know, occasionally, I teach at the College of Art in Wolverhampton, and..."

"I am not having those dick-head students do it," interrupted Laz.

"Hear me out. I agree. I wouldn't trust them to paint my outside lavatory by themselves, but I have a cunning plan, and I think it's nothing short of inspired. Do you remember, ages ago, when I was an advertising illustrator; I used to do some work for a company that manufactured Paint by Numbers?"

"Yes. I don't like where this is going."

"Have faith! Listen! I intend to create for you a Paint by Numbers Sistine Chapel roof. If I had to lie on that scaffolding and paint the ceiling the way old Michelangelo did it, it would take me, conservatively, two to three years, which, at my hourly rate, is, well, extortionate. I put my rates up recently too."

"Put them up?" questioned Laz, with a nasty hint of incredulity in his voice. "I thought they were up already. They've *always* been up!"

David couldn't allow that to go by without comment.

"Quality is expensive, and I'm the best, though I'm usually far too modest to admit it. Why not go and ask Rolf Harris to do it instead? He'll charge you twice as much, probably, and you still wouldn't be able to guess what it was when he was finished. Now shut up and listen. My idea is to scale down the ceiling and paint the finished design in my studio, let's say no more than three feet wide. That will mean I spend around three or four weeks painting it instead of three or four years. Then I'll place a sheet of tracing paper over it and break it down into precise line-work and numbers, just like I used to do for Artikraft Products years ago. We can use thirty colours, which is plenty, I reckon."

"Go on," said Laz, quietly. "You interest me strangely."

"Good! Next we have the numbered line-work tracing enlarged onto great big sheets – there's a company I know that produce massive blueprints who can handle that. Then, once the ceiling is prepared and undercoated, the students tape the sheets to it and trace down the lines and numbers, under my supervision of course. When it's done, we simply have thirty pots of acrylic paint mixed up to match my colour swatch, and number the pots. For example; number 1, light flesh, number 2, dark flesh, number 3, light blue sky, number 4, dark..."

"Yes, I've got it," snapped Laz, searching around for another cigarette – he was incredibly short-tempered until he'd had at least six. "And then what?"

"Easy. Then my chain-gang take a section each and begin neatly filling in the areas with the relevant colour - they can manage that, for God's sake, they're taking a Bachelor of Arts degree after all. Anybody can fill in little segments neatly - well, apart from you that is. The beauty of the idea is that, from the ground, which I presume is some distance away from the ceiling, it being a chapel, you won't be able to tell that it's actually Paint by Numbers. The drawing of the figures will be spot-on, because it's all been traced from my original, so

11

there's no dodgy student draughtsmanship. The colours, likewise, will be pretty much bang-on to my original design too. We simply organize this in the college holidays, hand-pick six or seven students with the required number of brain cells – that might be hard, I admit – and pay them peanuts for two week's work, which should see it off I reckon."

"And you guarantee that it'll look the business from down below?" asked Laz, slowly warming to the idea, now that he could see his budget being slashed dramatically.

"Absolutely! You won't be able to tell it from the real one. The diners will sit at their candle-lit tables, gazing up at the majestic heavenly firmament above them, fully stocked with winged angels, semi-naked blokes reaching out to each other, wrestling and writhing and what have you, women reclining on fluffy clouds, God, Adam and Eve; the whole of creation. I'll just steal the best bits from Michelangelo's version. If that doesn't make the punters go gooey-eyed, fall in love, propose to each other over a good Chianti and then order tons of *calamari in padella con limone e pangrattato,* then I don't know what will."

"Brilliant. I actually think that'll work."

"I know it will. I'll charge you for six week's work, instead of three years, and we'll bung the students some beer money and tell them it's a not-to-be-missed artistic experience that'll look good on their CVs. That should do it. If they're anywhere near as naïve as I was when I went there, they'll fall for it, and hopefully not literally. You'll have to make sure the scaffold is safe. I'd find it hard to explain to the Head of Faculty if I accidentally killed seven of his students. Maybe we could equip them with parachutes."

"No need," replied Laz. "Students need to be culled. It's a harsh fact of life. We'd be doing everyone a favour if a few fell off. It's called collateral damage I think. Anyway, when do you reckon we could start?"

David consulted his diary. "Well, the summer holidays start in four weeks, so I'll pop into the college and head-hunt the best ones for starters. There's no point anyone turning up for duty until I've finished the design work, or you've got the ceiling prepared. What's it like at the moment?"

Laz explained that the ceiling looked as if it had been renovated at some point, and only needed a good rub down and a coat of acrylic primer, which pleased David no end. The last thing he wanted was for his handiwork to shell off after a few months and drop into the *risotto ai funghi* below. Leonardo had experienced a similar problem, David recalled, when he painted the Last Supper in Milan.

Luckily, the usually in-demand artist had just finished a huge restoration project at Birmingham Art Gallery and had deliberately not taken on too much work for the following month, as he sorely needed to take his foot off the gas pedal and take things easy for a while. That said, he was happy to forego this intentional fallow period to help out his old friend, but before he could begin, he had to drive to Wales to see a wealthy Arab gentleman who had requested a quote for repairing a valuable painting that had been damaged. The man was a wealthy racehorse owner who also owned a Stubbs original (amongst many other important works of art) and several wives. Apparently, one of them had taken exception to his obvious preference for his latest addition to the harem, and had made him aware of this grievance by flinging a pineapple, two saucepans and a carriage clock at him in quick succession. Being an agile young Arab millionaire, as opposed to the usual fat, lethargic variety, he had managed to side-step these improvised scud missiles, but the Stubbs racehorse, being a mere oil painting of a horse and not the real thing, just stood there and suffered the full force of the smaller saucepan's handle on its well-toned mahogany torso, if indeed horses possess torsos. The damage was a nasty five-inch gash that would have almost certainly resulted in the poor thing being put down, had it been a real horse. Luckily, being an oil paint horse, the wealthy Arab, after he had cursed and stamped around a bit, enquired at the National Gallery and been advised to contact a talented art restorer from the West Midlands. It was this rather long-winded tale that was being related to Laz now, and a fly on the wall at the Homer residence would have noted that the proprietor was stifling a yawn and wondering to himself what all this had got to do with him. Trying his level best to show something approaching interest, Laz asked David why he was travelling to Wales, of all places, to see an Arab.

"Ah, apparently he's there for two days, staying at The Millennium Hotel on business, and he wondered if I could meet him there. He's bringing the Stubbs with him, so I can see how bad the damage is."

"Last time I went to Wales it was shut!" said Laz dryly. "Lord knows why he'd want to go there. I'll see you when you get back then. We can drive down to Tutton and take a look at my chapel."

"I'd love to," said David. "I need to get a feel for the place and see what I'm up against. I'm curious as to where it is too. I know Tutton fairly well, but I can't picture it. I'm actually moving the studio out of our house and taking a unit on the Edgecliff Hall estate in Tutton. The owner's renovated the old stable block and turned it into very smart business units, so I've bagged one. As soon as I get back from Wales, I'm moving my stuff in."

"Well you won't have far to go to see me then," laughed Laz. "I've just bought the Edgecliff Hall chapel!"

CHAPTER 3

Smelly Trev

David was not happy. He had just returned from a wild goose chase in Wales - a complete waste of a valuable day. He'd arrived nice and early at his destination, parked on the pay and display by the beach and asked the lady at the nearby Tourist Information Centre where the Millennium Hotel was situated. It had come as a considerable shock when she informed him that there was no such hotel in the vicinity. David's first instinct was to tell the woman that she was talking out of the back of her head. It was, after all, not the first time he had been badly advised or misdirected by a local. Back in Stourbridge, he had once asked a gentleman who professed to have lived there for ninety or so years, for the directions to a social club where David was to meet a friend, only to be told that no such club existed in that town. The man was categorical. He even said that he would swear as much in a court of law, and added a rather idiotic comment about sacrificing his daughter's life if he were wrong about it. Then he asked if David's friend had perchance meant to say Enville, or Wollescote, or Hagley, or maybe even Stourport. By this time, David had virtually lost the will to live, and his mind was beginning to wander off, as was his habit when bored or disenchanted. As he stood there, shuffling from foot to foot, with the old chap's monotonous diatribe still droning on in the background, he idly gazed around him, taking in his surroundings and stifling a yawn. It was then that he noticed, just behind where the wizened old fellow was standing, a large neon sign bearing the legend, Stourbridge Sports and Social Club.

In fairness to the Information Centre lady, reasoned David, she was at least a trained professional and not some passing village idiot. She should have known her area fairly well, given her job description. He therefore decided to broaden his search to include Barmouth, Tywyn and Machynlleth, just in case the horse-fancying polygamist sheik had got a bit mixed up, but again, this drew a complete blank. Totally perplexed now, David began to question his own sanity. Was he perhaps saying Millennium when he actually meant Mausoleum, or Magnolia or Molineux? He asked the long-suffering lady to check hotels In Wales that began with an M, and when that failed to provide a result, he began to doubt that M was the first letter after all, and asked her to trawl through all the 'A's, in the vain hope that he'd know it when he heard it. The lady undoubtedly had the patience of a saint, but even saints have their limits, and this latest suggestion of David's was the last straw. She made her excuses, pounced on a newly arrived customer and virtually begged to let her help him, leaving poor David alone with his thoughts, which, as usual, were many and varied. After another ten minutes of dithering, he left the centre, strode over to the pay and display car park and gave his Mercedes coupe an almighty boot up the rear, instantly wiping at least five hundred pounds off the asking price. He jumped in, slamming the door shut noisily after him, screeched off the car park homeward bound, effing and blinding and occasionally punching the steering wheel as he did so. His misery was compounded when a traffic cop stopped him in Welshpool and issued him with a sixty pounds fine and three points on his licence for doing over seventy miles per hour in a cul-de-sac.

Three hours later, he pulled onto his gravel drive in a cloud of yellow dust and dashed into his house in order to try and answer the phone before it cut off. It was the Arab gentleman himself, tetchily asking where David was, as he had been in the hotel lobby for hours with a huge, battle-scarred Stubbs original under his arm. After a short but deeply embarrassing exchange, David replaced the receiver. Then he picked it up again and whacked himself forcibly across the brow with it, Basil Fawlty-style, before replacing it for the second time.

There were times when he was prone to bouts of extreme self-loathing, and this was one of them. One would have thought that after a lifetime of scatterbrained behaviour he would have learnt to accept it, but it still clearly upset him. The problem, in a round-about way, was that David was such a gifted artist. He had dedicated his entire life to perfecting his various artistic skills, but this had come at a price. He could now paint like Vermeer and write like Jerome K. Jerome. He could even play guitar a bit like Eric Clapton, but he had chosen to bury his head in the sand when it came to virtually everything else in life. He had no idea what seven sixes equalled, or for that matter, eleven nines, and he couldn't remember a pin number to save his life. He didn't have a clue how much money he had in the bank, or how to fill in a tax form. Without his children's help, he couldn't even operate the video recorder or use his mobile phone. He didn't know anything about chemistry, physics or biology, and he didn't know much about geography either, or he'd have realized that the Arab gentleman was staying at a hotel in Abu Dhabi, and not Aberdovey.

Once he had calmed down a little, David was able to see that he was perhaps being too hard on himself, and that it was a mistake that anyone could have made. For a start, the line had been bad, which didn't help. And who did this Sheik think he was, expecting art restorers to drop everything and fly halfway across the world at the drop of a turban, or whatever it was they wore, just to assess whether a painting of a racehorse could be patched up or should be sent to the knacker's yard. Unfortunately, it mattered little who was to blame for the misunderstanding, because the outcome remained the same. This was another expensive restoration project David could kiss goodbye to, at a time when he could have done with the money.

The best thing to take his mind off this latest debacle, he concluded, after sinking the morale-restoring cup of tea that his wife, Suzanne, had made for him, was a spot of physical work. He decided to load up the van he had hired for two days and ferry the contents of his home studio over to Edgecliff Hall Mews, where his new premises were situated.

Edgecliff Hall was a rather splendid old country house dating back to the early sixteenth century. It was situated near to the sleepy village of Tutton on Stour, near Kinver, just within South Staffordshire, and came with many hundreds of acres of farmland, two well-stocked lakes, several fields overrun with incontinent sheep, stables full of expensive racehorses, a cricket ground, several tied cottages and a recently converted mews. The place was owned by a Major Winterfold, whom David had never met, ably assisted by his elder sister, Claudia, whom he had. It was the seriously horsey and frightfully posh Claudia who ran the day-to-day affairs of the estate, which included renting out the properties in the newly converted mews.

There were twelve units in total, near to the entrance of the estate and arranged in a long line, with their own parking spaces and a small communal garden area to the rear. Whoever had been in charge of the renovation and subsequent promotion of the place had done a very good job, and already most of the units were occupied. There was a rocking horse maker – compulsory in such developments, and a violin maker, (likewise), an outfit that sold traditional boiled sweets which rotted your teeth just like Grandma's used to do, a man who turned wood (into what he didn't specify), a small antiques centre, a farm shop cum delicatessen, a graphologist, a private investigator and David.

As David pulled up outside in his white van, he couldn't help thinking that he and the private investigator didn't quite fit in. They were hardly your typical twee craft centre retailers, after all. David specialized in restoring insanely expensive and often famous works of art for the likes of the National Gallery, which placed him well beyond the means of the average punter on a day trip from West Bromwich. It was also difficult to envisage hoards of tourists flocking to the private investigator's place to have him spy on their errant wives or husbands. David had said as much to Claudia when he first viewed the unit, and she had replied that her brother wasn't fussed who used the buildings as long as they coughed up the rent each month. Running a huge country estate was a nightmare, she explained, and they had to rake it in where they could, which was why they'd taken the decision to renovate the mews in the first place. As far as she was concerned, Sweeney Todd could rent a unit with a view to selling Home-Made Pies, and she'd be happy.

David's other reservation was security. His home boasted a state of the art alarm system, insisted upon by all of the prestige galleries around the world that he worked for. Many preferred him to work in situ at their premises, but this was not always possible, due to the many items of specialist equipment David needed to have at his disposal. Nowadays, Van Goghs, Monets and the like were sent in armoured vans with security guards to have blemishes touched up or scratches repaired, and it was always a nerve-wracking time when they were left at his house for days on end. For obvious reasons, David never explained, other than to his closet friends, the precise nature of his work. As far as they were concerned, he just repaired pictures. He conveniently forgot to mention that some of them cost more than the entire Edgecliff Estate. Now that he had moved out of the Fortress of Solitude, (as he called his home studio) the alarm system would have to be relocated also.

It was June, hotter than hell, and not the ideal day to move into new premises. David was already sweating and so far he

19

had only lugged his desk, swivel chair and the plant his mother gave him into the empty room. There was a whole van full of stuff to unload yet, and he was drained. Claudia, who had spotted him struggling on his own, sent over a slow-witted, monosyllabic youth by the name of Brett to help him. Brett was a pupil from the nearby school who was doing his 'work experience' stint on the estate, and from what David could gather during their brief acquaintance, the lad was probably not going to be a nuclear physicist when he grew up.

Three weary hours later, virtually everything was inside, if not in position, and David's mouth now felt as if someone had emptied a carton of sand into it. He unpacked his brand new Debenham's Turbo 900 kettle and was just boiling water for a much-needed pot of tea when he became aware of a polite tap on the front door, almost unnoticed amidst the volcanic gurgling noises of the boiling water. He flicked off the kettle, which was only slightly noisier than a helicopter in a gale force wind, and called for whoever was without to come in.

A thin, seedy-looking individual of around thirty-five popped his head around the door and leered at David; a gesture that was probably intended to be a friendly smile. He was five feet ten inches tall, give or take an inch, with black, greasy hair and black stubble that seemed to grow in random tufts and would never have provided enough coverage to form a beard, had one been called for in a hurry. He was sweating profusely – a lot more than even David was – and his right hand was shaking quite badly. In spite of the temperature outside, he was wearing a grubby Mac that might have been dove grey or maybe even cream once, giving the impression that he had suddenly been surprised by the hot weather and hadn't had chance to change, even though it had been stifling for days.

David smiled sweetly back at him and asked him to come in, which he did, followed seconds later by his B.O. He spoke, and the body odour instantly lost pole position to the smell of stale beer that accompanied his words, forcing David to step back a foot, in spite of the fact that he was already a good yard or two away from him.

"Hello, I'm Trev from next door," he said. "Just thought I'd say hello and welcome you to Edgecliff Hall and ask you a small favour."

"Ah, the rocking horse man?" David enquired, even though, given his admittedly limited experience of rocking horse men, Trev didn't exactly fit the bill.

"Nah, the private investigator," replied Trev, with more than a hint of swagger, and then, just as David was about to launch into his next question, a remarkable thing happened. Suddenly, without any prior warning, Trev twitched violently and followed this immediately with a loud verbal ejaculation (thank God it was just verbal) which, to David's ears, sounded like the word CUT. A pedantic linguist, had he or she been in the room with them at the time, may well have preferred to spell it KUT, arguing that the 'K' seemed to sharpen the thing and make it more aggressive than the 'C', whilst admitting that none of this made a scrap of difference to the sound of the word when it was read out loud. Then, without seeming overly perturbed by this impediment, Trev continued.

"I'm goin' on holiday tomorrow for a fortnight, and I wondered if you'd mind – KUT! (There it went again) – looking after my office for me, sorting out the mail, doin' the answering machine messages, chucking the milk away when it turns into gorgonzola, sort of thing, if it's no trouble."

"Yes, of course," replied David, doing his best to be neighbourly. "What about the mail though? A lot of it might be private and confidential."

"Yeah. Might be I s'pose, but then they'll think nobody's bothered to answer it for two weeks and it might be urgent, so maybe the lesser of two weevils is to open it, and if it looks important, ring 'em and say you're my assistant or something, and that I'll be back in two weeks if they can wait that long. Use my phone o'course. If it's junk mail or unsolicited crap, just sling it. I'll have to trust you to be discreet, mate!"

David resisted the temptation to ask him what his last slave died of, and ploughed on.

"You'll have to show me how to use the answering machine. I'd hate to lose a load of messages by accident."

"No problem, erm…"

"David. David Day."

"Well David," said Trev, "If you've got a sec, we can do it now, that's if you're not busy."

David replied that, currently, thanks to the Abu-Dovey Debacle and the fact that Laz was still away in Bulgaria, there were Galapagos Island turtles that were considerably busier than him, if one excluded such prosaic tasks as arranging the furniture, setting up the computer, putting forty tons of art equipment in all the right drawers and trying to build a self-assembly bookshelf from Ikea. David followed him outside, grateful that Trev was taking most, though certainly not all of his B.O. with him. He made a mental note to pop by the local Makro in Halesowen and grab an air freshener at the earliest convenience - preferably something that brought to mind Canadian pine forests. The two men slipped into Trev's office, which was to the left of David's in a longish row, and instantly he was reminded of the Raymond Chandler novel, Farewell My Lovely that he was currently rereading. Trev had certainly spared all expense on furnishing the place. It looked like one of those living museums that recreate 1950s' houses, except for the choice magazines strewn across his teak-effect coffee table, which were probably still illegal back then.

There was a filthy green metal filing cabinet, a battered wooden desk with a health hazard telephone on it and a grubby calendar sponsored by a local car repair garage whose boss must have had a serious breast fixation. A threadbare, lumpy, Persian-style rug graced the floor, which David skirted en-route to Trev's desk, so as not to dirty his shoes. Other than those scant items, plus a pair of moth-eaten orange and brown floral curtains and a red vinyl-covered chair, the room was what is often referred to as minimal in concept. Even Phillip Marlowe, that most frugal and honest of private investigators, would have turned his nose up at it. It looked to David as if Trev had purchased the lot from a sink estate house clearance for no more than three quid. Even at that, he reckoned the man had been done.

Trev mumbled something apologetically about clients not liking plush offices because they smacked of large fees, and proceeded to show David how things worked, where his fridge was, and so on. They didn't look at his lavatory, which was a blessing, but Trev explained that, should David be caught short and needed to use it, the flusher was playing up and needed a big yank to make it work. David asked if John Wayne was big enough, but the comment sailed harmlessly about a foot above Trev's greasy, dandruff-encrusted head and into the ether. David was slowly beginning to form the opinion that Poirot and Miss Marple had nothing to worry about, competition-wise.

Trev rounded off the guided tour by telling his new assistant that there were a few things in his fridge that might come in handy, so he hadn't chucked them away. David thanked him profusely and made another mental note to clear the thing out first thing the following morning, after the pungent P.I. had buggered off to wherever he was going. For some reason, David suddenly had a strong image of him with his trousers rolled up, still wearing the filthy Mac and paddling alone in the sea at Blackpool, a fag hanging from his lower lip in jaunty, care-free fashion.

"What happens if someone actually turns up here looking for you, rather than phoning?" David asked. Already he could see this 'doing a small favour' for smelly Trev turning into a full-time unpaid secretarial job.

"Oh, just tell 'em I'm on holiday and they'll have to wait. If I lose a customer, so be it. Everybody needs a break don't they?"

"Well I don't at the moment," David smiled. "I could actually do with some work, to be honest. I've had a very busy year so far, but the diary's looking a bit empty now. I'm going to do a job for a mate of mine soon though. He wants me to paint his ceiling."

Trev grinned back at David, displaying the various gaps in his dental work, which made the insides of his mouth look like a scaled down prototype of Stonehenge.

"It's a funny old game you're in, mate; art and that. You 'ave to 'ave a university degree I s'pose, and know how to speak and write proper an' all I expect. I'm crap at all that, the verbs and adjutants and stuff, whatever *they* are."

"Adjectives."

"Yeah, additives I mean. I was never no good at all that when I was at school. That's why I decided to be a copper, but they wouldn't have me."

"So how did you end up being a P.I.? It all sounds very glamorous, I must admit."

"Nah, it ain't," Trev assured him, though quietly David had already gathered as much, given that Trev was one. "When I left school I worked at a college as a caretaker, lockin' up and doin' odd jobs and that…. KUT!"

Trev let fly with one of his strange vocal tics, which reminded David of Tourette's Syndrome but, so far at least, without the swearing. Once more, Trev soldiered gamely on, neither acknowledging nor apologizing for his latest outburst.

"…but they sacked me 'cause I went to the end of term party and got blind pissed and copped a feel of this student's tit. My Uncle Bill used to be a copper, and got retired early for gross misconduct, I think he said it was, so he set up as a private investigator, and I was on the dole at the time, so I started helping him out an' that. It's mainly divorce crap – you know, sitting in a car for hours on end trying to spot some woman's husband sneakin' into his girlfriend's flat for a shag, and then taking pictures of 'em with me old Nikon digital. Here, have one of these!"

He handed David a dog-eared business card which looked as if it had been set with real lead type from the John Bull printing set he'd had for Christmas in 1968. It read:

Trevor Jenkinson – Private Investigater

Unit 4, Edgecliff Mews,

Edgecliff Hall, Tutton on Stour, South Staffordshire

Telephone 01384 442881

All types or work undertaken. Discreshion ashured.

David smiled one of his private, superior smiles and pocketed it quickly, before he had chance to burst out laughing. Trev then handed him a bunch of keys and explained which one opened what. David briefly examined them, wondering to himself which one unlocked the man's private brewery.

"So where are you off on holiday?" he eventually asked him, hoping that it was far enough away to get rid of his skunk-like aroma.

"Never you mind," Trev grinned, tapping his purple nose. "I'll send you a postcard."

And with that, they wrapped up their business. Trev took off in his rusty green Vauxhall with the one blue door, and David repaired to his new office to fumigate the place, hoping that his mother's rather delicate plant hadn't succumbed and keeled over.

He laboured building his Ikea shelves until around four-thirty, bathed in sweat and swearing like a trooper, as was his custom when undertaking any DIY tasks. He threw the Allen key, which had stayed hexagonal for all of thirty seconds, into the waste paper bin in a fit of pique and resorted to brute force and a hammer instead, which got him absolutely nowhere apart from a few steps nearer to his first stroke. Finally, he stood up with a heartfelt groan, rubbing his severely bruised, creaky joints to encourage the blood to circulate once more. Several of the small chromium screws from bag 'K' were still embedded into his kneecap, which partly explained why he was in so much agony.

David staggered back a foot or two in order to admire his handiwork, only to discover that shelves 'A' and 'B' and bracket 'D' had been fixed upside down and back to front, which meant that all the rough chipboard edges without the imitation ash veneer were now showing, and it was at this juncture that he decided enough was enough. He begrudgingly resolved to dismantle the whole lot and start again first thing in the morning when his mind was clearer.

It was still a tad too early for David to call it a day without feeling guilty, but a much lighter task was now called for if he was to avoid total collapse. After eventually electing to blast a few token squirts of Mr Sheen hither and thither, half-heartedly spreading it around with a dirty yellow duster just like his wife, Suzanne always did, he decided to knock it on the head until the morning. Mentally drained and physically exhausted, but experiencing the golden inner glow that only honest toil can engender, he locked his front door and stood quietly outside admiring his new place of work with a genuine sense of pride.

It was just about the only thing he had the energy left to do, thanks to the still-oppressive heat. The sky was no longer the cloudless, bright cobalt blue it had been all day, and now it had become heavy and foreboding. A spirited wind, like the ones that always feature in spooky films about the supernatural, began to whip up the fallen leaves, moaning eerily as it did so, and David felt the hairs on the back of his neck stand to attention. The atmosphere on the estate became suddenly highly charged and quite magical - surreal, almost, with the broody, dark purple sky juxtaposed against the orange glow of the old brick buildings, and somewhere, many miles away, a thunderstorm was brewing. David could hear the distant rumble, which made him feel invigorated and alive once more, albeit temporarily. Since he was a small child, thunder storms had always had that effect on him. His grandmother, Bertha, on the other hand, had she still been alive, would probably have been hiding under the kitchen table.

Once he had enjoyed his brief ethereal moment, David decided to revisit Trev's palatial office suite in order to empty his malodorous fridge before it started growing weird cultures that might take over the world and make the Ebola virus look like the common cold in comparison. If Trev's personal hygiene was any indication, everything would have been well past its sell-by date since 1987 anyway. He let himself in and made his way to the rusting appliance, theatrically crossing himself like a Roman Catholic priest about to perform an exorcism as he did so. Surprisingly, it wasn't all that bad, if one discounted the mouldy pork pie that appeared to be growing a malformed green head. David gingerly removed the offending item, along with half a bottle of semi-skimmed, semi-solid milk (or semi-skilled as Bertha often called it) and a block of cheese which might have been cheddar once, but now resembled stilton, ready to sling into the waste bins outside. The numerous cans of cheap cider David left in situ.

Mission accomplished, he was about to exit stage left when he suddenly felt the urge to pee, caused no doubt by the fifteen-odd cups of tea that he'd consumed to counteract the dust he'd inhaled whilst Spring-cleaning. Too lazy to dash out onto the walkway, fiddle with his Chubb lock and sprint, clutching his groin, to his own lavatory, David elected to avail himself of the facilities, offering up a silent prayer that Trev's lavvy was up to scratch. He pushed open the door that led to the cluttered back room and stepped over or around the black bin bags, the mop bucket, the dismantled old bike, the assorted cardboard boxes and the shrink-wrapped toilet rolls that the man had left all over the place, desperate now to relieve himself. He fell over a garden strimmer and head-butted the lavatory door open in the nick of time, feverishly struggling with his zip and turning the air blue with his language. David flipped up Trev's deluxe black plastic lavatory seat with no more than a second to spare and emptied himself of something approaching eight gallons over the next two minutes, sighing ecstatically and becoming ever so slightly cross-eyed as he did so. Then he did that idiotic thing that most folks do, if they are honest and admit to it. He looked down to examine his waste products, even though he knew full well what he'd be seeing (he always looked at what he had blown into his handkerchief too). Maybe it was for reassurance – a mini health check, just on the off-chance that it might one day be the wrong colour or blood-streaked or something. Whatever the reason, David decided to take a good look before he flushed it away, and what he saw, floating around in his thankfully normal-coloured urine, was something he had never, ever seen before, and wasn't that keen on seeing again.

CHAPTER 4

A Phillip Marlowe Moment

David tried to kid himself that he was going round to Trev's place again just to empty the freezer compartment, which he'd forgotten all about in his haste to dispose of the deadly pork pie. In reality, he wanted to visit the lavatory once more just to make sure that he'd actually seen what he *thought* he'd seen – that it wasn't just a hallucination, or a trick of the light.

It was neither. The thing was lying there, submerged in the yellow water, just as it had been on the previous evening. He flushed the cistern but it still stubbornly refused to budge. Unsure how to proceed, David stumbled out of the cluttered little back room and back into the office, which looked every bit as stylish as it had done the previous afternoon.

He opened the fridge and tugged at the small blue door that was situated above the main cool-box area. It was welded shut with caked-up ice, and couldn't be persuaded to reveal its secrets. He grabbed an old spoon from Trev's tea tray and began hacking at it, his fingers turning numb with frostbite as he did so. Finally it gave way, and David was able to wrench the door open, immediately wishing that he hadn't succeeded. Inside the tiny freezer compartment was a solitary fish finger with rather fetching green mould spots, which had most probably been there since the ice age. Oh yes, and a severed hand.

He would have preferred a little time to himself in order to allow this to sink in properly, but at that precise moment the doorbell rang and he nearly jumped out of his skin. He hastily closed the freezer compartment, slammed the rusting old fridge shut, swallowed his pounding heart and headed for the door. He opened it, his hands shaking even more than Trev's had done, and was greeted by a tall, sunburnt gentleman of around forty-five dressed in a checked shirt, green corduroy trousers and an old but expensive-looking pair of tan-coloured brogues. He had a lightly freckled face and wiry, sand-coloured hair that had been cut precisely but not all that fashionably. It was the kind of hairstyle that Prince Charles would have asked for thirty-odd years ago, when the new mobile barber turned up at the palace, and, once instructed, the barber would never again have had his brief changed or modified. For a moment, David actually thought that Rory Bremner, the satirical mimic, had come a-calling in need of Trev's razor-sharp mind and legendary, if misspelt *discreshion*, but a second glance confirmed that the gentleman was nothing more than a half-decent look-alike; a mere Rory Bremner impressionist, if you will. David greeted him with a cheery good morning and asked him to enter, feeling rather ashamed of what was on offer inside. The man duly marched in – march being the *mot juste* - and David felt strangely compelled to retreat backwards in unison towards Trev's tatty utility desk, ending up sat on the corner of it. He asked how he could help, his heart still bumping dysrhythmically against his ribcage.

"Do you know who I am?" the man asked, apropos of nothing.

"No," David replied, slightly taken aback by hearing his least-favourite expression, "but isn't it a little early in our relationship to be launching into all that threatening stuff?"

"Oh God, I didn't m-mean…." The man stammered, flushing slightly. "No, I didn't mean, do *you know* who I am? I literally meant, do you know who I am, sort of thing, if you get my drift."

"Ah! That's a hell of a lot clearer now," David replied, and then, for good measure, adding, "What, have you forgotten who you are or something?"

The gentleman soldiered gamely on, digging deeper and deeper foxholes for himself. "S-Sorry, I meant, do you know me? Have we met recently?"

"What, can't you remember?"

He shot David a troubled look.

"Well, that's the thing, you see. I'm afraid I can't! I suffer from a condition called prosopagnosia, unfortunately, amongst other things. It's a bit of a complex brain disorder commonly known as face blindness, which prevents us from telling faces apart, even with close friends and family sometimes. It's quite common actually. About one in fifty people have it, to varying degrees. Mine's pretty severe, which is bloody embarrassing, as you can imagine. A woman stops me in the street and asks if I'd like to go for a coffee, and I say 'awfully nice of you, but you're a bit old for me, love,' and she replies, 'It's me, your mother, dimwit!'"

David stifled a smirk. "Jeez! That's an unusual one; never heard of that before. Well, to the best of my knowledge, I don't know you, but I did think you were Rory Bremner for a split second."

"Oh!" the gentleman frowned, politely ignoring David's flippant comment, "that's odd, because I was absolutely convinced that I called by and spoke to you last week about something rather private, but obviously I wouldn't have remembered your face. I was expecting you to remember mine though, unless of course you have prosopagnosia too."

David's head was spinning now, though to be fair to him, there *was* a severed human hand waiting for him in the freezer, and that can often distract a fellow.

"Let's start again," David suggested, doing his best to be cheery. "Firstly, I'm not the chap you saw in this office, if indeed you did call at this office in the first place. I'm just helping out because he's on holiday for a fortnight."

"So I *might* have been here then?" asked the gentleman hopefully. "I distinctly remember that this place had a certain, erm, atmosphere, shall we say, and I just presumed you were the proprietor."

David was horrified that the major was confusing him with Trev on any level – looks, personal hygiene, intellect, occupation, literacy or anything else he could think of. He felt that a full explanation was necessary, so he raised his hand and interrupted the man, mid-flow. David assured him that he wasn't going mad and invited him to take a seat. His instinct told him this was going to take time to unravel.

"This propaganda thing you have…."

"Prosopagnosia."

"Yes, that. Does it also affect your memory then?"

"No," the gentleman assured him. "That's yet another completely separate problem of mine. Look, I think it's best if I start at the beginning, don't you? My name is Major Simon Winterfold, ex of the army; now your landlord. I own Edgecliff Hall."

If David had known where his forelock was, or indeed what it was, he'd have tugged at it. Instead, the two men shook hands, wiped the slate clean and made a fresh start.

"I recently inherited the old place from my late father," explained the major, "and I love it – who wouldn't? - But it swallows my money like my old 'E' Type swallows petrol. If there was a Betty Ford Clinic for vehicles, that thing would be a permanent resident, and the house makes my car look like a teetotaller, if you follow me. That's why I had a lot of the surplus outbuildings converted into offices and so on – to rake a bit of cash in from the estate. Before that I was serving in Iraq, to name but one top holiday location."

David nodded in sympathy, smiled generously at the major's little witticisms and added what he hoped was a serious, respectful, patriotic look at the end that probably looked to the major more like a bad case of trapped wind.

"That was until a landmine blew my spine through my tin hat. Now I've gone from career soldier to country squire, courtesy of this."

He tapped the bottom of his right leg, which was, unless the man had calf muscles like Arnold Schwarzenegger's, patently prosthetic.

"I bet it comes in useful for planting potatoes," David added sympathetically. "Mind you, they've got realistic feet attached nowadays I suppose, not like the old Long John Silver prototype. Unless, of course, the foot section screws off."

David decided it was best to cease this train of thought as he sensed the major was getting restless.

"It's a bugger," Major Winterfold replied resignedly, graciously resisting the temptation to unscrew his leg and stove David's skull in with it, "but far worse is the mental stuff – the flashbacks, the bad dreams, the insomnia and the, erm… the…."

"Memory loss?" suggested David.

"How did you know about that?" the major asked, incredulously. "That's absolutely correct. The blast seems to have wiped sections of my memory completely. The docs reckon it was the bit of shrapnel that they had to remove from my head that caused it. That and the shock. What with all that *and* the blessed prosopagnosia which I had anyway, I'm a bloody mess."

David offered the major a cup of tea, wisely popping next door to his own office to gather up the equipment and ingredients. He didn't want poor Major Winterfold adding cholera to his list of ailments, after all - he seemed to have enough on his plate. As the mighty Turbo 9000 whooshed into action, the major resumed the conversation, with David trying desperately to hear him over the noise. He imagined that the ex soldier must have been used to yelling instructions to his men over the noise of incoming Chinook helicopters in Baghdad, so it didn't seem to faze him.

"So it's best I wait until the other chap gets back from his holidays, then?" he bellowed, his hands cupped either side of this mouth. Mercifully, at this juncture the kettle turned itself off, job done, and David began making the tea.

And then he did an inexplicable thing. Maybe it was because business was slow next door, or because he was just plain nosy. Perhaps it was because he'd been reading his Raymond Chandler books again, and was full of some romantic notion of the brave, incorruptible private eye (as opposed to Trev's seedy, deeply unattractive, easily corrupted version). It could even have been that he was a little bit fed up with painting or restoring pictures eight hours a day, day in, day out. Whatever the reason, David found himself saying:

"No sense waiting two weeks if something is worrying you, Major Winterfold. Why don't you tell me all about your problem, in complete confidence, and I'll start looking into it right away, if you instruct me to, of course. If it turns out that you've already explained everything to my, erm, colleague, Trevor, well, no harm done! He wouldn't have started working on it yet anyway, I should imagine, what with his holiday and everything."

The major agreed. He looked like a man who had a lot to get off his chest, so David invited him to take the floor and give him chapter and verse. Predictably, possessing as he did the memory of a shell-shocked one-legged goldfish, he found this somewhat hard going.

"It's the, erm, house, you see," he began falteringly. "Well, I know the old recall mechanism isn't what it ought to be, but I'm convinced I'm right about this. I think someone is tampering with things."

"What, stealing the cutlery and stuff?" David asked, making notes on a scrap of borrowed paper with Trev's badly chewed biro. For those interested in the minutiae, he wrote down the words TAMPERING, and STUFF.

"No, not exactly," replied the major, his countenance modulating from the previous 'troubled' to 'deeply troubled'. "Look, I might well be going off my trolley…"

David quickly scribbled MAJOR OFF TROLLEY? Shielding it with his left hand like a young child does during a maths exam when he thinks his neighbour is copying, and then looked him in the eye again with an earnest expression.

"…but things don't look….well, *right*, if you follow me."

"No. Not yet."

"The oil painting of my great grandfather by what's-his-bloody-name, for example. It doesn't follow me round the room like it used to."

"An oil painting has been following you round the room?" David queried, surreptitiously double-underlining the words OFF TROLLEY as they spoke.

"Sergeant, that's him. His eyes, I meant."

"Your sergeant's eyes follow you around the room? Are you sure this isn't some form of post traumatic stress disorder you're experiencing? Did your sergeant maybe get killed or..."

"Sir Malcolm Sergeant, I meant," interrupted the major. "The artist was Sir Malcolm Sergeant."

"I doubt it," David replied. "He was a famous orchestral conductor. Do you mean John Singer Sargent by any chance?" He poured the tea, suddenly embarrassed that he had corrected the man. If Major Winterfold was annoyed at this, he didn't show it, possibly because he owed a real Sargent, presumably worth a few million, and all David owned was a good knowledge of artist's names.

"Sorry," the major replied, banging his brow gently with the palm of his right hand, "you're absolutely correct, but the point is; great grandfather doesn't look at me everywhere I go anymore."

"I see," said David, but clearly he didn't, though he *was* beginning to get the impression that the major had a somewhat overprotective great grandfather.

"And the Chippendale sideboard isn't quite as tall as it once was," Major Winterfold added, sipping his tea nonchalantly, as if what he'd just said made complete sense.

David studiously made further notes, his tongue sticking out at a jaunty angle.

"The Constable looks different to me too," the honest soldier added, nibbling one of David's HobNobs.

"Maybe he's changed his hairstyle," David suggested, as he scanned the room for an escape route. "These young lads do so on a regular basis nowadays. Was he round your place investigating the cross-eyed Sargent by any chance?"

"My Constable painting, I mean. Before my last tour of duty, I could have sworn that there were two peasants and one cow, not two cows and a peasant."

David weighed this carefully. "Are all the paintings in your place done by people in the forces?"

Major Winterfold smiled weakly. "We are very privileged to own several works by famous artists, and no, we don't have a watercolour by Colonel yet, but I'm working on it! Look, I know this all sounds crazy, but ever since I came back, I've been getting these really odd feelings about things. Like they're not how I remembered them. Not that my memory is to be trusted. Then there's the old box in my safe. My sister Claudia, who works as my P.A., reckons that nothing is missing from it, but I'm sure there is. The trouble is, I'm not absolutely sure what it might be. It's somewhere in the back of my mind, so I'm hoping it'll come back to me soon. I've stepped up security now, what with the spate of thefts around the estate, and yet another attempted rape."

"Rape?" David asked, shocked, and writing down the words THEFTS and RAPE as he did so.

"Yes. Very nasty business. One of our farm girls was assaulted on the estate three weeks ago. The cops haven't arrested anyone as yet. She's okay, but obviously shaken up."

David poured the major another tea, sat down again and expelled a giant sigh. "So far, according to my notes, your great granddad won't look at you anymore, the Chippendale's shrunk and one of your Constable's cows has swallowed a passing peasant. Oh yes, and an intruder broke in and decided not to bother stealing anything, or at least, he might have done but you don't know what it is. To be frank, I'm just wondering what I'm supposed to do about any of it, if anything actually *needs* doing, that is. The thefts and the attempted rape are the only really tangible crimes you've described so far, and the police are looking into those, I presume. Everything else stems from your admittedly shaky memories of things before Iraq. Do you understand my predicament, Major?"

"Of course," replied the major resignedly. "I suppose it does all sound a bit daft, put like that. You chaps prefer something a bit more black and white, eh?"

"Ideally, yes, like, my wife is missing, or someone nicked all my spoons, or one of my prize racehorses has been nobbled; that sort of thing." David had only been a private eye for five minutes, but already he was getting the hang of it.

Major Winterfold stared at the ceiling and scratched his head, wondering where to go next with the most surreal conversation he'd had in years. David saved him the trouble.

"Look, I'll tell you what," he said, sensing that things had reached an impasse, "why don't I call round tomorrow morning and you can give me a guided tour of the old place? Maybe, between us, we can sort things out. Something might just leap out at me when I'm actually there. Show me these paintings and items of furniture for a start, and then, if anything seems fishy, I'll take a nose around. How's that?"

The major stood up, shook David's hand, thanked him profusely and told him he'd be expecting him at ten. That was, of course, if he actually remembered that the artist-cum-private eye was coming and the forgetful major hadn't gone out shooting rabbits instead. David let him out, locked the door and immediately strode over to the fridge, his wild eyes darting this way and that as he did so. It was like a scene from an absurd scary movie, where the hero finds himself in a house of horrors. There was still the unspeakable thing basking in the lavatory to contend with, and even worse, a frozen human body part stuck to the side of the freezer compartment. It was obvious to the meanest intelligence that Trev must have had a hand in it, so to speak; the man was cool, that was for sure. He was brazen and completely unconcerned about being caught, from what David could make out, which suggested that he was almost certainly off his rocker; a psycho killer on the loose. David's mind was reeling. Who was Trev's handless victim? What on earth was the unspeakable thing in the loo and was it connected in any way? Would Trev smash open the front door at any moment, casting an ominous long shadow and holding a bloodied machete, intent on hacking the hapless artist into prime cuts of meat for his home larder unit? David felt as if he'd suddenly been swept up from his cosy rural surroundings at Edgecliff Hall Mews and transported to the set of Steven King's 'The Shining 2', with Smelly Trev reviving the part previously played by Jack Nicholson.

David had to phone the police, and fast. He turned away from the fridge of horrors – he didn't really fancy taking another peek anyway - and made his way to the desk. He opened the drawer with trembling hand in search of clues, but found instead only a dirty 1994 copy of Yellow Pages and several deceased woodlice. Musing as to whether Trev had done for them as well, David grabbed the phone and was in the process of dialling 999 when he spotted Trev's open diary. He replaced the receiver and flicked through the recent pages, looking for something – anything - that might shed some light on what had gone on in this evil place. Mostly, the diary entries were brief, prosaic reminders to pick up a serviced vehicle, meet some client or other on a pub car park or keep an appointment with the doctor.

Then David saw it, and his blood ran cold. It was as if a hidden demonic violinist in Trev's office had suddenly begun playing that awful, shrieking piece that accompanied the infamous stabbing sequence in Psycho. He felt the hairs stand up on the back of his neck again, 'like quills on the fretful porpentine' as Shakespeare so memorably put it, even if he couldn't spell for toffee.

He quickly turned back to the beginning of the month with clumsy, sweating hands, in search of more damning evidence, and soon found it. On the third of May, Trevor had written, 'I can't fight the urges today' in a spidery scrawl. David feverishly flicked the pages over to the seventh of the month, where he discovered the ominous warning, 'Urges getting stronger. I am not coping.'

And just after that, the page that had chilled David's blood in the first place. On Thursday 14th of May, Trev had scrawled across the page in vivid red ink:

I AM THE RAPIST.

CHAPTER 5

Laz Returns!

Surprisingly, David didn't sleep well that night. Usually that happened when the weather was oppressively hot, or if he had eaten too late, or had too much to drink, or if there was a lot on his mind, or maybe if he'd found a severed hand in the fridge.

After locking up he drove home through the dark country lanes, skittishly glancing in his rear-view mirror every twenty seconds for psycho killers hiding on his back seat. Suzanne was out doing her keep fit and Lauren and James, his children, were at his mother's house watching a video, so he sought sanctuary in Giovanni's Italian Restaurant, where he ate too late, drank far too much (for medicinal purposes) and fretted about the human hand in the fridge, in the order named. With hindsight, he should have realized that he had collected the full set, making insomnia inevitable, and maybe swallowed a couple of the blue pills that his friend and G.P., Doctor John Frith had prescribed for such occasions. He didn't, and consequently he witnessed every lonesome minute tick by at a snail's pace. It was, therefore, a grey and twitchy David Day who drove down the long gravel path that led to the hall the next morning. Most people of a certain age will remember those old-fashioned circus entertainers who juggled diabolos whilst simultaneously spinning scores of plates on top of flimsy poles. Well, that was what the inside of David's head felt like. One minute, a fellow is bored senseless through lack of activity and trying to relieve the tedium with a spot of Ikea shelf building, and the next, he's become a private detective. Not any old private detective, David mused, but one with unspeakable things down his psychopathic neighbour's lavatory, severed body parts residing in his fridge and mad clients with virtually no brain cells left that functioned correctly. Then there was the shrinking antique furniture, the oil paintings that seemed to have developed a mind of their own, and the crazed rapist. Having slept on it, or rather, not slept on it, David had formulated a plan. He would get to his new studio, ring the police to come and fetch the hand, and then pop over to see the major. This, he felt sure, would be a wild goose chase of Abu-Dovey proportions, but he felt duty-bound to at least see the man and take a look around before walking away and leaving things to the professionals. And by professionals, he meant the police and not the nutcase next door, who was probably taking his fortnight's vacation in some death camp or other, chopping up the inmates and turning them into sausages.

As David's Mercedes crunched onto the car park gravel and came to a halt, he spotted the large black Range Rover with the private number plate LAZ 48. Being an astute private eye, David knew immediately that his old friend was back from Bulgaria. Laz opened the driver's door, jumped out and sauntered over to greet David halfway, frantically chewing gum like a football manager on the touchline when his team is eleven-nil down.

David smiled, shook hands and asked if Laz was still chewing on the remnants of the Bulgarian furniture manufacturer's ear, such was the ferocity of his friend's legendary bollockings. He was, therefore, rather disappointed to discover that it was just a Wrigley's 'Juicy Fruit'.

"I thought I'd show you round my new chapel, if you've got a few minutes," said Laz. "It's further down by the main house."

42

"I know," replied David, "I saw it yesterday, and it looks fantastic from the outside, I have to admit. I met the owner yesterday too, and he was explaining to me why he's had to convert the mews and sell off the buildings he doesn't want, or should I say, can't afford to keep. The old place is very expensive to run."

"Well, his loss is my gain, old pal!" grinned Laz. "Let's go and have a look, so you know what you're up against."

David explained that he only had ten minutes, as he was expected at the hall, or at least, he hoped he was. The two men jumped into Laz's vehicle (Laz refused to walk further than six feet, which explained his burgeoning waistline) and drove the two hundred yards to the back of the hall.

The old chapel was indeed picturesque. It was small, by church standards, but still large enough to create an intimate, exclusive restaurant. The exterior was Italianate in style, and reminded David of ones he'd seen in and around Florence, rather than the typical English fifteenth and sixteenth century country churches scattered around the countryside. Laz pulled the door keys from his coat pocket and proudly opened up to give David a sneak preview. The interior smelled a little damp, and sorely needed some love and attention, but it was as Laz had described it - full of potential. David looked heavenwards and saw his blank canvas for the first time. Mercifully, the ceiling was in extremely good condition and not too big, but that said, it was still a mammoth task, and one that would have undoubtedly taken him two years, had he undertaken the work single-handedly, to Michelangelo's standard. As he stood there in a reverie, just taking it all in, the best he could manage was a simple 'Phewee!'

"What do you think?" asked Laz.

"Magnificent!" replied David, still in a daze. "It's obviously listed, so you can't just barge in and rip it to bits."

Laz confirmed this, but didn't see it as a problem. He'd sought advice from the right people; nothing structural needed changing and he hadn't figured on adding a white plastic conservatory. Everything was sound, and the powers that be didn't mind David painting the ceiling, as long as he didn't start tearing it down in a fit of pique, as artists are wont to do when things aren't going right for them. The work would begin the following week, and as far as Laz was concerned, David could get cracking on his designs right away. David pondered a little more in studious silence, and then outlined his battle plan. First, he would photograph the ceiling panels and scale them down to a workable painting size. Once that was done, he would pop along to the Birmingham University Art Library and find the biggest and best pictures he could of the Sistine Chapel ceiling. Then, he would use the 'best bits' of Michelangelo's work and drastically revamp them to fit.

David apologized for his flying visit and headed for the huge, carved wood front door.

"Oh, how did your trip to Wales go, by the way?" asked Laz, and there was something about the way his friend head-butted the chapel door on the way out that told him maybe all was not well.

A few minutes later, having rung the brass doorbell, David stood at the front door of Edgecliff Hall, rubbing his throbbing brow and wincing. After what seemed like a year, but was probably just the time it took some faithful old retainer to walk from one end of the Hall to the other, the door creaked open, and David was confronted by an ancient gentleman dressed like an Edwardian butler. In fact, this gentleman looked like a cartoon butler; more like a butler than anyone had a right to look. Had Hollywood been casting for the role of an old butler for a new feature film, this man would have won the job hands down. David gave him the once over, and estimated that he must have been hired when the hall was first built, making him, conservatively, five hundred years old. The elderly gentleman

44

smiled and asked David's name and business, which seemed to use up a lot of his energy, and then asked David to follow him inside, which virtually used up the remainder. After a walk of no longer than twenty yards that took the best part of twenty minutes, the butler tapped at a door with a shaking, Parkinson's hand and was asked to enter, which he and David duly did.

Major Simon Winterfold was seated at an old desk, looking at what appeared to be invoices. On seeing David, he stood to attention, hobbled around the desk and shook David's hand firmly. The butler, whose name was Horace, began to make his unsteady way back whence he came, when Major Winterfold called after him, asking if the old fellow would be kind enough to provide tea and biscuits for the guest. That was, of course, if David could afford to wait that long.

"Pleased you could come," smiled the major. "Take a seat, and call me Simon, by the way."

"Pleased you could remember who I was," grinned David cheekily.

"Ah! Well I just consulted the old diary you see," explained the major. "I actually remembered to write it down, which is good for me, so I knew you were coming. I've got another chap coming to see me soon about the sale of the old chapel. I've met you both before and I couldn't recognize either of you again if my life depended on it! Your face is familiar now, but I couldn't categorically say that you were the chap I saw at the mews yesterday. I just presume you are because you said you were coming at ten, and it's now ten. Oh yes, and I can tell the voice, which helps."

"How are you with body shapes?" asked David, intrigued by this unusual affliction. "I'm going to be awfully hurt if you mix me up with that fat bugger!"

The major roared with laughter. "Well, either you know him well, or you're very rude, that's all I can say."

45

"The former, I'm glad to say," replied David. "I just saw him outside, showing the place off to me. He's my oldest friend, and we spend most of our time insulting each other. We're both forty-eight, but when we're together, we act as if we were just eight. If you think *I* was harsh, you should hear what he says about me!"

"I will do when he arrives later," laughed Major Winterfold. "It's a lovely old chapel isn't it? I hate having to let it go, but, as I said yesterday, this estate needs to generate some cash, and I like the sound of what Mr Homer is planning to do with the old place. Apparently, he has an artistic genius friend who will transform the ceiling. He reckons the chap is a scatterbrained, unworldly loony, but incredibly gifted."

"Does he now?" frowned David. He was about to probe the major more deeply about this latest comment, but another tap on the door signalled the unexpectedly early arrival of Horace and his tea tray. David leapt up from his seat to open the door, realizing that the major could no longer manage the one hundred metres in eleven seconds either. Horace shuffled in at a snail's pace, his silver tray clattering noisily, with various items falling off as he gamely made his way to the table in a new personal best of less than six minutes. By the time he had laid the tray down, most of the tea was swilling around in the tray itself, and half of the sugar and milk and one of the spoons were on the Persian rug. Horace began to bend down very slowly and creakily in order to retrieve the spoon, but David begged him not to worry, assuring the wizened old fellow him that he could do it. Once Horace had eventually departed, David turned his attention back to the chapel.

"I'm very interested in old houses," he began. "What's the history of this place and the chapel then?

The major was happy to launch into his favourite subject.

"Well, the house was built in 1509, the same year that Henry the Eighth became king. It was built by a chap named Edward

Winterfold, who was my great, great, great, great, great, great....well, you get the idea. He was a wealthy businessman; a cloth merchant who owned three galleons, by all accounts, and spent time in Italy, buying and selling his wares. He was a Roman Catholic. I think you had to be in those days or someone would come along and take your head off, after they'd set fire to you for a bit first and removed your guts."

David winced. "Such a forgiving religion in those days! I've just remembered why I chose to be an atheist and humanist."

"Quite! So anyway, old Edward amassed a sizeable fortune and built this house in Tutton, and also an Italianate chapel, to save him having to catch the bus into Kinver for a bit of a pray I suppose. He even installed his own Roman Catholic priest by the name of Umberto di Buonarroti Simoni. My parents always said they named me after him. I suppose in those days, it must have been a status symbol to have your own pet Italian priest on the premises."

"Yes," laughed David, as he sipped what Horace had left of his tea. "So Laz's idea isn't even original. There was an Italian at the old chapel five hundred years ago."

"Absolutely!" replied the major, nibbling a Rich Tea biscuit. "And then old Henry the Eighth decided to smash all the churches up and nick all their treasures a bit later on, the bugger! Thankfully, he didn't bother to visit Tutton on Stour because it didn't show up on his A to Z, so our little gem is still here today!"

David thanked Simon for his brief history lesson and decided it was high time he wore his private eye hat. He still had to phone the police, tidy his new office, build his Ikea shelves again and look something up in his medical book before he returned home that evening, so he needed to press on. Simon began by opening the ornate Victorian safe next to his desk. He reached down and took out a large brown, tooled leather box file, which he placed on his desk top. Inside was a pile of very

47

old, musty letters and documents tied up with a piece of string, which he carefully undid. He handed David the top document.

"These have been here for hundreds of years. There's all sorts of stuff – deeds, bills, letters and so on. Some date back to when the house was built. There are even letters with wax seals in here written by Edward Winterfold."

David was fascinated. Ever since childhood, he'd loved old documents in boxes. To him, it was like treasure.

"So what's worrying you about these?" he asked.

Simon sighed the sigh of a man who wasn't quite sure where to begin.

"Look, I know my memory is hopeless, but I remember that there was other stuff in here. Pictures I think, of hands. I keep this locked up in this safe, but the hands are missing."

David swallowed deeply. "I know exactly what you mean," he sighed, as the vision in Trev's fridge came back to haunt him. "Okay, that's one thing that's troubling you. What else?"

Simon invited David to join him for a guided tour of the house, with the major pointing out items of interest as they walked. First up was the Sargent painting of Simon's great grandfather, above the fireplace in the Green Room.

"Call me mad if you like," said Simon, ruffling up his hair, "but before Iraq, the eyes used to follow me around the room, and now they don't."

David walked around the room, viewing the painting from different angles. Eventually he concluded that, no, it didn't, but then again, he couldn't vouch for the fact that it did in the first place. The major reluctantly had to agree. The test was hardly scientific.

Next they moved to the Yellow Room, where the Constable was situated. It was a large painting hanging above a

Chippendale sideboard, depicting a country scene with a lake. In the middle distance, two cows were being chivvied along by a peasant with a stick.

"Ah! The Constable!" exclaimed David, impressed. "And you reckon there's a peasant missing, presumed eaten by this extra cow."

"Yes, I know it sounds silly, but before Iraq, I distinctly remember two peasants, and I think there was only one cow in those days."

David smiled a sad smile. "I suppose nothing was the same after Iraq was it?"

Simon tapped the Chippendale sideboard, by way of changing the subject.

"Look here! This thing always came up to exactly here on me, when I stood by it. Lord knows why I remember that when I can barely remember anything some days, but I do. *Now* look. Either I've had a growth spurt or it's shrunk, wouldn't you say?"

David knelt down and examined the legs. Not the major's legs, but the ones on the sideboard. This was mainly to make him appear thorough, rather than for any forensic reason. Besides, he couldn't really envisage a burglar breaking into a country house in order to shorten the legs of a sideboard. There would be no percentage in it whatsoever.

"Again," he concluded, as he struggled back to his feet. "Like the pictures, I never saw them pre-Iraq, so it's hard to comment. Do you mind?" David carefully lifted the Constable painting away from the wall, and with the major's help, looked at the back of it.

"Hmm! Interesting," he whispered to himself, lost in thought. "Look, I have to go now, but leave this with me. I'll do a bit of digging and get back to you. Meanwhile, if a man comes to see you in half an hour with greying curly black hair, a Frank Zappa moustache and beard combination and a biggish stomach, tell him the price has just gone up by fifty grand and try to keep your face straight."

David thanked the major for his time, the history lesson and the house tour, and promised to report back as soon as he could. He declined Horace's kind offer to see him out, explaining that he needed to get back to his studio before the following Wednesday. He was just rushing past the stables when he was intercepted by Claudia. The tall ruddy-faced, jodhpur-wearing filly was also wearing a worried frown.

"Ah, David, the very man. I wanted a discreet word, if you don't mind."

David asked her to continue, having assured her that he was the very soul of discretion, when he wasn't gossiping to everyone and anyone about anything, which was most of the time.

"It's about my brother, Simon," she continued, nervously glancing this way and that as she spoke. "As you know, apart from being his older sibling, I'm also my brother's personal assistant, and I'm very protective of him. Since he had his accident in the army, he hasn't been, well, like his old self, if you follow me. The injury to his leg was bad enough, but the head injury was the one that buggered things up. He's a lovely chap, but nowadays he's forgetful, and...how can I say this tactfully...he gets a bit mixed up. Having bloody prosopagnosia as well doesn't help. I'm sure he's mentioned that to you, unless of course he forgot, which is quite possible. Anyway, he was asking that strange smelly man who rented the unit by you - the private eye fellow - about things that were worrying him at the house. I know because he mentioned it to me. This smelly chap's probably dismissed my brother's claims as total hogwash, quite rightly, and gone on holiday, and now Simon's been talking to you as well, though heaven knows what it's got

50

to do with an art restorer, no offence! You see, this is the problem with my brother. He swears blind that you are a private investigator, and I keep telling him that you're not. I understand that you've probably come here this morning more out of embarrassment than anything else, because you didn't know how to say no, but rest assured. I would just forget all about it now, because I know he will! It's okay for you; you can walk away, but I have to listen to his deranged ramblings every day. I've lived here since I was a baby, and the blasted Constable has always had a 'two cows to one peasant' ratio as far as I can recall, not that I go around counting peasants. He thinks the old sideboard's shrunk, but it's probably just because he's had to wear special built-up heels following his accident. That old box of letters has been here forever – he was always getting them out and looking at them when we were kids. I always remember him getting a real ticking off, because he went and hacked the bottom of one old document off with a pair of scissors. Apparently, it had one of those red wax seals on it, just like a pirate's letter he said, and he took it to his prep school for the show and tell table! Father went mental, and after the hoo-ha died down, poor little Simon left a sweet little note in the box saying 'sorry daddy', which melted the old bugger's heart, God bless him, and all was okay again. I can't say I know the contents of the box intimately, but I'd be very surprised if anything was missing. No-one apart from him ever goes near the thing. And as to granddad's eyes following you around the room, I have nothing constructive to add there. That's just barking! Now, it's very kind of you to spare Simon your valuable time, David, but please, the best thing you can do is tell him everything's fine and quietly disappear, just like that smelly chap did."

"I completely understand," replied David, looking her squarely in the eye. "The misunderstanding arose because the smelly chap, as you call him - and God, you are right there – asked me to look after his place while he went to Benidorm or wherever – I shall find out when his postcard arrives – and while I was in there, pottering about, Simon arrived and mistook me for Trev, which has to be the biggest insult ever! However, I instantly forgave him because of his propaganda thing."

"Prosopagnosia."

"Exactly. His propospagnolia. So he mistook me for Trev, and reminded me that I hadn't been to see him yet, and, to be honest, I just fancied a guided tour of your lovely old house, so I turned up this morning, just to be sociable. I haven't got the least intention of following anything up, because, as you rightly say, I'm a picture restorer and artist, not a private eye, and I know smelly Trev isn't going to either because he mentioned it to me before he left, so don't worry, and I'm sorry that your poor brother is in the state he's in. It must be a nightmare for you."

"It is," sighed Claudia, "what with father dying and the bills mounting up as well. Now, if you'll excuse me, I'm very busy."

And with that, she turned on her heels and returned to her horses. David smiled a wry smile. He had just heard a phrase that always made him react that way, and having not seen an episode of 'Columbo' or 'I Spy' for absolutely ages, it was very amusing to hear it again.

With a new spring in his step, he marched back down the gravel drive towards his new studio, whistling a jaunty tune and admiring the cloudless blue sky of a perfect English Summer's day.

"And if you believe that bollocks, you'll believe anything!" he said out loud to no-one in particular.

CHAPTER 6

The Deadly Albino

David had just finished building his Ikea bookshelf for the third time when the doorbell rang. He rose unsteadily, rubbed some feeling back into his creaking knees and hobbled to the door. He opened it and was confronted by two policemen, one small and ugly, the other tall and uglier. David stood blinking in the strong sunshine, and did a double-take that Stan Laurel would have been proud of.

"Oh Jesus Christ! Oh spare me! Please tell me it's not you!" he groaned.

"Mornin' Dave," grinned the smaller one.

"Mornin' Dave," grinned the taller one. "Can we come in?"

David pushed the door open wide and silently gestured for them to follow him.

"Donald and Pongo, lovely to see you again! Are you pair the only coppers *at* Stourbridge Station, or are you just assigned to me for life?"

"Nice to see you again, Dave," said Donald, the smaller, more talkative, marginally less thick one. "I was only saying to Pongo the other day, life's dull now that we don't see our Dave any more, didn't I Pongo, and lo and behold, the old team are back again. What is it this time? Exploding mini clubman? Art forgery? Egyptian mummies terrifying the residents of Tutton? Lesbian assassins running amok in Devon? Australian Chief Superintendent from Scotland Yard stolen the Ashes from Lord's?"

David slumped into his old leather chesterfield and sighed his trademark sigh – the one he reserved for when the two dimmest policemen in the universe descended on him, ate his biscuits, drank his tea and generally made his life a misery.

"Surely you two must be coming up for retirement now?" he asked, hopefully. "Bacon sandwich, or is that considered cannibalism with you lot?"

"Thought you'd never ask, mate!" replied Pongo. "And Donald's packed in taking sugar because of his waistline, so don't go and forget will you?"

David unpacked his frying pan, and began to rummage around in his spotless new fridge for a pack of bacon. He knew there was little point in resistance, so he just got on with it. Meanwhile, Donald magnanimously filled the Turbo 900 at the sink.

"So what's the problem, Dave?" he asked. "Our receptionist said you'd found something grisly in your next-door neighbour's fridge, but you didn't want to go into detail on the phone."

David explained about Smelly Trev, and what had happened two nights previously, and he could see that the two policemen were becoming excited. A nice, juicy, human butchery job must have made a welcome change from harassing innocent motorists with speed cameras, or fining them for having half a tyre on the pavement. By the time David had mentioned the 'rapist' entry in Trev's diary, the officers were virtually salivating, unless of course it was just the smell of the bacon cooking that was getting to them.

54

This was proven to be the case, in David's mind at least, when they elected to sit and eat breakfast on David's settee, swilled down with three cups of tea each, before venturing forth to inspect the crime scene.

"So tell me more about this frozen severed hand," asked Pongo, as David was eventually requested to unlock Trev's office door.

"Well, it's a hand, and it's severed, you cretin. It's also frozen, it being in the freezer compartment of a bloody fridge."

"Yes, but is it a human hand. Are you sure?" asked Pongo.

"I don't know," sneered David, "maybe it's just a pig's hand, or a cow's hand, and our Trev was aiming to have it for his dinner. Maybe it was one of those farm hands. There are lots of them around here. Perhaps it was just five fish fingers getting together - of *course* it was a frigging human hand, what other sort are there?"

"It could have been a monkey's hand," chipped in Donald tetchily.

David stared at him in disbelief, and refused to dignify Donald's suggestion with any kind of response. The three gathered around the stained, malodorous fridge, and David invited Donald to open it.

"You open it," suggested Donald.

"No," replied David simply.

Donald tentatively pulled at the door as if he half expected the hand to leap out at him, while Pongo nestled reassuringly just behind his partner. The seal around the door was a strong one, however, and the door refused to budge. Donald pulled again, harder this time, and the door shot open, causing both officers to leap backwards in unison.

"It's not there," observed Donald.

"That's because it's in that little freezer compartment at the top," explained David, eyes heavenward.

Donald wrenched the blue door open and shone his torch inside.

"It's not there either," he confirmed, mightily relieved.

"WHAT?" yelled David. "Shift, let me see."

Donald, for once, was right. There was no severed hand.

"Right, come here!" said David, storming into the lavatory. Donald and Pongo followed, Pongo falling heavily over an old bike frame en route.

David pushed open the lavatory door and invited them to look into the bowl.

"What's THAT then?" he demanded.

Pongo volunteered this time. "It's a nice clean khasi, Dave."

David peered into the abyss. Pongo was right. There was nothing there. Frustrated now, David charged out of the cramped little store room and began throwing things around on Trev's desk. The desk diary was missing. This was all very embarrassing.

"I swear I'm telling the truth!" begged David, tearing what was left of his hair out.

"Here we go again," sighed Donald.

"Look," David ranted, pacing the room like Basil Fawlty was prone to do in times of stress, and in imminent danger of succumbing to a stroke. "I know what I saw. It wasn't a bloody trick of the light, Pongo, before you open your stupid trap. I am not mad. You pair know me, and you have to admit that, even when things didn't make sense in the past, I always ended up being right. Am I right? Am I?"

Donald put his flat cap back on his head, while Pongo collected up his things.

"See you soon, Dave," said Donald, heading for the door. "We'll leave you to lock up."

And with that, they left. David stormed back to his new studio, slamming the door behind him, and marched over to his computer, thanking the Lord that James, his young son, had found time in his busy schedule to set it up for him. He clicked the Google icon on his desktop and waited for it to open. Then he typed in the words 'white faeces' and pressed 'search'.

David sat silently absorbing the various websites that Google had found for him, sometimes making notes as he did so. Then he closed the site down, pushed back his chair and rubbed some life back into his tired forty-eight-year-old face. He couldn't for the life of him explain what had gone on in Trev's house of horrors, but one thing was for sure. Whoever had left the giant white turd in Trev's lavatory was a very sick man.

David sat at his computer table for some twenty minutes afterwards, just thinking, thinking, and thinking some more. He wasn't going mad, he knew that, and he had seen what he had seen. Someone had been into Trev's office the night before, cleaned a lavatory, removed a severed hand and a diary and disappeared into the night with them. Trev was away on holiday, or so he would have David believe. If he *wasn't* on a beach in Benidorm, then where was he? Had he been packing, ready to leave for the airport, maybe, when he suddenly realized that he'd left his favourite white turd and severed hand behind – essential for the Spanish beach holiday – and dashed back to collect them? And if it wasn't Trev, who on earth would have a reason to want to break in and do it. This last thought had suddenly opened other doors too, so to speak. Trev's lock had not been tampered with, and there were no signs of forced entry around the back either. Whoever did steal the evidence had to have a key, because the keys that Trev gave to David had never left his side since.

The more David pondered the conundrum, the more questions arose. Whose hand was it? Whose albino stool was it? Trev had a full compliment of hands, because David had seen them, shaking with delirium tremens, but the faeces could well have belonged to him. Had he not warned David that the lavatory didn't flush too well, and here was the proof. Smelly Trev did white poos, just like the dogs used to do when David was a little boy in Brierley Bank. That was down to their diet, apparently, which included bones to munch on, which provided lots of calcium, which in turn did funny things to faeces. The modern dog didn't go in for that sort of thing anymore; most of them now preferring *Penne Arrabiata* or Chicken and Rabbit *risotto* with a sprig of fresh parsley instead, if the TV ads were a true reflection. White poo in humans, however, was far more serious. It indicated that the poo's owner needed immediate medical attention. There were several causes, all potentially life-threatening, but one that had leapt out from the pages of Google and hit David in the eye was liver failure caused by excessive alcohol consumption. This one had Trev written all over it.

Then there was the little matter of the diary. Had Trev realized that he had incriminated himself by writing about his urges, and confessing that he was the rapist? He had allowed a complete stranger to take over his office, foolishly forgetting that people had a habit of being nosy, and peeking at other people's private scribblings. It was now beginning to make sense. The prime reason for returning was to dispose of the hand, naturally. Leaving it there was just damned careless. Then, as he scanned the room to double check that he hadn't done anything else stupid, he sees the diary, flicks through it, and spirits it away when he remembers what he'd written in it. Finally, he decides to take a leak before disappearing whence he came, visits the loo and sees that one of his Albino floaters is still there. Either he attacks it with a stick and flushes it away, or horror of horrors, he takes it with him.

David knew that he needed to inform the police of his suspicions. He also knew that they now wouldn't believe him. Needing some fresh air in a hurry, he grabbed his keys, locked up and sped off in his car; destination Birmingham University's Art Library. As Claudia had pointed out, he was, after all, an art restorer, and not a private investigator, and he had to earn a living.

David needed to borrow some very detailed reproductions of the Sistine Chapel roof if he was to do a good job – not the small, grubby, out of focus versions that his local library offered. He also wanted to borrow books on Constable and John Singer Sargent, just for fun.

CHAPTER 7

Nothing beats a Good Book

Laz's rags to riches story had been one worth retelling, so he often did so. In spite of a powerful intellect, he had managed to fail his Eleven Plus exam, and had subsequently been sentenced to spend his teenage years incarcerated in the hell-hole that we shall call Slag Bank Secondary Modern, by way of protecting the innocent. Here he grew his hair even longer, learnt to play rock guitar and smoked cigarettes that had a distinctive aroma and were not strictly legal. The reason for Laz failing his Eleven Plus is not on record, but if asked, he explained that the reason for doing likewise with his CSEs (Secondary School Factory Fodder Children weren't allowed to take GCEs) was that he was at the Isle of Wight Festival with a bunch of hippies and Hell's Angels at the time, and couldn't make it, man.

After school, Laz found himself a job as a car mechanic, but was hampered by the fact that he didn't know how to mend cars (though he could drive one very quickly, if required to). After suffering this filthy job for several years – just long enough to rake together the funds for a nice guitar and a dodgy Mark 2 Ford Cortina, he found himself a job on the track at British Leyland, hampered only by the fact that he didn't know how to build cars either (though he was adept at sneaking the bits out in his lunchbox and down his trouser leg, just as Johnny Cash had taught him to do, to musical accompaniment).

It was towards the end of his 'career' as a mechanic that he met David, a good-goody Grammar School boy with a satchel, a posh blazer and a clarinet case tucked under his arm. They say that opposites attract, and so it was with these two. Before long, they were playing in rock bands together and laughing themselves silly each evening in Laz's old car.

Meanwhile, Laz had left Leyland, and set up as a house clearance specialist with his Brummie business partner, Sammy Chinn, which in turn led to them being asked to supply bric-a-brac for pub chains. If someone needed a moose's head for a Beefeater restaurant in Slough, Laz or Sammy could get one. Quite how, no-one knew. The pub managers just hoped that he and Sammy weren't actually decapitating the local moose population in order to meet deadlines. Quite soon they had amassed huge stocks of junk, and were forced to move into a massive warehouse in order to store and catalogue it all. One could never ask for the wrong thing at Laz's place. There were whole rows of 1930s' football boots, top hats, fancy mirrors and sideboards, acres of Tiffany lamps and sheds full of Negro jockey figures, jockeying for position amongst the chaise longues, enamel advertising signs and old fashioned mangles. Each day, framed butterfly and moth collections with wings missing would be despatched for some pub refurbishment contract or other, along with badly-stuffed pike, trout, ferrets, pheasants and badgers in glass cases that had seen better days. Laz had more ditchwater-dull but outwardly decorative Victorian books than the British Library, more agricultural equipment than New Zealand and more old-fashioned woodwork tools than Barry Bucknell.

Then he tired of bric-a-brac and moved seamlessly into handling the refurbishment contracts himself. Laz and his partner went their separate ways; Sammy Chinn taking his flea-infested stuffed antelope heads with him. Soon Laz began to manufacture his own seating, pub and restaurant tables, bar fronts and the like – you name it and he could build it, or else

61

get some bloke in Bulgaria to do it for him. Now he was forty-eight and had a successful business, which meant he was also pretty well off - conservatively around ten times better off than David, the talented grammar school and art college boy with all the lovely academic qualifications.

Laz was in his cluttered office, poring over plans, fiddling around with fabrics and leafing through lighting catalogues when the phone rang. It was David, back from Birmingham, loaded down with heavy art books, and of all the academic books available, art books were by far the heaviest, in both senses of the word.

"Hello Laz, I've got some great reference material here for you to look at. Michelangelo's ceiling was massive compared to yours, as you're aware, so obviously we'll have to be selective. I fancy using the famous panel as your centrepiece - you know, the one they use for the South Bank Show; God and Adam, I think it was, with their hands reaching out to each other. I reckon we'll also have room for The Creation of Eve, The Expulsion from the Garden of Eden, and maybe The Flood. What do you reckon?"

"I haven't got the foggiest idea what you're on about," admitted Laz, "but as long as it's got lots of naked folks writhing about together with their willies hanging out, a few angels and a nice blue sky with rays of sunlight streaming through it, I'll be happy."

David assured him that it would be so, and hung up. He put his Michelangelo books to one side and began to idly flick through his Constable book instead. Over at the hall, if one will recall, he had asked Simon to help him lift the painting away from the wall so that he could examine the stretchers. They didn't, to David's expert eye, look quite old enough to have been on a Constable painting; nor did they look like the ones he had encountered when he had restored other Constables for the

National Gallery. This wasn't conclusive proof of anything though, which is why he'd borrowed the library book, the most comprehensive book on the works of Constable that existed. Breathless with anticipation, he checked the index for an obscure, minor painting entitled 'View of Matthew Cox's Farm, Flatford', and to his absolute delight, found that it was included, with a reproduction on page 79. David skimmed through the pages impatiently, and finally found what he was looking for.

"Well I never!" he whispered. "Well I never!" The reproduction was quite small, and the figures within the painting minute, as they were only ever intended to add a smudge of colour and a focal point to the far right field in the scene. However, with the aid of his powerful desk-mounted magnifying glass, David could tell that Simon was right. Constables 'View of Matthew Cox's Farm, Flatford' clearly showed one cow and two peasants. The painting at Edgecliff Hall was a fake. Either that or the one in the book was, and he thought that most unlikely.

David tossed the book aside and excitedly began to read the list of reproductions in the John Singer Sargent book, which proved frustrating, as the book was nearly four inches thick and weighed half a ton. Then, just as he was about to give up, he found it.

Portrait of Sir Henry Winterfold of Edgecliff Hall, South Staffordshire. Oil on canvas. 4 feet by 3 feet 6 inches. Private Collection. Circa 1894.

David found the page. It was, joy of joys, a full page reproduction this time. He set the book down against the wall and walked a few paces to the right side of it. Henry Winterfold was still looking at him, with his suspicious, beady eyes. David strode over to the left of the picture and tried again. Voila! The old curmudgeon was still giving him the once-over. Whoever had copied the painting had done a first class job, that was for sure, but he had positioned the pupils incorrectly. They were only perhaps a fraction out when compared to the original, but it had made all the difference - they no longer followed the viewer. Major Simon Winterfold may have possessed the memory of a concussed goldfish and lacked the ability to recognize his mother even if she was sat on his lap, but the man was no fool. And if he was right about two things, then the odds were with him being right about the other two. Either his sideboard had been hacked down to size out of spite by a very small burglar with a chip on his shoulder, or more likely, it too had been faked. That just left the box of old letters, and David was willing to place a substantial bet with Ladbrokes that there were some important pieces missing from that too. The only problem being, neither he nor the major knew what they were, other than some vague recollection of hands.

David's head was now in a state of turmoil. He had work to do, and a lot of it, but he'd been an artist for nearly thirty years, and consequently, he was feeling a little jaded, and not as enthused as he would have liked. On the other hand, he'd been a private eye for a few days, and it was all very thrilling and new. He desperately wanted to pursue the various lines of enquiry he'd unearthed, as he was famously impatient, but he knew in his heart of hearts that he must calm down, keep his cards close to his chest and begin work on the ceiling. Reluctantly, he cleared his drawing board and turned to the Michelangelo book, which made the Sargent book look like a pamphlet by comparison. He added yellow post-it notes to the relevant pages and lugged the book into his darkroom, testing his old hernia scar to the limit. He tentatively began to trace out small sections of the nine ceiling panels in order to see how he could interlock them, in order to create his new abbreviated version.

He'd been in the dark for no more than twenty minutes when the front doorbell rang, so he switched off his grant projector and rushed to answer the door. It was a courier with a large parcel under his arm, which he asked David to sign for. This he duly did, while commenting cheerfully on the lovely sunny day to the courier, who ignored him completely and walked back to his van.

This was strange. Not the fact that a courier had ignored him – that was quite normal. No, it was strange that a parcel, obviously containing a painting, judging by the shape, had been sent without prior warning. The many galleries he worked for always told him what was coming and when, and wanted to know the turnaround time too, well in advance. He hacked impatiently at the packaging with his Swann-Morton surgical scalpel and eventually pulled out a painting of a racehorse with a large tear in its side. Taped to the frame was a letter, which he opened. It read:

Dear Mr Day,

Please forgive my attitude the other day. I had no idea that there was a town in Wales with a similar name to the place I was staying at. With hindsight, it does seem rather cheeky to have expected you to drop everything and fly to my part of the world just to quote for restoring a painting. Sometimes, I forget how the other half live! My first wife often reminds me of this, in-between launching saucepans at me.

Ring me when you receive this, and I hope it can be invisibly repaired, as it is a favourite painting of mine. When you return it, I will lock it away in my private study to avoid a repetition of what happened, especially as I am contemplating taking on another wife quite soon, which always makes her agitated.

I am told that you are one of the finest restorers in the United Kingdom, by one of your bigger clients, Henry Tibbatts at the

National Gallery. Be assured that I will not quibble about the cost, as long as the result is good.

Oh yes, and how was Aberdovey? I hear that it is quite pleasant there in the summer, and excellent for windsurfing.

Best wishes,

Abdul Rashid

This was all very frustrating. David was, of course, grateful for the work, but it seemed to him that God was sitting up there on his cloud sending all manner of slings and arrows at him just for his own amusement. One minute there was nothing to do, and the next there was too much. He placed the Stubbs carefully against the wall and returned to his darkroom to wrestle with the Sistine Chapel ceiling for a while longer. He had been there for all of six minutes when his doorbell rang again. This time it was the alarm company, come to install his hi-tech security system. Barely able to stifle his heartfelt sigh, David let them in and returned to his dark sanctuary, to a backdrop of banging hammers, screeching electric drills and tuneless, whistled renditions of 'Gold' by Spandau Ballet. If David had had access to a service revolver, he would have been seriously tempted to end either his own life or that of the alarm company's electrician, depending on his whim at the time.

Not content with seeing one of his flock becoming deranged and suicidal, the white-bearded man on the cloud decided to throw yet another thunderbolt, this time in the guise of the local postman, who rang the doorbell, requiring the occupant to sign for a registered letter. David staggered across the office, drool dripping from the edge of his tightly clamped little mouth and his thinning hair looking madly unkempt. The postman, who was at least a cheerful soul, handed him the letter – a dreary document from David's accountant, plus an invitation to eat half-price at a Balti restaurant in Lye, a card from his local

Labour M.P. asking David to vote for him (fat chance), a misspelt leaflet from a man who was offering to chop David's trees down, and a postcard. The stressed art restorer threw them down onto his desk and was about to return to his darkroom for the umpteenth time when he remembered the postcard, and was curious to see who had sent it. On the front was a picture of the Grand Canyon with the caption, 'It's Goddamed hot here, y'all! David flipped it over, and saw that it had been sent by none other than Smelly Trev.

Trev began by explaining that he *didn't* wish David was there (amusing) because then there'd be no-one at Edgecliff Hall to look after things for him. This reminded David that, since the incident with the severed hand, he hadn't actually bothered to sort Trev's post or listen to his answering machine. Somehow, his heart hadn't been in it after that. The note continued on its semi-illiterate way, relating to David how wonderful Las Vegas was, how Trev had managed to win a bit on the one-armed bandits and how he'd nearly shit himself with fright when he took a helicopter trip into the Grand Canyon. All charming stuff, and signed by Trev at the bottom, followed by the words 'kiss kiss' which fair nearly turned David's stomach, courtesy of his notoriously vivid imagination.

As one can readily imagine, this postcard caused David's already overheated mind to self-combust. If Trev *was* in the States, as it now appeared, then who had removed his diary, his ghostly poo and his severed hand? David decided to pop next door and nose around again, just in case anything had changed in the interim. Somehow, he didn't feel particularly inclined to be Trev's little helper any more, partly because he was now too busy with his own troubles, and partly because certain health and safety issues had arisen since their agreement - namely David's health and safety. He earned a living with his hands, and was careful to always look after them. He didn't really fancy having one removed and stowed away with the Bird's Eye Cod steaks.

David left the alarm engineers to it and sneaked next door. Once inside, he made a beeline for the fridge. Nothing had been taken away or added since his last visit. Good! Next up on his whistle-stop tour was the lavatory, and again, he was pleased to report that albino stools were noticeable only by their absence. This just left the desk. A cursory glance revealed that it was as he had left it after Donald and Pongo had departed. David sat down on Trev's threadbare chair and pulled open the drawer. The ancient edition of Yellow pages was there, and the dead woodlice too. So was Trev's diary. If David was confused before, it was nothing to what he felt now. He and the Keystone Cops had looked for this diary on the desk top, and it wasn't there. They had not bothered to look in the drawer, because David had never put it in the drawer. He knew he hadn't.

Or had he? Did this explain why they didn't find it?

David snatched the diary from the drawer and turned to the page where Trev had talked about his urges. Then he flicked to the part where he admitted to being the rapist, and David suddenly had an awful thought. Was the severed hand a trophy? Had Trev killed a previous victim and removed a part of her to keep? He quickly turned over several more pages and was met by a new entry. This was strange. The pages after Trev's dramatic confession had been blank. David remembered that because he'd looked when he first discovered the diary, hoping to find more gory details. There weren't any. Only now, there were.

The entry for Friday 5th June - the day Trev handed over the keys to David, now stated, in Trev's own hand:

This cannot go on. I am unable to fight these urges to attack women. It is only a matter of time before I am apprehended, and the thought of life in jail is too much to bear. This is my full and frank confession. I am the Tutton Common rapist. I cannot live with what I have done to this latest woman, and many others before her, so I have no choice. I intend to commit suicide, and to whoever reads this, may I say that I am truly sorry.

Trevor Jenkinson

"Curiouser and curiouser!" thought David. He was now unsure whether he'd absent-mindedly placed the diary in the drawer after he first read it, but still *totally* convinced that the rest of the book had been empty, other than a few mundane appointments with garages, dentists and the like. Had he turned two pages at a time, perhaps, and missed it? It was possible of course. The entry had been written on the day Trev was leaving work to go on holiday, which made sense. He was riddled with guilt, and just pretending to go away for a break, when in fact he was leaving forever and planning to end it all. Was he having one last fling at the tables in Vegas first, perhaps? Did he intend to fly halfway into the Grand Canyon and fling himself out of the chopper? David shuddered at the thought.

But something wasn't quite right. Something small and vague and ill-defined was wriggling around in the back of David's brain. It was the same small, annoying, ill-defined wriggly thing that told him not to write off Major Simon as a shell-shocked time-waster, and on that occasion, the vague wriggly thing had been spot-on.

David replaced the diary and locked up. He walked back into his own office to find the electrician still whistling snatches of Spandau Ballet's 'Gold', though thankfully his was, by the very nature of whistling, just an instrumental version. He'd got to the bit where Tony Hadley had bought a ticket to the world, but now he'd come back again and was about to demand that the truth be told, when another, even more irritating sound interrupted him. It was David's doorbell again.

69

By now, David had abandoned all hope of beginning Laz's job, and had resigned himself to trying again first thing the following morning. He opened the front door and found himself eye to eye with Major Simon Winterfold. He was clutching a wad of bright yellow A5 sized cards in his hand.

"Ah, good afternoon!" he smiled, "We haven't met I don't think, but I'm Major Winterfold, the owner of the estate, and we're planning a little informal get-together next Saturday, over at the hall, to officially welcome the businesses that have rented our mews units. I wondered if you'd like to come!"

He handed David one of the invites.

"Er, yes, thanks," replied David, "I'd love to."

"Great!" said the major, turning to go, "and if you see that nice chap from the private investigations firm next door, ask him along, would you? I just knocked the door but he wasn't in."

David gently closed the door and then gently closed his eyes, as if he were trying to block out the world. The electrician began to whistle Spandau Ballet's 'True', by way of a change, which was the last straw as far as David was concerned. There was only one thing that he could possibly do now, after the day he'd had.

He filled the Turbo 900 and switched it on.

CHAPTER 8

Enemies Reunited

David decided, after much soul searching, to begin the Stubbs renovation first, so that he wouldn't have to break off halfway through his giant Michelangelo project. This way it would be out of his hair, allowing him to concentrate on Laz's job without artistic distractions – he couldn't really do much about the other sort. That said, by David's current standards, it was a quiet week. No-one had left messages on Trev's phone, his post was all junk, and no-one had restocked his rancid fridge with limbs. There were no more ghostly additions to his diary, and no new albinos down the loo. Major Simon stayed away, and so did his sister. The alarm was now fitted and functional; Laz had been pacified and had reluctantly accepted the slight delay with the ceiling artwork. David was putting in a good solid eight hour shift and then going home to his wife and kids like a proper dad should. He was earning good money from a wealthy racehorse owner, and he was quite enjoying restoring the man's wealthy racehorse. With a supreme mental effort, David had purposely blocked out all the things that were deeply troubling him, and was getting on with the day-to-day stuff. Meanwhile, in the deep recesses of his mind, ideas and theories were bubbling and percolating. Muddy, unclear thoughts were being purified and filtered, ready for David's day of action.

The Stubbs looked perfect, though David said so himself. He had removed the surrounding varnish, micro-stitched and glued the torn canvas and repainted the affected area, before finally cleaning and re-varnishing the entire picture. He'd asked Laz to guess where the tear had been, and Laz couldn't tell - it was that good. It had to be when the bill was well over five thousand pounds, plus shipping. David would allow the varnish to dry properly and send the painting off the following week. Abdul, he felt sure, would be ecstatic. He might even throw in a sizeable tip. These Arabs were nothing if not generous.

It was now Friday, meaning that David could take a well-earned break over the weekend, always more satisfying after a good, productive week's work. Monday was the day he planned to begin work on Laz's job. It also meant the return of Trev, and David couldn't wait to welcome him back, if indeed the man planned to come back, or was even still alive. David had transferred Trev's incriminating diary to his own, locked drawer for safe keeping and had a few questions to ask the errant detective, preferably in the company of two of Her Majesty's dim but loyal servants, just in case things got rough. There were still a few things that just didn't add up though, and David's solution was to take a long walk before he headed home. He found that the exercise stimulated his mind – got the little endorphins working, whatever they were – and often, the solutions to difficult problems would just pop into his head as a result.

To this end, he decided to set off along the gravel path that skirted the hall and the two carp lakes, and eventually led to the first of several fields full of sheep, known by the locals, logically enough, as the Sheep Walks. He could wander over the vales and hills, lonely as a cloud, looking at hosts of daffodils, just as William Wordsworth presumably once did, and hopefully be inspired as a result. As David reached the summit, he began to realize what Maria Von Trapp must have seen in hill walking. The ground beneath him was a carpet of wild flowers and all around him the sheep gaily trotted about, bleating in a strangulated way as sheep are wont to do when a stranger comes amongst them. The view from the top of the Sheep Walks was panoramic; a three hundred and sixty degree affair that had it all. Country estates, mirror lakes, lonely farm houses, flora and fauna in abundance, a patchwork quilt of faraway fields and....a circle of grubby-looking caravans. This was a new feature, and not a particularly attractive one. The field at the bottom of the hill on the opposite side to the Edgecliff Hall estate looked as if its five-barred gate had been smashed down and discarded in the country lane, and its young crop churned up with ugly tyre tracks, courtesy of several rusting Range Rovers. If Wordsworth had come across this scene of devastation on his travels and recorded it as he saw it, mused David, that poem about daffodils wouldn't have sold a single copy. He strode down the hill, carefully avoiding sheep droppings the way a soldier avoids landmines, until he was at the bottom, with only a small country lane between him and the travellers.

He hid behind a large, ivy-clad tree and observed for a while, picking up a large, gnarled old branch that some previous walker had obviously used as a walking stick and later discarded. It wasn't long before his worst fears were realized. Talking to a pair of rough-looking women, both sporting black, scraped-back hairdos and giant hoop earrings, was none other than Johnny O'Driscoll, the travelling equivalent of Blackbeard the pirate. The effect that unexpectedly spotting O'Driscoll had on David was akin to being zapped in the privates without warning by an electric fence. If anything, it was worse. Johnny was older looking now, and his black, curly hair had turned a little grey, but David knew immediately who it was, and it filled him with a nameless fear. The two men had briefly met before in very trying circumstances, well before Laz's unfortunate 'Aeroplane Food' encounter, and David wasn't keen on ever meeting the man again.

Many years previously, when David had just left Wolverhampton College of Art, he had been offered a part-time job at Tutton's incredibly dull 'Museum of Local Life', helping to spruce up the dowdy exhibits in the vain hope that the public would one day actually choose to patronize the God-forsaken place. In fact, it was entirely down to David that the museum was eventually turned around and made to pay, thanks to him accidentally discovering an ancient Egyptian burial chamber beneath the museum's cellars, unlikely as that would sound if one were not fully cognizant of the facts.

During David's stay at the museum, a caravan belonging to the museum's proprietor was brazenly stolen by O'Driscoll and his gang of cut-throats, only to be stolen back by David at a motorway services on the M5. Somehow, David couldn't imagine that Johnny was the 'forgive and forget' type, so he intended to remain behind the old tree, clutching his gnarled stick and breathing only once every two minutes.

Even more worrying, the gang had a deserved reputation for ransacking stately homes. Indeed, several of Johnny's cronies had served prison sentences for the infamous country estate raids of the eighties, though Johnny himself, slippery as an eel, had so far escaped justice. Members of the gang would get inside information about the comings and goings of the house owners, usually from petrified domestic staff. When no-one was home, they would charge into the estate with fleets of old Range Rovers and strip the places of their treasures in minutes, just as they had stripped Laz's aeroplane. Paintings were stolen to order for unscrupulous collectors, as were statues, silverware, and anything else that wasn't bolted down. Even if it was, it stood little chance. Anyone returning home unexpectedly was beaten to a pulp, just to add injury to insult, and loyal dogs that barked found themselves picking shotgun pellets out of their backsides for their trouble. In short, a charming bunch of folks who gave the honest gypsies of the land a bad name, as usual. Irritatingly, everyone seemed to know who was responsible for the burglaries, but the hard evidence could not be found, and, surprise surprise, witnesses rarely volunteered information for fear of vicious reprisal. Raids on Johnny's various ramshackle sites turned up absolutely nothing – not so much as an incriminating monogrammed silver spoon in the cutlery drawer. And then the police had a breakthrough. They discovered a secret hangar, packed to the ceiling with treasure. Heirlooms were reunited with their overjoyed owners and a few of the gang received their just desserts. The country estate raids ceased, and everything went quiet for a while. Now it looked as if things were hotting up again, but maybe old Johnny, the cunning fox, was handling things differently nowadays, and certainly more ingeniously, if the faked paintings were his doing.

David turned on his heels and ran up the bank as fast as he could manage, squidging into dollop after dollop of revolting sheep poo as he did so. He forfeited his Maria Von Trapp moment at the summit in favour of the relative safety of Edgecliff Hall, arriving at the old tied cottages minutes later, breathless and with a nasty stitch in his side – something he hadn't experienced since school. He paused outside the first of the tiny cottages for a breather, laying his trusty walking stick against the wall beside him.

"How do!" said a voice.

David swung around to see a rustic gent leaning against his front door, chewing a straw. He was wearing a cow gown, jeans and wellies, and this stylish ensemble was topped off by a tatty straw hat. The man's features were virtually hidden by the biggest ginger beard David had ever seen. It looked as if it had been fashioned from shredded wheat and dyed with carrot juice.

"How do you do!" replied David, still out of breath. "David. David Day. You work here?"

"Ar!" said the man. Ginger. Ginger Tom they calls me. Oi does ard jarbs an' stuff. You?"

"Oh, I rent one of the mews offices just down there," explained David, perplexed as to why a local farmhand would speak as if he originated from Somerset. He had encountered this phenomenon before, when he briefly worked at Stanmore Castle, copying the owner's Monet painting for what David was wrongly led to believe were insurance purposes. The castle's odd-job man, Jethro, possessed an identical country bumpkin accent, even though he was born in Stourbridge, leading David to theorize that all farmers were specifically taught the dialect at agricultural college.

"Ah well," said the rustic gentleman, stretching, "Can't stop here chattin' all day can we? I gotta feed the cows."

He picked up a bucket so David picked up his stick, waved goodbye and continued his walk back to the mews car park. Then David heard a familiar sound that stopped him in his tracks. It was just a hint of a sound really, carried on the breeze, but it was enough to make him ponder. For fully one minute, he just stood there, his over-active mind whirring. He looked back at the rustic gentleman, who was still fiddling with his bucket. David scratched his chin and stared at the floor for another minute, and then he walked through the rustic man's old gate and up his tiny front garden's path.

"Evening, Trev," said David, holding on tightly to his gnarled stick for security reasons.

The rustic glanced up and said "Sorry, moi friend?"

"Hello Trev," repeated David, with a half-smile. Unless he was very much mistaken, rustic farm-hands didn't randomly shout 'KUT' as a rule, though of course, it was theoretically possible.

"You'd better come in," sighed Trev.

David was sat at Trev's old pine kitchen table, still holding onto his stick.

"I think you have a lot of explaining to do," he said, sipping his tea.

"I reckon I have," smiled Trev, "but this has to be highly confidential, right?

David gave his word, such as it was.

"Right," said Trev, followed by a subdued KUT and twitch combination, which seemed to upset him more than it had when the two had first met. "Look, I'm working undercover for the major. He suspects that something fishy is happening at the hall – that's all I can say at the moment. I told you I was going on holiday as part of my plan, so everyone would presume I was elsewhere, leaving me to dig around."

Trev's beer breath wafted across the table, causing David to turn his head away.

"This undercover work, it wouldn't involve paintings, sideboards and boxes of documents, would it? Or maybe rapists around the estate?"

David eyed Trev's twitchy face, looking for a reaction to the word rapist. None came.

"How did you know all that?"

"The major has prognosis, or whatever it's bloody well called. He can't remember faces to save his life. After he'd asked you, he called round to your office while I was tidying up – and it needed tidying up – and he thought I was your assistant and you were on holiday, so then he asked me as well."

"Bugger me!"

"Exactly."

"So naturally you told 'im you was an art restorer, not a private eye."

"Er, not quite. Look, I was bored and I fancied a nose around, thinking I could report back to you when you got back from Las Vegas, har har har! Only I knew you hadn't gone there."

Trev looked hurt. At least David thought he did. It was hard to tell through the preposterous ginger fuzz.

"No post card would arrive that quick," explained David, so whoever you got to send it for you sent it too bloody soon. The date was all wrong as well. Not very thorough was it?"

"That's my cousin for you," moaned Trev, removing the offending beard. "He's an idiot. I posted him that card and asked him to send it on the.... Look never mind. So what happened when you became a bloody detective for the day, Sherlock?"

"Never mind that as well," snapped David. "What's a human hand doing in your fridge, you psycho?"

"Oh shit!" said Trev, holding his brow in his hands.

"Yeah, shit. I called the police, you know that? I had you figured for a right nutter until I read the frigging paper this morning. 'Edgecliff Hall Farm Worker Fitted With Prosthetic Hand'. Derek Evans open brackets, 37, close brackets lost his hand in a combine harvester accident but doctors were unable to reattach it because they couldn't find the bugger. That's me paraphrasing."

"Oops!"

"Oops indeed. That, I presume, was because you'd got it."

Trev seemed to be wrestling with some inner demon. He twitched, let out a quick KUT that had been brewing up and tried his best to explain.

"Look, I was pissed up, taking the shortcut back to the office across the fields from the Fox pub. Least, I think it was a short cut. I never really know when I'm pissed. Anyway, I'd heard about the accident, 'cause everybody in the pub was on about how it had just happened. The air ambulance had already taken the bloke away when I got there so there was nothin' to see. They'd obviously searched high and low for his hand and come up with nothin', and time was of the essence, so they buggered off to Russell's Hall Hospital sharpish. So meanwhile, I'm staggerin' across this field, and I sees this mitt just lyin' there under a bush - the harvester must have flung it yards – so I pick it up and run back to bung it in the freezer, 'cause that's what you're supposed to do to preserve it, only being pissed, I forgot after that and left it there. The trouble is, they have this window of opportunity, as they call it, for sewing stuff back on, and I'd exceeded their sell-by date by two days. I meant to get rid of it before I went undercover, but I forgot. It must have been a nasty shock for you, Dave!"

"Not at all! Me and Suzanne keep transplant hearts and allsorts in ours - yes of course it was, you bloody imbecile! I nearly shit myself. I bet poor old Derek Evans open brackets, 37, close brackets is overjoyed about it as well, wouldn't you say?"

Trev pondered this as he slurped his tea. "What he doesn't know won't hurt him, I say."

"And then there's your diary. The diary full of horrible confessions that seems to disappear and then mysteriously materialize like the bloody Tardis."

"WHAT?"

"You know."

"I haven't got a bloody clue what you're on about, mate!"

David looked heavenwards and snorted air through his nose, like an irate bull. "So you didn't sneak back into your office and take it, write an even fuller confession in it, threatening to commit suicide, and then replace it?"

"What? What are fuck are you on about, confession to what? Look, I suddenly realized that the hand was still in the fridge, and I didn't want you passing out with fright, so I popped back and removed it, but there's nothin' in my diary I didn't want you to see."

"Ah, right, nothing except an admission that you tried to rape that farm girl recently."

Trev just gawped incredulously at David now, like a startled mackerel. Either he was an incredibly good actor - and if his country yokel was anything to go by, he wasn't - or he genuinely didn't have the foggiest idea what David was talking about. David found himself giving Trev the benefit of the doubt, and took a deep, steadying breath.

"So, let's get this straight. You didn't write about having urges you couldn't control then."

"Well yes, I did. I have this nervous thing; a bit like Tourettes Syndrome. You might have noticed."

"Er, yes, a bit, sort of."

"I have this incredible urge sometimes that I find it hard to control. It upsets me, so I drink a lot, and that calms me down. I might have been a bit upset and got it off my chest maybe, by writing it in the diary."

David weighed this. "Well, okay, fair enough. It must be difficult, but what about the page with bright red ink scrawled across it saying I AM THE RAPIST. How do you explain that?"

Trev looked nonplussed. "Well, I can't. I never wrote anything like that, mate."

"Oh yes you did," growled David. He snatched a biro from Trev's table, and wrote down what he'd seen in the diary on the corner of Trev's copy of the News of the World. "Like this!"

Trev studied it silently, scratching his black, greasy hair. Then, slowly, a huge grin spread across his face.

"David, mate, that's just my crap writing. It was meant to be '1a.m. Therapist'. It was my appointment with the speech therapist."

David snatched the newspaper from him and glared at it, flushing red with embarrassment. After taking a few moments to compose himself, he spoke.

"But, but no-one goes to see a therapist at one in the morning. Explain that then, if you can."

"Oh, right. I always get my a.m.s and my p.m.s mixed up, that's all. I meant lunchtime. Sorry."

David was now deep in thought again. After another considerable silence, he flashed Trev a concerned look.

"I wasn't sure about this, but now I am. At first, I wasn't absolutely certain if the diary had been taken by someone and then put back in the drawer instead of on the desk top where I left it, or if I'd just put it away in your drawer myself and forgotten that I'd done so. When I looked the second time, after I believed it to have been borrowed, there was a new entry in it that I hadn't noticed before. Again, I thought maybe I'd just missed it the first time, but as I say, now I'm sure I didn't. Something just wasn't right about it. The handwriting was just like yours, but the words weren't."

Trev was confused. "What did it say? Why would anyone else write in my diary?"

"That's what bugged me to start with," David replied. "You see, when I thought you were the Tutton rapist, after reading

81

your 'Therapist' entry, the new entry made sense, even though I was suspicious about the style. No offence, but your spelling's crap, and this new entry's spelling wasn't. However, now that I realize that you are clearly not the rapist, I'm puzzled as to why you would then confess to it later on in the diary, and threaten suicide."

"WHAT?"

"Suicide. It's a full confession. So if you didn't write it, who did?"

Trev was beginning to understand the full implications of this ghost writer's handiwork.

"I'm being fitted up."

David nodded gravely. "It certainly seems like it. Whoever broke into your place was almost certainly the real rapist. Lord knows what he was looking for. Maybe he suspected that you were on to him and he was looking through your stuff to see if you had anything on him. Who can say? If you'd been hired by Major Simon to investigate all the goings-on around this hell-hole, and he *knew* you had, it makes sense to check you out – see what you know; case the joint, as Phillip Marlowe would say. Imagine his delight when he reads your diary and sees entries about urges you can't control, and a page screaming 'I AM THE RAPIST in red ink. It's like Christmas has arrived early. All he has to do is borrow the book and add the final entry, the one that really stitches you up, and announces your imminent death. Neat, eh?"

Trev nodded. He knew where this was going. "So to finish things off nicely," he said thoughtfully, abandoning his luke-warm tea in favour of a fortifying can of lager, "he has to finish *me* off nicely. He's then off the hook, and I'm not only blamed for being the rapist, but I'm also dead. Marvellous!"

"And if he attempts to bump you off, he has to do it first thing Monday morning when you get back to work from your break. Think about it. He's set you up by means of your diary. If he doesn't do you in right away, he's giving you time to skim through it, find the bogus page, destroy it and then be watching your back, right? So if he makes a move it has to be Monday first thing."

"Great!" grunted Trev, polishing off his can. "Why me? What have I done to deserve this?"

"Well, this is pure guesswork of course, but I reckon he knows you're snooping around, and maybe feels the noose is tightening."

"Well he's wrong about the noose tightening," replied Trev. "The major has asked me to investigate several things that have been going on around here, but it's early days, and there ain't much to report yet. As far as I can see, the thefts - old farm vehicles and lead from the roofs mainly - well, I reckon we can both guess who's responsible for that, can't we? Now I know that O'Driscoll's lot are here, I'll concentrate on that angle. As to his paintings and his sideboard and stuff, well, he's obviously lost the plot, poor sod. How can I take any of that seriously? I *was* asked to do some digging into this rapist case, because the major doesn't like to think some nutter is prowling around on his estate. He has quite a few women working here, so he's worried. This bloke's struck several times, usually picking on young women rambling over the Sheep Walks or in quiet country lanes, all within a mile or so of here, but so far I haven't had chance to do anything, apart from take loads of covert photos of any dodgy-looking liaisons I see. So no, I'm not ready to reveal who the bastard is in the oak panelled bloody library, like Hercule Poirot always does."

"Ah yes," said David, wagging his finger, "but this rapist chap doesn't *know* that you're clueless. He spots the private eye snooping around, maybe even hears some gossip about it in the local pub, and he's worried the net's closing in so he plans to get rid of you and set you up for the assaults as well. And you do fit the bill, if you don't mind me saying so. You look a bit, well, grubby and unshaven and you drink too much. No offence."

"Cheers, grunted Trev. "Lots taken."

After listening to Trev's analysis, David quickly came to the conclusion that he was much further down the line than the sozzled private investigator was. By the sound of it, so far all *he'd* done was take photographs of everyone that lived or worked within a five mile radius of the hall. Either that or the bugger was being cagey. David, consequently, thought it only fair to share what he'd learnt, for the greater good, even if Trev wasn't doing likewise. He told Trev about his visit to the hall, his subsequent trip to the library, and the discovery that the major was actually correct about his paintings subtly changing. Trev was greatly impressed, even offering David an instant partnership deal, which David politely refused. He was happy, he explained, for Trev to get all the credit, so long as justice was done.

It was obvious to the meanest intelligence, and Trev *was* the meanest intelligence, that these works of art were copied so that the originals could be removed. Each painting was worth a small fortune, and so was the Chippendale sideboard, so the subterfuge was worthwhile, if mightily difficult to achieve. In fact, there weren't many artists capable of such quality forgery, David being one of them. In his career, he had encountered a few others; Bert Jolliffe springing to mind, but he was long gone, and also Harry Millichip, current whereabouts unknown, but a good bet was Winson Green Prison.

Whoever was doing this, argued David, had to have inside knowledge. It took a long time to source an old stretcher and canvas of the right period, copy a picture, age it and then varnish it. It took even longer to make a fake Chippendale sideboard. Surely, those who lived at the house would notice the gap in the wall decoration and the tell-tale rectangular faded section of wallpaper. And surely, if the sideboard where the cutlery was kept simply vanished one day, eyebrows would be raised.

Major Simon had been away for long periods of time, getting his limbs blown off in Iraq for his pains, so this could have happened during his absence. His sister had remained at the house though. Maybe it was time for Trev or David to have a little chat with her. However, before that could be arranged, the two had to formulate a plan of action for Monday morning. This they duly did, and finally David stood up to go.

"Look after yourself, Trev," he said, shaking his co-conspirator's hand. "Watch your back."

"Don't worry about me, I'm invincible!" smiled Trev.

David paused for a moment, his body language suggesting that he was about to broach an awkward subject. "Er, look, Trev, there's something else. I was in your lavatory."

"And?"

"I know about the white turds."

"Eh? Are they a band or something?"

David shook his head sadly. "Come on, you know what I'm on about."

Trev frowned. "No, I don't, no."

"You do. You do white turds, and I've looked it up on Google. Now that's a sentence I never thought I'd have to say. Listen, the truth is, you're not just in danger from the rapist. You have a serious health problem too. White shit means that you probably have cirrhosis of the liver caused through drinking too much. You need urgent medical help. I don't know how to tell you this, but it can be fatal."

Trev looked David in the eye. "Dave, come with me please. I want you to see something."

David followed Trev through the tiny kitchen and upstairs to the bathroom.

"Can you stay there please?" Trev asked him, before going into the bathroom and locking the door behind him. David stood on the landing waiting impatiently for Trev to re-emerge. Meanwhile, behind the closed door, he could hear sounds that he had no desire to hear. Finally, the door opened again, and Trev invited David inside. Against his better judgement, David accepted. The nick-name Smelly Trev had always been well deserved, but never more so than now. It was all that David could do to stop himself gagging.

"Look down there," Trev ordered him.

David winced, but bravely did so.

"Wow!" he observed, acid tears welling in his eyes. "I'm so pleased for you, really! It's the most beautiful, Burnt Sienna colour. That's fantastic!"

CHAPTER 9

The Sting

It was eight-thirty, Monday morning and David was already in his office, peering through a slit in the blinds. The car park was empty. He was just wondering if he'd given up valuable sleeping time for no good reason when a blue Jaguar saloon car glided onto the car park and hid itself under the huge spreading chestnut tree at the far end. The driver pulled a grey fedora hat down low across his face and began to read, or at least pretend to read, the Daily Mail.

David gulped audibly, finished his much-needed tea and strode out of his studio and across the car park in the direction of the Jag. He tapped the driver's window. Nothing happened. He tapped it again, and this time it lowered. The man, who looked more sheepish than a Sheep Walks' sheep, looked up slowly. He was slightly chubby and around fifty years old, with piercing, steely blue eyes, a greying goatee beard and frameless spectacles.

"Hello there!" said David, smiling a sickly smile. He felt like a swan, all graceful above the water line but paddling furiously below it, only with David, he wasn't so much paddling as clenching his anal sphincter to avoid accidents.

"What do you want?" asked the man sharply.

"Sorry to bother you," David continued, "but you're the graphologist chap from the end but one unit, aren't you? I know it's a cheek, but could you just take a peek at my handwriting and tell me what you can glean from it? I'll gladly pay you. I find it fascinating!"

"You'll have to excuse me," the man growled, "I'm very busy."

There was that sentence again. That was twice David had heard it in the space of a week.

"Oh, go on, please!" he begged. "It'll only take you a second. I'll bung you twenty quid. Thirty quid then. Go on! If you're waiting for the bloke next door, he never arrives till after nine. Was it him you were after?"

"Erm, no, it wasn't. Very quickly then. Five minutes is all I have."

David accompanied the man to the studio, opened the door and ushered him in.

"Tea?"

"No thank you. Can we get on with this please?"

"Absolutely! Have that seat there, behind my desk if you like. Here, take a look at this."

David slid Trev's diary across the table. It was open at the confessional page.

"What do you make of it then? The deep downward strokes on the R show a need to exert power over women, I'm told. Note the flamboyant curl of the A, and the slightly shaky P. And that's a sign of egotism isn't it, that circle over the I? Check out that wiggly S - that's a sign of sexual frustration I think, and that T...."

Throughout David's ramble, the graphologist had slowly turned incandescent with rage, and was now burning laser holes in David's face with his cold blue eyes.

"What are you talking about?" he snarled.

"You know full well," said David, with an eerie calm to his voice now. "You wrote this to pin the blame on Trevor Jenkinson for the rapes and attempted rapes that you have perpetrated…"

"Shut your mouth now, or I will shut it for you," interrupted the graphologist. He reached into his pocket and pulled out a craft knife with a lethal-looking blade – the kind of blade that would have made a real mess of Trevor's wrists, once the chloroform had done its work. "I don't know how you worked that out, but it won't do you any good now."

He rose to his feet suddenly, causing a terrified David to lurch backwards in his chair, overturning it. David's head hit the quarry-tiled floor with a bang, and he saw stars. Then, as he looked up at his attacker, a strange thing happened. David's nasty bump on the head must have caused instant delirium, because a horse had suddenly appeared in mid-air behind the graphologist's head, and, bizarrely, it was galloping sideways towards David at high speed. Then the graphologist seemed to somehow disappear inside the horse, before the horse, in turn, disappeared and the graphologist emerged again, looking confused. This look of confusion was short-lived, however, because a split second later, the man appeared to be fast asleep with a Debenham's Turbo 900 kettle on his head.

The next minute or so was a blur, but eventually David was aware of Trev helping him to his feet, and also of a collapsed man wearing a Stubbs painting around his shoulders, lying in a puddle of water next to a busted kettle.

"Oh bloody hell no!" wailed David, as soon as the mists had cleared. "Not the Stubbs. Please not the Stubbs!"

Trev took this as no more than a touch of insanity caused by the crack on the head. He turned his attention to the comatose graphologist now.

"Take that yer bastard! I got it all on my Dictaphone so you're dead meat, buster!" he yelled, his adrenalin still pumping.

"I didn't know you used your Dictaphone," groaned David, rubbing the back of his head. "Personally, I just use my finger. Okay, it's an old joke but I'm probably concussed. You can't expect too much."

Trev knelt down, removed the deadly blade and began to wrap his victim up in gaffer tape. For some reason, David was reminded of a spider wrapping up a lunchtime fly in his web. The whole thing was quite surreal. Once the man was secured, Trev searched his pockets. He removed what he identified as a skeleton key, which explained how the man was able to get into Trev's office so easily. Trev handed it to David and asked him to look after it carefully.

"Dave, you're wasted as an artist, man," he grinned, still high as a kite. "You should have been a detective. Your instinct was spot-on. Now we need to phone Plod right away."

But David wasn't paying attention any more. He was staring blankly at a ruined Stubbs original that was due back in Saudi in a week or so. No-one could repair it anymore. It was totalled. Yesterday it was worth millions. Now it was worth about as much as a rancid horse-burger from a Parisian street vendor, and that was only because the frame was still intact.

"Why'd you have to whack him with the Stubbs, Trev?" David croaked, his voice barely audible. "The kettle would have sufficed, and I bloody hated that kettle."

Trev patiently explained that he was calmly observing and recording proceedings through the darkroom keyhole when the graphologist suddenly pulled the craft knife, giving him a split second to act. The Stubbs, he continued, was the first thing he could lay his hands on, and the kettle the second, so it was rather churlish of David to criticize Trev's choice of blunt instrument after he had been good enough to save David's life. Put like this, David could hardly continue to whinge about it. Instead, to take his mind off the ruined painting, he phoned Stourbridge police and asked to be put through to either Donald or Pongo. Luckily, Donald was intercepted just as he was about to leave the station, and seconds later he was on the other end of the line.

"Donald," said David, his voice tremulous with nerves, "you need to get down here straight away. Trevor Jenkinson, the private investigator and I have caught the Tutton rapist. We've got him tied up here, and he's coming round as we speak."

"David, you're at it again," sighed Donald. "Is this another of your cock and bull stories? We can't just drop everything to dash over you know. Look at last time. We could have done you for wasting police time if we were that way inclined. Severed hands, secret diaries, white turds – I don't know how you think of it all, I really don't. Now you say you've got the rapist, and when me and Pongo get there, you'll probably tell us we've just missed him, on account of he's just popped out to get twenty Benson and Hedges. Have you ever heard the story about the boy who cried 'woof'?

"It's wolf, not woof, you cretin."

"Well that doesn't make sense. It's a story about a big dog that terrorizes the sheep, surely."

"It was a bloody wolf. Have you never actually read a book? Look, never mind that; we have this bloke here, and you need to get your ass down here now, or all hell could break loose."

Donald said that he would round up Pongo, who was in the canteen, and drive down with the blue lights flashing, but warned that this had better be the truth. He also tersely reminded David that kidnapping innocent people and tying them up constituted a long jail sentence, before putting the phone down.

The graphologist was indeed returning to the land of the living, albeit slowly. He seemed disorientated, as anyone who'd been attacked with a Stubbs oil painting and a Debenham's Turbo 900 kettle in quick succession would have been. The studio phone rang, causing David to leap at least three feet in the air. He grabbed the receiver on the way down. It was Laz, asking him for a progress report on the ceiling painting.

"I'll phone you back in ten minutes," promised David, still all of a shake. "I've got a graphologist tied up in my studio and he's waking up."

There followed a lengthy silence.

"David," asked Laz, eventually. "Are you a sexual deviant?"

"No," David assured him, "but he is. I'll ring you back. Bye!"

"Help! Help! Help me!" screamed the graphologist suddenly. He seemed to be in a state of severe shock, and was becoming hysterical. Trev bent down and slapped him hard across the face, not so much in an attempt to bring him to his senses, but more so as to hurt him again. This seemed to do the trick, and the man sat silently, staring at the wall after that. Minutes later, the wail of the police siren rent the air, signalling that Donald and Pongo had arrived. Pongo, who had been interrupted halfway through his breakfast, ran towards the studio front door looking flustered and holding a paper plate with half a sausage sandwich on it.

David and Trev met them at the door, closing it on their captive to drown his protests, and gave the officers their version of events. Trev handed over the Dictaphone as vital evidence, along with the craft knife (for fingerprinting purposes) and the diary. Seconds later, the graphologist, or Bernard Such, as he was also known, was roughly manhandled into the police car, with Pongo making sure that he accidentally whacked his prisoner's head on the rear door frame as he did so.

When all the fuss had died down and the police had gone, the two men returned to David's office to calm down over a nice cup of tea. At least, that was their intention, but unfortunately, the kettle was no longer capable of performing the solitary task that it was designed for. Trev suggested a celebratory beer instead, but David, who never touched alcohol before the sun had gone over the yardarm (whatever that was) declined. As one of those private eyes who favoured a more flexible approach vis-à-vis yardarms, Trev popped next door and grabbed a couple of cans.

"I can't wait to ring the major and tell him that I've ticked off one of the main items on his hit list," he grinned, slurping noisily and burping occasionally in David's direction.

"*We've* ticked off," David corrected, "and you should ring Donald and Pongo while you're at it, and get them to check that bloke's shit. Tell Donald to go through it with a fine-toothed shit comb. If it isn't white, I'll eat my hat. There was one snuggled up in your disgusting khasi and I naturally presumed it belonged to you. He must have got in, nicked the diary and nature called. I've heard burglars often experience an overwhelming urge to defecate during burglaries. It's a well-known syndrome. Trouble was, he didn't know your flusher was knackered, so he must have popped back at some later stage, to write that bogus entry I suppose, nicked off to use the loo again, seen his previous effort staring up at him and retrieved it. Nice job!"

"If what you say is right about the state of his turds, he's got more than just a long jail sentence to worry about. It's made me think about cutting down, I can tell you!"

"Yeah!" replied David. "I can see you've already started. It's me that should be getting drunk anyway, to ease my pain. Do you know what that horse painting was worth? I use the past tense advisedly."

Trev took at stab at it. "Two hundred and fifty quid?"

David shook his head. "Try several million. That's a bit nearer."

Trev sprayed lager across the floor. "WHAT?"

"You heard me. I restore famous paintings quite often. Monets, Constables, you name it. That one belongs to a rich Arab who's expecting it back anytime soon. It had a small tear, which I repaired beautifully. Now it has a graphologist-sized hole in it. I'm finished. Career over. Hand me the service revolver, razor blade and paracetamol."

Trev was beginning to realize what he'd done, and was feeling terrible about it.

"Could you get it copied, maybe?" he asked, a trifle naïvely.

David composed himself and tried to explain. Art wasn't Trev's subject, and David didn't want to sneer at his lack of knowledge, especially after the chap had saved his life.

"Look, to copy a Stubbs, or anything for that matter…well, it can be copied of course. Any artist can copy it with varying degrees of quality, and from half a mile away, it'll look okay, but when we're talking the premier league like this, you need master forgers, and they are about as common as Hollywood stars who haven't had facelifts. There's literally a dozen or so people worldwide who specialize in that kind of thing, and half of those are crooks. I'll tell you who's good enough to pull it off. Me! I have the skill, and I've done it before to get me out of the shit, but it would take a month and I don't have a month. I have to begin my mate Laz's restaurant project today, or he'll never forgive me. This is a massive thing for him, and he's thrown every penny he has into it I reckon, so taking a month out is a non-starter."

"Why don't you ask the antiques chap at the other end of the mews?" asked Trev. "He used to be one of the experts on the Antiques Roadshow you know. I bet he'll know an art forger."

David shook his head and bit his lip simultaneously – and Suzanne said he couldn't multi-task!

"I could, I suppose – there's no harm in asking. If he did know someone, they'd have to be top quality, which means expensive as hell, and then there's the morality of it to consider. I don't know if I could live with myself, cheating some poor bloke in Saudi who's done nothing against me. I've been raised by my mom and dad to be honest, and I am. Besides, if I got caught, I'd end up in jail. I've got a wife and kids and a nice house. I don't want to end up a convict, taking communal showers and being perpetually scared to bend down to pick up the soap for fear of some hairy-arsed psycho buggering me."

"All fair points," agreed Trev. "So where are you going to get the several million quid from, or are you insured? Not that Mustapha Fagg will be bothered about the insurance. He's rich already. He'll be seething mad with you for destroying his beloved picture. He'll have you stoned to death in the village square and feed your bollocks to the crows. My way, he gets a shiny new painting with a tear that's been repaired so beautifully that he can't even find where it used to be. He's no expert so he won't notice that it's not exactly identical, because odds on he never looked too close before. Remember, he's not *expecting* a forgery. It won't even cross his mind. If it looks a bit different, just tell him it's been revarnished and cleaned. He'll be as happy as Larry."

"You don't know Larry!" sighed David. "At the moment, he's not the least bit happy. Look, I'll ask this antiques expert – he might just have come across someone who could handle it. I doubt it though. If that draws a blank, I may have to forge it myself and get someone else to draft out my Sistine chapel ceiling design. That might be easier to arrange, come to think about it. You say the Arab chap won't suspect, but look at our Major Simon Winterfold. He can tell that his artwork's not quite the same, can't he, and he's got bloody prognostication! I reckon the best bet is to somehow pacify Laz, do the horse picture myself and hope for the best. Or, I could come clean and phone the Arab."

"And suffer the death of a thousand cuts. I say start with the antiques bloke. Meanwhile, put the Arab off with some artistic bullshit about the oil paint taking ages to dry or whatever. That's my advice. Now I'm off for a walk to the hall to tell the major the good news. And cheer up, mate. We did well just now. We'll probably make the Stourbridge News!"

Trev exited stage left, leaving David alone with his thoughts. The phone rang again. It was Laz, thanking David profusely for not phoning him back after he'd promised to. David apologized, explaining that Monday mornings were always busy, what with one thing and another. Laz asked David how the design was going, and David assured him that he was a long way down the line and things were looking good. What he actually meant was that so far he'd only managed to get a long way down the first pencil line and it was looking as good as a solitary pencil line could. If there was one thing he didn't need at that juncture, it was a Bulgarian Furniture Maker-style going over from his hot-tempered friend. David cleaned up the mess, locked the battered Stubbs in his darkroom and then took a stroll down the mews to find the antiques man. Having missed out on the mews get-together at the weekend and taken his family to Giovanni's instead, he thought it was high time he got to know the inmates in this veritable nest of vipers.

CHAPTER 10

Another Busy Man

David walked into the Antique Centre, setting off a tinkly bell that was even more irritating than his own. There was no-one around, so he took a leaflet from the small pie-crust table near the door and studied it. There was a photo on the front of a distinguished, grey-haired gentleman of around sixty, wearing half-moon glasses near to the end of his nose, as is *de rigueur* for the respectable antiques dealer about town. Even worse, they were fitted with a gold chain, in the style made unpopular by camp comedian, Larry Grayson. Below the neck, the gentleman in the picture sported a pink shirt with matching tie and a loud pinstripe three-piece suit with flamboyant pink hankie thrust into the left breast pocket. He was handling a piece of fine china, his pudgy, liver-spotted hands weighed down with sovereign rings, gold chains and a chunky Rolex watch. Either side of him, punters looked on with awe, and appeared to be hanging on his every word. Beneath the photograph, the caption read:

Raymond at the BBC's Antiques Roadshow. Worcester 1986.

David shuddered melodramatically, and replaced the leaflet where he'd found it.

At this point, the self-same gent, now dressed in a lemon yellow Pringle golf cardigan and dicky-bow combination emerged from his private quarters and smiled a slimy, superior smile. David said good morning and introduced himself as the art restorer who'd recently moved in. The gentleman said that David's reputation preceded him, and he offered his limp, overly manicured, gilded hand to be shaken. David duly did so with all the enthusiasm of a father about to change his first nappy, and then backed off quickly before the gentleman's aftershave overpowered him. His full name, according to the leaflet at any rate, was Raymond de Winter.

"Any connection with the Winterfolds who own the hall," enquired David.

"None whatsoever," Raymond replied. He pronounced the W and the H the wrong way round, the way newsreader Trevor McDonald always did. In only two words, David could already tell that this fragrant character had possibly the poshest accent he'd ever heard, with the possible exception of Brian Sewell, the art critic.

"However," Raymond continued, "Claudia Winterfold, Major Winterfold's elder sister and I do plan to marry next spring, so the question of her new surname continues to cause much consternation. She is reluctant to lose her name, as it can be traced back to even before the hall was built in 1509. A double-barrelled version would come out (Raymond pronounced 'out' as 'ite') as Winterfold de Winter, which I rather like."

David had nothing constructive to add to this, so he just smiled sweetly. Day was as economical and unostentatious a surname as one could get, which pleased him no end. His beloved parents, coming from a lowly council house background, couldn't even afford to give him a middle name.

"So hye can I help you?" asked Raymond.

Luckily, David had already concocted a very plausible story to feed to the snooty antiques dealer. After all, he could hardly tell him the truth, and by so doing, instantly ruin his spotless reputation in the art industry.

Many years previously, when David was a young and naïve art student (as opposed to the middle-aged and naïve professional artist he was now), he had been duped by a conman named Lord Hickman into copying the bent aristocrat's Monet, for 'insurance purposes'. He had explained to David that he preferred to leave the original in his vault and display the forgery at his castle, just in case some light-fingered tourist took a shine to it. The unscrupulous lord, in reality, was planning to steal the painting, which his wife owned, leaving her with the fake, and afterwards disappear abroad with his mistress.

Painful though the memories had been to David's pride, they now provided him with the perfect story. He explained to Raymond that a rich client of his owned a Stubbs which had been attacked by a madman with a craft knife while it was on display at the client's stately home in Berkshire. This client had now been persuaded by his insurers to create a fake for the wall, and once David had repaired the original, it was to remain, like Lord Hickman's Monet, safely locked away. David would ordinarily have preferred to create the faked picture himself of course, but a busy schedule made this impossible.

The only trouble with David's story was that if Raymond de Winter *did* have a pet forger on his books, this man would naturally need to see the painting in order to fake it, and once he had seen the trashed Stubbs, he would realize straight away that a repair was downright impossible, and that David was telling lies. Luckily, David had an ace up his sleeve. Whenever he had completed a repair that he was especially proud of, he always took a high resolution flatbed scan of the picture with his state of the art darkroom equipment, so that he would have something to keep for his portfolio once the original was returned to its owner. It wasn't as good as working from the original, but beggars, as they say, can't be choosers. A print from the high quality scan would have to do.

All this would have been fine and dandy if Raymond de Winter knew an expert forger. He didn't.

"I have a reputation within the industry, Mr Day," he explained, looking down his nose at the artist both literally and metaphorically through his ridiculous half-moon specs. "I don't know if you are aware, but I was once an Antiques Roadshow expert - I no longer appear on the programme due to my work commitments – and as such, I have to be most careful. I understand that the forgery work would not be in any way dishonest, if one excludes the fact that your client is misleading the general public, but if I were to rub shoulders with international forgers, can you *imagine* the rumours that would fly around? (Raymond pronounced this last word as 'arinde') So I'm awfully sorry, Mr Day, but I can't help you on this occasion. Now, if you'll forgive me…"

"I know," interrupted David, "you're very busy." He turned on his heels and left the antiques centre, setting off the annoying tinkly doorbell again.

So Raymond was betrothed to Claudia, was he? This was all very interesting and incestuous. Unfortunately, David had no time left to investigate this further. He would have to let Trev get on with it now, while he reluctantly concentrated on his own career, or what was left of it. He returned to his studio and emailed his rich Arab, explaining that, whilst the painstaking restoration was going very well, it was taking considerably longer than expected. That, David felt, would stall the man until he could sort things out. In the meantime, there was no point in worrying. He had to put the blinkers on and begin work on Laz's ceiling, difficult as it was to do. To this end, he strode purposefully into his darkroom and began where he'd left off.

* * *

Trev, meanwhile, was hiding behind an ivy-clad tree at the far side of the Sheep Walks, pointing the telephoto lens of his Nikon digital camera at a group of caravans across the country lane. His already whiffy bodily odours had been considerably augmented by the collection of black sheep turds stuck to the bottom of his brogues, and thanks to another sweltering day and the long uphill walk, he was now beginning to sweat profusely inside his grubby gabardine Mac. He took off his coat, slung it onto the well-fertilized grass, and resumed his photography, blissfully unaware of the three travellers striding across the Sheep Walks behind him.

* * *

David, for once, had had a productive day. He had suffered no interruptions and had been able to forge ahead with Laz's work to the point where he believed, given a fair wind, he could finish the initial rough layout by the following evening. Once Laz had given his stamp of approval – and he surely would – David could begin painting the finished artwork on Wednesday morning. Like all good artists, David knew when to stop, and that time had come. He washed his brushes, emitted a self-satisfied groan, and stood up to stretch his legs. Tonight was the night he had to take his son, James, to his cricket practice, something David loved doing as he was a bit of a cricketer himself, and regularly turned out for nearby Enville's third team, in the absence of a fourth team, when they were truly desperate.

The day had got off to a hell of a start. He and Trev had caught the Tutton rapist and trashed a multi-million pound painting before half nine. It was difficult to describe to people how that made him feel – an uneasy mixture of euphoric and suicidal. The hard work had been therapeutic though, and helped to engender a slightly more optimistic frame of mind. He'd enjoy his bit of cricket now, sat in the golden glow of a summer's evening with a glass of Shiraz, idly gazing at James and the other young lads dressed in their whites, smacking red cork balls about and having fun. Ah, the sound of leather on willow. There was nothing like it to calm a person down, David felt. It was far better than the sound of Stubbs on graphologist, that was for sure. Trev was right though, bless him. The Arab chap wouldn't be looking for a fake. It wouldn't enter his head. He'd probably never even had a really good, close look at the thing. Okay, it was a disaster, but the world was looking slightly brighter now. David would find a forger from somewhere. He had hundreds of contacts, after all. Maybe the National Gallery knew of one, and if they didn't, there were loads of other big city galleries that David had worked for. Surely one of them knew somebody. He'd get on the blower first thing the following morning and sort it, so that he could continue with Laz's job safe in the knowledge that the Stubbs was being dealt with.

David headed for the door, and home. As he opened it, he suddenly found himself face to face with Major Simon Winterfold, who came within a toucher of rapping sharply on David's nose. Once both men had recovered from the shock, the major was first to speak.

"David?"

"Yes."

"The art restorer who I wrongly thought was a private detective?"

"Correct, though I did sort of confuse you a bit, I admit."

"Not at all, I'm just pleased that I got it right. I'm getting better at this recognition malarkey I think. Erm, look, can I come in please? I have some awful news."

David asked him in and offered him a seat, which the major politely refused.

"I think you might need one though," he said, biting his lower lip anxiously. "It's your mate Trevor, the *real* private detective. There's no easy way to say this. He's been beaten senseless and left for dead over the Sheep Walks. One of my farm hands found him. He called an ambulance, but the poor fellow was so badly injured, and lying in such an inaccessible spot that they had to send the air ambulance instead. My chap said he didn't look good, and the paramedics looked pretty worried. For all they knew, he might have been unconscious a long time. I just thought you'd like to know."

David slumped into his chair and put his head in his hands. He'd moved to the mews from home because he and Suzanne needed more room and the house was getting a little noisy, now that the kids were getting older.

"You'll be able to concentrate better at the mews," Suzanne had told him. "There'll be fewer distractions."

There hadn't been a solitary peaceful day since he'd arrived there.

"Oh yes," added the major quietly. "My chap found this nearby. It's his digital camera. They've smashed it to pieces, but here, the SIM card's still intact, if you need to see what he was working on."

CHAPTER 11

The best things come in small packages

David knew he should be working on Laz's job with his blinkers on, avoiding all distractions, but the tiny little SIM card kept calling out to him from the desk nearby. It said in a wee plaintive, sorrowful voice, "David, download me! David download me! You owe it to Trev to download me!"

David was too jittery to work anyway. He'd phoned the hospital first thing, but the doctor couldn't or wouldn't help him because David wasn't family. If Trev had any family, David didn't know where they lived, so he'd reached what is commonly referred to as a brick wall, or an impasse, if one is marginally less common. He then asked the doctor if he could maybe visit, but the doctor said that Trev was in a very bad way, and was far too ill to even acknowledge, let alone receive visitors. David thanked the doctor for this assessment of Trev's health that only seconds before he was told he couldn't be given. Okay, it wasn't in depth, but it told him everything he needed to know. Trev was in serious trouble.

It was all very ironic. Earlier the same day, 'invincible' Trev had coolly, if expensively, disarmed the graphologist, and in doing so, surely saved David's life. A few hours later, someone was trying their best to save his. David abandoned his artwork and began the process of downloading the SIM card. A few minutes later, hundreds of thumbnail images from the camera were spilling out in neat rows onto David's computer. He began to patiently sift through them all, looking for clues. There were pictures of Claudia with the slimy Raymond, snapped from afar through a car window, and several of unidentified farm workers, grooms, stable girls and the like, going about their business. Trev had even revealed his softer side with a few shots of the local mallard ducks on the sparkling, sunlit lake, and a nice back-lit portrait of a handsome racehorse.

Then David spotted something interesting. It was a series of shots taken with Trev's motor drive – the device that enables a photographer to hold the shutter down and fire off shots in rapid succession, like a machine gun. It had created a sequential effect, a little like looking at stills from a movie film. The quality was not so good, but it was definitely Raymond, at the back of his antique centre by the recycling bins, and he was handing over an envelope to another gentleman. David reached for his magnifying glass and took a closer look. He knew that face. It had aged a bit since he'd last seen it, but there was no disguising such an ugly mug.

"Oh my prophetic soul!" he whispered excitedly, as he went through the sequence again. "Trev, God bless you. You are a genius, and you probably don't know it. Well done, my son. Now bloody well hang in there."

And then, suddenly, David began to cry. Maybe it was his own little soliloquy that had touched a nerve, or maybe it was delayed shock after the day's traumatic events. It was almost certainly exacerbated by the recent death of his beloved father, the memory of which was still all too painful. Whatever the catalyst had been, he offered up a silent prayer to the God he professed not to believe in for poor old Trevor to pull through. Wiping his eyes on his sleeve and desperately trying to compose himself, he also vowed to seek revenge on the sewer rats that had done this to his new-found comrade. "La vendetta è un piatto che va mangiato freddo," he whispered to himself, with a very uncharacteristic snarl to his voice. He resumed his work, struggling to see the small thumbnails through his blurred, moistened eyes. A trawl through the next hundred or so images revealed nothing of real interest, and then, eureka! He hit pay dirt. The final pictures were of Johnny O'Driscoll's makeshift caravan site. Some were just of farm vehicles, which Trev presumably suspected had been stolen from Major Simon. One was of two men with what looked like roofing lead in wheelbarrows. Then, the next three images were just violent smears of colour. This was obviously the moment when Trev had been attacked, but it was the final two shots that had excited David. The composition would have come in for some harsh criticism at the Dudley Annual Photographic Exhibition (Dudley Museum and Art Gallery, entry free, programmes £1.50), but there was no disputing that Trev had, admittedly by accident, captured his three attackers beautifully. It was a perfect study of animal aggression, arguably enhanced by the rather strange camera angle. Remarkably, thanks to the automatic digital camera, it was in sharp focus too – a manual film camera almost certainly wouldn't have been. Anyone seeing the shot would know who these three gorillas were instantly; it was that good. The only problem was that the travellers had now disappeared, according to the major, leaving behind, as ever, a field strewn with rubbish.

David rang the police station and informed the desk sergeant that he had discovered a photograph of Trev's attackers. The sergeant thanked David for his efforts and said that he'd send Donald and Pongo around for it as soon as possible. He also hinted that he and Trev might well be nominated for an award for catching the rapist, who had now confessed. David told the sergeant that he hoped and prayed it wouldn't have to be awarded posthumously, in Trev's case.

* * *

In spite of the fact that his head was spinning, David somehow managed to spend the rest of his day quietly painting.

106

Originally, he had planned to spend it ringing around the galleries in search of a forger, but something he had seen on the computer had changed all that. He put his brushes down at six, and then phoned home to say he'd be a little late. He took a stroll around the estate until seven, and then returned to his studio, via Raymond's place. Raymond had gone home. It was time to take a nose around, Phillip Marlowe-style. Turning his collar up for no obvious reason, other than because Humphrey Bogart always did it, David glanced this way and that. No-one was about. He took his hand out of his pocket and looked at his watch. He put his hand back in his pocket. He still didn't know what time it was. He produced the graphologist's skeleton key and tried it in the lock. Voila! It actually worked. David had imagined that these things were but a figment of the crime writer's imagination. Until that morning, he had no idea they actually existed, and had certainly never met anyone who owned one. He pushed the door open, and the loud, tinkling bell almost induced a coronary. He closed the door quickly and tip-toed into the shop, bashing into the pie-crust table and scattering Raymond's leaflets across the floor. The next few minutes were spent on his hands and knees, cursing under his breath as he retrieved them from under old chests of drawers and Welsh dressers. It seemed incredible how things that fell on the floor could travel miles. David had dropped a wine glass on his ceramic-tiled kitchen floor a year previously, and was still picking up stray bits even now.

It was summer, which meant it was still light, and not the ideal time for a trainee burglar to be attempting his maiden break-in. He made his way to the back of the shop, where he could hide behind things if anyone happened to wander by. All of the mews buildings had a main front room and two smaller back rooms, one of which contained a lavatory. David used his other room as a darkroom, and Raymond used his as a private office. David opened the door and walked in. He closed the door behind him, turned on the light and began to rummage around in the desk. Bingo! Raymond's book of business phone numbers and addresses. He skimmed through it until he reached the 'M's, and there, in bold black and white, was the person he was looking for, as he suspected it would be. He scribbled the name and number down on a scrap of paper and pocketed it. Then he pulled out the deep bottom drawer of Raymond's desk. It contained a large folder. Inside was a sheet of A2 cartridge paper folded to A3. David opened it. Within were several sheets of very old paper, inscribed with faded brown ink. The handwriting was of a different age and difficult to read, for two reasons. Firstly, it was extremely ornate, with flourishes and swirls. Secondly, it was in Italian. David leafed through the pages and found a small scrap of paper with naïve, childlike handwriting. It said: 'Sorry Daddy. Please don't shout at me any more, love Simon'. David felt the tears well up in his eyes again, but this was not the best time to get maudlin about lost fathers. He continued his search, and found underneath the old letter several ancient sheets of drawing paper. They were the rough sketch sheets of an artist, and full of terra cotta-coloured drawings of hands; some twenty or more in total, all in different positions. Beneath each study was a simple reference letter, presumably so that the artist could identify the various gestures. This appeared to be no more than a comprehensive reference library of hand positions – the type of thing that artists though the ages have all created in order to get the hands right in their paintings. David smiled to himself. Some things never changed, which was quite comforting. Hands, in his opinion, were still the hardest things for an artist to draw properly. He photographed each sheet individually with his digital camera, and then placed the old drawings and the letter back inside the drawer. It was time to make himself scarce for two reasons, the second being that it was coq-au-vin night.

CHAPTER 12

My Kingdom for a Horse

Almost a week had passed since David's first ever burglary, and, as usual, he was beavering away in his studio like a man possessed. He had stripped the battered Stubbs original from its stretchers and replaced it with an old canvas he'd found from the same period. After sanding it down and priming it to hide the hideous Victorian schmaltz beneath, he completed the under-painting, which he was pleased with, though of course, it was still early days.

The week before, whilst nosing around in Raymond's shop, if one will recall, David had found an interesting phone number. It was the number of one Harry Millichip, renowned art forger. This was more than interesting. Raymond de Winter, the ex-Antiques Road Show expert himself, assured David that he knew no art forgers, adding that he would not have associated with such pond life even if he did know them, for professional reasons - the man had his reputation to think of, after all. Why then, wondered David as he studied the photographs on Trev's SIM card, was Raymond snapped handing Harry Millichip an envelope at the back of the antiques centre? And why then, he wondered as he flicked through Raymond's address book later that day, was Harry's number there?

Equally troubling was the old folder. Major Simon was right yet again. He was convinced that several old sheets full of hand studies had gone missing, and now here was Raymond with a nice collection of old and beautifully executed hand drawings. Unless Simon had actually given them to Raymond and then forgotten he'd done so – which in fairness to Raymond, was quite possible, they had clearly been stolen. The vision of Harry Millichip claiming his grubby envelope put it beyond doubt. Simon had two forged pictures hanging on his wall, and Harry forged pictures for a living. The old hand drawings could even have been his next task. It didn't take Phillip Marlowe to work out what was going on, and it was almost certain that Simon's sister Claudia was in on it, which, if proven to be the case, was nothing short of despicable.

David prepared himself to apply the next layer of oil paint to his canvas. Those following the plot carefully and making notes would have realized by now that he was painting the Stubbs copy himself, and doing so seemingly without a care in the world, when only days previously he was to be observed running around like a headless chicken, trying to locate and employ international art forgers. These plot-followers would have smiled a self-satisfied smile when they reached the point in the story where David came across the number of Harry Millichip in Raymond's address book, and pronounced to anyone who was interested, that odds on, the Stubbs was about to be taken care of by Harry, leaving David free to continue with Laz's work.

Had they then been bold enough to place a bet with Ladbrokes, they would have lost their money. David, for all his faults, which were many and varied, had a strict moral code, if one excluded breaking and entering and lying to Laz. He didn't wish to pay Harry Millichip to forge a picture in order to deceive the wealthy Arab businessman. Harry had forged a career out of forging, so to speak, and every penny he'd earned

110

had been illegal. The thought of continuing this trend stuck in David's throat. He also didn't fancy parting with barrow loads of money to pay for this to happen, so instead, David put a proposition to Mr Millichip – an offer he couldn't refuse, as a fictional Italian Mafia boss with cotton wool in his cheeks once said.

David had already done most of the donkey work. He'd completed the rough layout of his ceiling painting, and had all the reference material to back it up. He simply asked Harry Millichip to paint the finished picture for him, free of charge, out of the kindness of his heart. When Harry insisted that his heart didn't have any kindness in it and instead demanded ten thousand pounds, David casually let it slip out that he knew about Harry's recent copies of a John Constable landscape and a John Singer Sargent portrait, and if David's work wasn't done free of charge, the police would get to know about them too. He also added rather tartly that Harry had carelessly miscounted the cows and peasants, and misjudged the sitter's pupils as well, which just wasn't good enough. For such a high calibre forger, it was downright sloppy. David may have even added a few 'tut tut's for good measure, just to rub it in. He explained that anyone as lax as that couldn't be trusted on a Stubbs that had to be just so, so Harry could do the Michelangelo ceiling design instead. In fairness to Harry, the renaissance was his forte, and all the initial design work had been done, which made the job considerably easier for him. A man with his skills could easily knock it off in two or three weeks, tops, and in return, David would forget all about Harry's illegal work on the Edgecliff Hall pictures. David also warned Harry not to breathe a word of this to his employer, Raymond, or else the cops would definitely be breathing down his neck.

Harry knew when he was beat. The only thing he could do was paint David's picture as well and as quickly as possible, so that he could get back to doing what he did best. It was, therefore, a broken and subdued art forger that reminded David to post him the initial designs and photocopied reference material, prior to replacing the receiver, a few days previously.

David was in a surprisingly buoyant mood for another reason too. On Sunday, he had taken his son, James, to the book fair, which was and still is held every third Sunday of the month in the nearby Kinver Community Centre, to the delight of the two hundred or so people in England who still read them. He had been looking at second-hand art books on a gentleman's stand and wondering if he could manage to carry three to his car without risking a hernia, when a BBC publication caught his eye. The gentleman had wanted four pounds fifty for the book, and after much haggling, David managed to talk him down to four pounds twenty-six. It was entitled, 'Antiques Road Show – The first 21Years'. Over a cup of tea and a slice of cake in the café area, a highly excited David browsed through the book while James went off in search of old Beano annuals to add to his collection. Imagine David's joy when he found, at the back of the book, a comprehensive list of every single Road Show expert that had ever been on the programme, and then imagine the expression on his face when he discovered that Raymond de Winter wasn't to be found on that list.

That afternoon, David rang Harry Millichip again. Harry's mood, on recognizing the voice at the other end, was not what one would describe as euphoric.

"More blackmail is it?" he growled.

"Au contraire, Harry," replied David chirpily. "In fact, I've have a big change of heart."

"Oh yeah?"

"Yeah. I couldn't see you spend three weeks of your time painting a freebie. It's just not fair, and besides, your heart wouldn't be in it and you'd probably come up with a mediocre picture as a result. To this end, I've decided to pay you a grand for your efforts, just to show willing."

Harry seemed to perk up a little on hearing this news. He was still a long way away from euphoric, however. It wasn't a fortune, after all, when one had estimated the job to be worth ten grand, but it was something, and not to be sniffed at.

"But," added David, "it comes with strings attached."

Harry groaned. One sensed that he had immediately slipped backwards into the slough of despond.

"Look, I'll tell you what. One and a half grand, final offer, if you find out about this Antiques Road Show bloke, Raymond, who I know you forged the paintings for."

"What d'yer want to know about him?" asked Harry flatly.

"For a start, is he kosher? Is that his real name? Spill the beans and I'll pay you what I said, and no holding back now. I won't tell him you told me – and that's a promise."

"Deal," said Harry resignedly. "His real name's Ray Bingham. Bingo for short. He's a confidence trickster from Stepney. He's never been on the friggin' Road Show in his life, apart from as a punter, which is what that picture on his leaflet shows, hence the big Road Show sign behind him. The camera never lies, eh? He's brilliant at that posh accent, but his real one's more like Alan Sugar than Brian Sewell. He's one for the ladies as well. Been engaged eight times to my knowledge, always to rich birds, but they always end up poorer after he's been there. Is that enough?"

"Plenty!" smiled David. "Now do me a good paint job and the money's yours."

David put the phone down, looking suitably smug. He'd fully intended to reward Harry anyway. Crooked as Harry was, David didn't like to take advantage of a fellow artist more than he had to. He knew what it was like. He'd endured twenty-five years or more of being screwed left right and centre and he didn't enjoy having to do it to others, even if they were as bent as Harry.

This last piece in the jigsaw was all he'd been waiting for. David decided that it was time to take a quick tea break up at the hall, if Major Simon's butler, Horace, could manage to keep some of it in the cups.

* * *

Major Simon was in, and once he'd remembered who David was, he welcomed him into the yellow room for tea like a long-lost brother. He didn't quite say, "Come into my arms, my beamish boy!" but it was a close-run thing. After all, he and poor old Trev had already solved the rapist case between them, and taken a great weight off the major's mind. Once the initial greetings were out of the way, Simon asked how Trev was faring. David explained that he had asked his two copper acquaintances to see if they could find out for him, which they had duly done. It wasn't great news. His skull and jaw were fractured and he was in a very poor state. The doctors were keeping him sedated, and just hoping that he'd eventually pull through. They'd let everyone know if and when he was well enough to accept visitors.

Donald and Pongo had news of Bernard the graphologist too. His stools, confirmed Pongo, were indeed white, and the police doctors had taken a look at him. He was currently in hospital having treatment, so that hopefully he'd become well enough to lock up for life. It appeared that Bernard actually blamed his illness for the sex attacks. Bitter and twisted because of his potentially fatal condition, he had been trying to satisfy his cravings and get his fill of young women before his miserable life ended. Many of his victims, it turned out, had been clients of his, curious to learn what their handwriting told him about them. He had informed the ones he fancied that their scribblings indicated 'a free spirit lurking beneath a layer of

114

respectability - someone who secretly craved wild sexual encounters with strangers'. If the women were at all receptive to this nonsense, he'd then suggest a date, which not one of them took him up on. It appeared that Bernard just didn't have what the ladies wanted - even those who really did have secret cravings for wild sexual encounters, so instead, deeply frustrated by his lack of success, he decided to don the balaclava, chloroform them senseless and take what he wanted by force instead.

Horace arrived, his tea tray clinking and clattering, with Earl Grey splashing around all over the place. Claudia popped her head around the door to say hello, and was about to leave for the stables when David asked if she could stay for a few minutes. She let Horace out, closed the door behind him and grabbed a seat, her brow corrugated by a large frown.

"Sounds intriguing!" she smiled, somewhat nervously.

"It is!" replied David. "I've been doing some digging for you both, in Trev's absence."

Claudia flashed him a withering look that said; "Didn't I specifically ask you not to?"

David gave her a return look that he hoped would say, "Awfully sorry, but I couldn't help myself." He cleared his throat and launched into it.

"Simon, you asked me about your paintings, your sideboard and an old box. I have to be honest here. Trevor Jenkinson thought you were talking gibberish and so did Claudia here, and who could blame them? The only thing is, you were dead right. Your Constable and your Sargent are undoubtedly fakes."

Simon laid his china cup down rather forcibly onto his desk and stared at David intensely. Claudia, who was sipping tea at

115

the time David delivered his killer line, ended up with most of it in her lungs and began to splutter and choke. Once David had slapped her on the back a couple of times and she had restored her composure, he continued.

"Your Chippendale sideboard is almost certainly a fake but I can't prove that yet, and there *were* some old drawings of hands in that box, because I've found them. I have photographs here to show you."

David glanced across at Claudia to gauge her reaction to this last comment, in exactly the same way that Horatio observed Claudius when Hamlet staged the play mirroring his uncle's evil deeds. All David saw in Claudia, however, was mild surprise and nothing even approaching guilt.

Major Simon and Claudia both had urgent questions, but David raised a hand and begged them to remain silent while he explained what he'd discovered.

This, he feared, was going to be awkward.

Fairly confident now that Claudia was innocent, he broke the news as gently as he could, which wasn't very. How could it be? Her betrothed was a con artist who had robbed many wealthy women, and she was the latest sucker. Raymond had had the pictures forged and stolen the originals. If they were lucky, he still had them. If they weren't, he didn't. It was almost certain that the sideboard had suffered the same fate. So far, all that David could recover was a pile of old hand studies, a letter with the bottom hacked off and a note attached in its place saying 'Sorry Daddy.' Scant consolation indeed.

Major Simon looked ashen. Losing millions of pounds in one fell swoop could do that to a fellow. Claudia, meanwhile, sobbed brokenly.

"The thing I don't get," said David, ploughing on regardless, "is how this bloke could have borrowed these things for the length of time it would have taken to copy them?"

116

"I was in Iraq, remember?" sighed Simon, staring out of the window at nothing in particular. "You were here though, Claudia. You must have noticed the bloody things had gone."

"But that's just it, Simon," sniffled Claudia. "They *were* here!" I've only ever been away for the odd weekend to the point to point. It couldn't have been done in such a short space of time, surely!"

"Did Raymond go with you?" asked David.

"No, he hates horse racing, the bastard," sobbed Claudia blowing her nose loudly.

"I must admit, this did confuse me," confessed David. "At first, I thought you were complicit in all this, and while Simon was away, you'd let Raymond take the pictures for a month. I've probably just watched too many old episodes of Columbo, but whenever someone in that show says, 'And now, officer, if you'll excuse me, I'm very busy,' I know right away that he or she is the villain. It's a dead giveaway - works every time. Well, you said that very line to me the first time we met, and so did Raymond and that graphologist chap, so naturally, it made me suspicious of you all. Very stupid, I know, and I can see now that this was nonsense of course, but it does enter your head, and I'm sorry for doubting you. All Raymond needed was a free weekend or two, if you think about it; time to photograph the pictures and snap the sideboard from all angles, take a lot of measurements. I've just done exactly the same thing with a Stubbs original only this week – taken a very good quality photo, I mean. It's never as good as working from the real thing, but beggars can't be choosers, as I probably say far too often. That explains why the Constable and the Sargent aren't quite up to Harry Millichip's usual standard – he's the one who forged them, by the way. As to the old drawings, they were in Raymond's desk, and as far as I know, he doesn't yet know they've gone. I suggest we call the cops and have him arrested. Hopefully, they'll beat out of him where the originals are and get them back for you. I'm sorry, Claudia. There was no easy way to break this to you."

Claudia issued forth with one more, mighty, shuddering sob, and then tried her best to re-introduce the stiff upper lip motif. Men were alright, after all, but they'd never replace horses. Major Simon thanked David profusely for his incredible forensic work up to that point. The potential loss of the heirlooms, let alone the thought of their worth, had momentarily unmanned him and he was clearly battling around sixty separate emotions simultaneously, but, like his sister, he was made of sterner stuff – he was a soldier, after all. He cleared his throat and rang the police, who must have been thinking that if they purged Edgecliff Hall Mews, the crime figures for the whole of England would surely decrease by half. They promised that someone would be round within the hour, and advised Simon to allow the antiques dealer to continue his business in the interim, so as not to arouse suspicion. Simon put his head in his hands and groaned a heartfelt groan. As if things weren't bad enough around the estate, what with his farmhands losing their hands on his farm, travellers stealing the lead from his roofs and leaving half-dead private eyes in their wake. Now a sizable percentage of his mews tenants were either in jail or on the run from the law and his sister was going steady with a chap who would steal the gold from her teeth while she had a nap. Simon was wondering whether he should have CRB-checked the old lady who ran the traditional sweet shop now. She was probably an undercover Al Qaeda terrorist in disguise, with a stock room full of exploding humbugs.

* * *

David was back at the easel when he heard the police car crunch onto the gravel car park next to his studio. It was, predictably, Donald and Pongo.

"Put that new kettle on then, Dave!" said Donald by way of a greeting, as David opened the studio door.

"Shouldn't you pair be arresting the bloke down the other end of the mews?" hissed David, fearful of alerting the scorpion in their midst.

"That's why we're here, mate," Donald assured him, "but he's done a bunk; a moonlight flit. He's shovelled what he could manage by himself into his van and buggered off sharpish – he's not even bothered to shut the front door. So we've come round for a quick cuppa before we go back to the station."

"Oh God!" moaned David. "This is terrible! That means we may never be able to find Major Winterfold's paintings or his sideboard. Who could have warned him that we were onto him? When I broke into his shop, nothing was touched. I deliberately took photos of the stolen folder so as not to alert him to…."

"You broke into his shop?" asked Pongo, helping himself to a chocolate biscuit from David's tin.

"Well, yes, but…"

"That's a serious offence, Dave."

"And so is taking biscuits without consent. I did it because I suspected this arsehole of ripping the major off for millions, yes millions of pounds, and now he's done a runner. We're sunk."

Donald radioed back to base and asked for his fellow officers to keep an eye out for Raymond's white van. David excused himself and dashed down to the antiques centre to see if the con man had taken the old hand drawings. Mercifully, he hadn't. They were where David had left them. And then, as he stood in silence, thinking things through in Raymond's empty office, a thought occurred to him. Why had Raymond stolen the pictures in the first place? He'd switched the oil paintings for obvious reasons, and likewise the sideboard, if indeed it *was* a fake, but why would he steal a letter and a pile of old

119

drawings from the box? Did he know something about them that Simon, Claudia and David didn't know? The drawings were very old and beautifully executed, that was for sure, and the old letter was intriguing, largely due to the fact that it was in Italian, and not English like the other documents in the box. Were the drawings worth serious money maybe, and Simon hadn't realized what he'd got. The style was of the renaissance period, and even sketchbook studies could fetch a fortune if they had been done by a premier league renaissance artist. Maybe David should borrow them and show them to his old friend and employer, Henry Tibbatts at the National Gallery in London. He might know what they were, and what they were worth. As for the letter, there would surely be a professor at Birmingham University who could translate it. Alternatively, David could ask his friend Giovanni to have a stab at it, but he knew it wouldn't be simple. The writing was full of ornate flourishes for a start. Also, Italy in those days was really a collection of autonomous regions, often at war with each other, and probably speaking many different dialects. The letter would have been, approximately speaking, the Italian equivalent of a Tudor manuscript in terms of its age and the floweriness of the language. It was no wonder that Simon's father had never succeeded in translating it, assuming he'd even tried.

David retrieved the folder and trotted back to his studio to find Pongo fast asleep on his chesterfield settee, much to Donald's embarrassment.

"He's done it again, Dave," he sighed, shaking his head in disbelief. "Every time he eats a whole packet of biscuits, he nods off. It's called something but I can't remember what it is. It's not narcolepsy is it?"

"How about greedy bastarditis? Is that it?" asked David, peeved. He hadn't had chance to eat a single biscuit himself, and now they were all gone.

Donald gave his sidekick a kick in the side, which made Pongo wake with a start. He leapt unsteadily to his feet and instantaneously broke wind, loudly and pungently - another of his many fascinating medical abnormalities, and indeed, the one that earned him his nickname. The two returned to their vehicle, promising to immediately cast a dragnet for Raymond. This gave David no reason to be optimistic whatsoever. If Simon ever saw his paintings again, it would be a miracle.

CHAPTER 13

When Harry met David

Three Weeks Later

Laz popped his head around the door, and shouted, "Huy!" at the top of his voice.

David's mahl stick clattered to the floor and his laden brush smeared an ugly brown stripe through the racehorse's face.

"You bloody cretin!" he shouted. "You NEVER do that to an artist when he's bloody concentrating. Now look what I've done!"

"Oops! Sorry Dave. I'll get the kettle on."

Laz, who was wearing a Hi-Vis jacket and a bright yellow hard hat, duly did so. He then flopped onto the chesterfield and stretched out, making himself at home. David carefully wiped away the streak of paint with the edge of his rag and abandoned adding his finishing touches to the painting. There was only an hour left on it now before it was completed – always a nervous and impatient time for an artist. He filled his new Geoff Hill's Electrical Superstore Laser 'Maestro' kettle and took it to the sink. Why did everything from sports trainers to the humble household appliance have to resemble an intergalactic spaceship, he wondered to himself, as he filled the kettle to the 'Max' line. When he got it home and unpacked it, he was half expecting it to come with a fifty page instruction manual and a remote control.

"So why are you dressed like Bob the Builder?" he asked his friend.

"We're on site now, so you'll be seeing a lot of me over the next month. I expect that fridge to be well stocked with bacon, sausages and eggs. We builders need a second breakfast around half-ten. And another thing," added Laz, "Where is it?"

"Where's what, exactly?"

"My design. Why are you painting what looks suspiciously like a horse, when you should surely be working on a naked bloke with his willy hanging out, sat on a cloud?"

David bit his lip. "Ah, well, erm... I can't stand people seeing my paintings until they're finished. I'm very touchy about it actually. It's almost done; it's in the darkroom. I just needed a break from it, and they say a change is as good as a rest, so I thought I'd finish this one for an hour and then get back to it."

"No shitting me, it's nearly finished?"

"Yep!"

"How's it looking?"

"Erm, you know me, I hate talking about my own stuff. Wait and see."

"When? When can I see it? I'm excited!"

David assured Laz that it would be ready that afternoon, IF he'd kindly bugger off and allow him time on his own to add the finishing touches. The longer he stayed there, dossing around on the settee, the longer it would be. Laz got the hint and duly disappeared *sans* tea, back to the chapel, where he could get in his builders' way instead.

As David continued to work on his Stubbs the door burst open again, sending his laden brush across the horse's face for the second time. He mouthed a silent expletive and looked up towards the door. It was Harry Millichip. He had a huge sheet of watercolour board under his arm, neatly covered with a paper dust cover to protect it. Had he arrived seconds earlier while Laz was still in situ, it could have been most embarrassing.

"Lock that door behind you," David asked him, "and drop it on the table here. Is it good?"

"You bet!" smiled Harry. He lifted the dust cover and revealed the painting with a flourish, the way a French waiter lifts his silver dome to proudly reveal his latest minimalist gastronomic creation. He may even have added a 'Voila' for good measure.

David studied it silently, his hand cupping his chin. "That's superb, I have to say. I couldn't have done it better myself. "

"Damn right you couldn't," agreed Harry, quietly relieved.

"Laz will be over the moon with this. It's exactly as I hoped you'd interpret it from my rough design. Well done. It's just such a shame that you won't be getting paid for it."

"WHAT?" snapped Harry.

"Won't be getting paid. You warned Raymond that we were onto him, allowing him to scarper with the originals. Major Winterfold has lost his two most precious heirlooms now, thanks to you. The trail's gone cold, and Raymond Bingham could be anywhere. He could have sold the originals to some unscrupulous art dealer in Europe. The major, who I like a lot, by the way, is absolutely heartbroken."

"Look," said Harry, "I'm sorry, I really am, but I was still owed money for the second painting. I was getting ten grand each and that's a lot for me. If I'd have shopped him, your cops would have arrested him the next day and I'd have lost my money. I *had* to warn him, didn't I?"

"I see," said David, annoyed. "And did you get your second ten grand?"

"Yeah, after a lot of persuasion, he coughed up. Look, I can make amends now I've been paid. I could really do with that one and a half grand, mate. This took three weeks solid, and I need the money for something very important to me. What if I tell you where Ray is?"

"Keep talking."

"Tell you what. I'll tell you where Ray is, as long as you don't tell him who told you. And I'll tell you where I think he's keeping the originals. How's that?"

"A deal, but you'd better not be taking the piss, or I'll have you locked up. I know your phone number, remember."

Harry looked heavenwards and ran his hands through his hair. He looked a troubled man. "Okay, listen. Do you know Jubilee Row, on the council estate a mile or so past Tutton Common?"

"Yes, I do. It's a shithole."

"I agree. Well Ray was renting the end terrace in Jubilee Row, number 56. It's a dump, but it was cheap, and he was only a mile or two from the hall, so it was handy for seeing what's her face, Camilla."

"Claudia."

"Her. Ray's about to disappear for pastures new anytime soon, so you'll have to hurry up. I'm pretty sure he still has the originals stashed away there. He was trying to set up a meeting with a fat old German bloke called Herr Grunstrasse, who's a bent art dealer.

"Jeez!" exclaimed David. "I actually know who that is! Is he still alive? I was responsible for having him sent to prison back in the seventies. He was the chap that Lord Hickman was trying to peddle his stolen Monet to, only it was a fake, and it was still a bit wet! Then I got him and Hickman sent to prison again in the eighties, this time for fencing a stolen Holbein drawing. We caught them red-handed at Twopenny Green aerodrome, just down the road from here, as they were exchanging the goods for money. Well I never! You'd think after all that incarceration, he'd have seen the error of his ways wouldn't you?"

"You would think so," agreed Harry, who was no better, "but this time, hopefully you'll get the originals back well before old Grunstrasse can get to see them, if you act quickly."

David warned Harry that he had better be telling the truth, and handed him his envelope. If Harry warned Ray this time, the police would definitely be paying the crooked forger a visit. Harry thanked David and headed for the door.

"And what now for Harry Millichip?" asked David. "No chance of going straight, I suppose?"

"Funny you should mention that," smiled Harry. "I have a job to deliver on Friday in Evesham and another on Saturday in Wolverhampton, which will both earn me lots of money, and I've made up my mind that enough is enough. They'll top up my savings nicely, and then I'll have enough to retire, if I'm careful. I've got no wife or family any more, so I've sold up, and on Tuesday next week I'm getting a taxi to Manchester Airport en-route for New Zealand to start a new, legit life down under, running a café and gallery in the Bay of Islands. There'll be no more faking pictures to order for shitbags like Ray Bingham, or anyone else. If I ever pick up a brush again, it'll be to sit in a field and paint the view for myself. Maybe I might even become a name in my own right. I won't be earning mega-bucks any more for my pictures, but there'll be no stress and I'll be happy."

David was pleased for him. They parted amicably, fellow professionals on different sides of the tracks, but in a way, comrades all the same. He warned Harry one last time about betraying him by tipping off Raymond, but it was abundantly clear that Harry wasn't a fan of the bogus antiques dealer, and more to the point, he wanted nothing to interfere with his new life abroad.

Once Harry had gone, David immediately telephoned the police and told them of Raymond's whereabouts. The duty sergeant promised him that a surveillance operation would be mounted at the Jubilee Row address, and if and when the paintings were retrieved, David would be the first to know. It was the least the man could do for Tutton on Stour's leading crime fighter, he added.

David grabbed Harry's ceiling design and headed for the old chapel. Laz was outside studying a blueprint when he saw his friend striding towards him with a big beaming smile on his face. They adjourned to Laz's vehicle to look at the results. Laz was impressed. What he saw had made his day. In fact, he even remarked that David had excelled himself. Laz had never seen David paint quite so beautifully. David sat quietly and took it all in. Several conflicting emotions jockeyed for pole position in his head. The more praise Laz heaped upon him, the quieter and more contemplative David appeared to become, leaving Laz to reflect that artists, as a species, were very weird indeed.

Once Laz had had his fill, David prized the design out of his reluctant hands and took it back to the safety of his studio. He still had to create the complex overlay which broke down the image into fine lines and numbers, and he needed to get on with it, but first he had to visit Wolverhampton College of Art to see his old Head of Department, John Auberton. John was an amiable, grey haired, toothy Welshman in his sixties with a grin that was far larger than the legal limit. He welcomed his ex student with a manly bear hug, followed by a handshake that lasted some ten minutes. Pleasantries concluded, David got down to business. David needed a handful of B.A. students – seven maximum - that he could trust to do a good job. They'd be paid an honest wage for two or three weeks of the summer holidays, and when the project was finished, they could use photographs of the incredible ceiling they'd created in their final degree show portfolios. It was a win-win situation, David assured him.

John promised to have a word with them that afternoon and select the best volunteers on David's behalf. They would be told to report to Edgecliff Hall on the first Monday of the holidays at nine a.m. with a packed lunch, wearing old working clothes, and should be prepared to stay until at least five p.m.

"The only foreseeable problem," added John, "is that a lot of them are from other parts of the country, and naturally they like to return home to see their folks in the summer break. I suppose this might mean my grabbing the best of the rest, if you follow me."

"Oh well," said David. "So be it. They're only doing a glorified paint by numbers after all. It's hardly taxing for a student studying for a degree, you would think. All I ask is that you don't send me anyone like that Tim Beasley chap. Remember him?"

How could he forget? John sighed so heavily at the mention of the lad's name that David thought he might completely deflate, like a punctured balloon. Tim Beasley could have that effect on a person. He had been at the college several years previously, and was not only completely devoid of talent, but also seriously accident-prone. At that time, David had been asked by the National Gallery to restore a small Van Gogh original that had been damaged by a madman who had scrawled a phallic symbol on it with a thick black marker pen.

The painting was subsequently stolen from David's studio, and the thief, realizing that the picture had little value in its current state, made the HUGE mistake of commissioning Tim Beasley, an 'art student', to remove the offending scribble. This, Beasley planned to do with the aid of a stiff scrubbing brush and a tin of Vim, and it was only a chance comment to David while he was teaching at the college that prevented a masterpiece from being ruined beyond repair. Tim also managed to single-handedly burn down the local cricket pavilion and concuss both the first team captain and the lady who did the teas, which prompted David to christen him Jonah, after the character in the Beano (and later the Dandy) who managed to sink every ship that he served on.

"I don't know how to break this to you," said John, after an almighty mental effort. "He's still here. He was asked, nay begged, to leave the course not long after you encountered him, because he just wasn't up to it. He spent three whole terms doing a pencil drawing of Gary Glitter, remember? You told him you could have done it in an afternoon, and yours would have resembled Gary Glitter as well. And why Gary bloody Glitter of all people? It was cross-eyed and looked more like Elvis, or possibly a werewolf I thought. Anyway, he patently wasn't in any way artistic, so we advised him to try something else. He spent six years with a company that makes garden sheds, and left just after the place mysteriously got flooded. He then came back and begged to be given another chance to finish his degree. He said he'd been practising night and day, and he showed me some stuff he'd done which, in fairness, showed signs of slight improvement, i.e. his Marilyn Monroe didn't resemble Boris Karloff, so me being a big soft-headed buffoon, I let him come back to try and finish what he'd started. So far, touch MDF, he hasn't damaged anything, if you discount the day the drinks machine in the canteen exploded, and we can't prove that one."

"Well, it's your business how you choose to destroy the art college," said David, "but I don't want him turning up at the hall – got that? This chapel had lasted five hundred years so far."

John assured David that Tim Beasley would not make the cut, but all the same, David left the building with an inexplicable sense of foreboding. There was an image fixed in his mind of legendary Beano artist, Leo Baxendale's priceless creation, Jonah, striding up the gangplank with his kitbag slung over his shoulder, and the other shipmates screaming, 'AAARRGH! IT'S 'IM.'

CHAPTER 14

Henry makes a Big Impression

Major Simon Winterfold was a little happier than he had been in recent times. David had solved virtually all the crimes in Tutton on Stour in the space of a few weeks, and the news from the hospital was that Trev, though still poorly, was expected to survive. The police, again thanks to David, had arrested Ray Bingham at the Jubilee Row address, and retrieved two paintings which were once again safely back on the wall, but now positioned side by side in the Yellow Room, with the fakes still propped against the wall beneath them. The peasant to cow ratio had been restored, and great grandfather was once more following the major everywhere he went. It was almost as if the major's guardian angel had returned to look after him. Even better, Ray had confessed to his crimes, but denied any involvement in the Chippendale sideboard mystery. It turned out that Claudia's theory was, on that occasion, absolutely correct. The height differential had been caused by Simon's injury and his specially built-up shoes, and nothing more sinister. Things, the major was convinced, were on the up. Unless Brian the rocking horse maker had a secret penchant for dismembering old ladies and burying them under the paving slabs, and Miriam at the farm shop was really Miriam the Tutton Poisoner, it appeared that the Edgecliff Mews crime wave was finally at an end.

It was, therefore, a revitalized Major Simon Winterfold that thanked Horace the butler and asked him to show Mr Tibbatts in.

Henry Tibbatts, curator of the National Gallery, had come on a state visit to see his old friend David and intended to kill two birds with one stone by viewing the two paintings at the same time. He warned his chauffeur, Jeremy, that he may well be quite a time, and advised him to get some lunch at the Cat Inn, nearby, warning him to lay off the Tutton Ale, as he wished to return to Trafalgar Square in one piece. Thanks to a convenient piece of synchronicity, artist and curator fetched up on the front steps of the hall at exactly the same time, and were now entering Simon's office.

Once the greetings and handshakes were dispensed with and Simon had reminded himself who David was, he got down to business. In truth, he was keen to hear what his two heirlooms might fetch, and was conscious of feeling a little like one of those members of the public on the Antiques Roadshow who sit with glazed expression through the expert's monotonous diatribe, eager to get to the nitty gritty. He was reluctant to get rid of the pictures, as they had been in the family for a long time, but times were hard, the estate still wasn't pulling its weight, and having a couple of million quid sitting on one's wall doing nothing was a luxury he couldn't afford. Besides, he argued to himself, he could always revert to hanging Harry Millichip's fakes on the wall, and no-one would be the wiser!

Fearing that Horace would take so long to deliver the refreshments that Henry would already be on his way back to London, Claudia stepped in, desirous of meeting their honoured guest. She tapped the door politely and entered with the tea and biscuits, her already ruddy outdoor face flushing even more so as she glanced at Henry Tibbatts – a man of around fifty who had the features of a world war two fighter pilot, if fighter pilots can be said to have standardized features.

132

Henry thanked her for his HobNob and she blushed some more.

"Do you get to this neck of the woods often?" she enquired, by way of breaking the ice.

"I do, actually," replied Henry. "I go to Cheltenham occasionally for the Gold Cup, and Worcester races now and again, when the gallery permits!"

"You like horses then?"

"How did you guess? I have two myself. They eat me out of house and home, them and my ex wife."

Claudia just gazed at him and seemed lost for words. Eventually, she stumbled out with her tray, having temporarily forgotten how to work the door handle.

Simon suggested that they take a look at the pictures, and then maybe pop to the Cat for lunch. To this end, the three men walked into the nearby Yellow Room. Henry, who was now becoming extremely excited, albeit in his restrained, curator-like way, strode over to the far wall and began to examine the pictures in detail.

"And these are the Millichip fakes, propped up against the wall?" he checked. David nodded.

Henry, previously so talkative, now fell silent. He paced a bit, clutching his chin. He picked at his left ear with his forefinger. He scratched his fighter pilot head. Then, more in keeping with the pilot of a Lancaster than a Spitfire, he dropped the massive bombshell.

"I really don't know how to tell you this, Simon, but all four of these are fakes."

* * *

Lunch at the Cat was a terse, silent affair, at least until Claudia arrived. Simon, understandably, was wallowing in the depths of despair, and David wasn't much better. There was no logic to it whatsoever, and David was struggling to understand what had gone on, and the wider implications thereof.

Having examined the four pictures for himself after Henry dropped his deadly load, David was swift to concur. They were indeed fakes, but interestingly, the two that the police retrieved had the eyes that followed the viewer around the room and the correct peasant to cow ratio. Did this then mean that the pictures that Simon had grown up with had been fakes all along? If they were, when had they been faked? Had Simon's father arranged the subterfuge years back to pay off a debt or two, maybe? And how ironic that Simon was planning to sell off the family silver, only to find that someone had got there ahead of him.

The conversation, since the arrival of Simon's sister, had subtly divided into two. Simon and David seemed to be experiencing a private hell made for just them and had become virtually monosyllabic, whilst Claudia and Henry appeared to be getting on with it like a house on fire. Meanwhile, Jeremy the chauffeur, who was feeling a little left out of things, sat quietly in the corner swallowing pint after pint of Tutton Ale. It was only when he slid off his red leatherette-topped stool and into the fireplace that anyone noticed him.

This rather neatly drew proceedings to a close. Jeremy was helped to his feet and given a stern telling off from Henry, backed up by the barmaid, who reckoned that Southerners, being Southerners, always underestimated the potency of Tutton Ale. Simon suggested that Henry and Jeremy stayed the night, in any two of the ten bedrooms that took their fancy, and went home the next morning after a good breakfast.

Claudia asked Henry if he'd care to visit her stables, which he said he'd be delighted to do, leaving Jeremy sleeping it off in the

Green Room on an antique chaise longue. Meanwhile, Simon and David slumped onto a nearby settee and groaned in unison.

"There's something not right here!" frowned David. "I need a walk!" and with that, he excused himself and took off along the gravel path to the Sheep Walks in search of inspiration. He passed Henry and Claudia and waved to them, but they were far too wrapped up in their conversation to notice him. He paced across the hill and down the other side to where Johnny O'Driscoll's camp had been, and where Trev had been so brutally attacked. It was yet another warm day, but the sky was now an ominous purple colour again, signalling that another thunderstorm was imminent. David, hot and tired, sat on a stile and tried to think. For five minutes or so nothing came, but then, it hit him like a bolt from the blue. It was so simple, it was brilliant.

Harry Millichip was delivering a job to Evesham. If David remembered correctly, it was the following day, Friday. This job was going to make him a load of money; enough to top up his pension, he'd said, so that he could retire to New Zealand the following week. The Bay of Islands - it sounded lovely.

Harry had faked two versions of *both* paintings. One pair that Raymond presumed were the originals, which Harry had secretly planted on the Green and Yellow Room walls, and another pair for Raymond to substitute them for. Brilliant! Raymond duly absconded with two fakes which he was going to try and sell to Herr Grunstrasse, Simon was left with two more fakes on the wall, and meanwhile, Harry has got away scot-free with the real originals, and no-one has even noticed. Consequently, there's no heat on him whatsoever; he does the deal with his very own unscrupulous art dealer, whoever that may be, and the following week, he's begun his new life down under.

All this, of course, was mere conjecture, but it sounded right to David. Harry, the cheeky bugger, had even given David clues during their last conversation, and David had wished him well and even topped up his blasted pension scheme to the tune of one and a half grand. David rose from the stile, lashed out at a nearby tree in anger with his foot and instantly wished he hadn't when it began to throb horribly. He stared across the lane at the wheat field that still bore the scars of O'Driscoll's brief stay, and a thought occurred to him. It was a long shot, but his instinct *had* been serving him well of late.

O'Driscoll was an Evesham man. That was where he came from, if indeed a traveller can be said to come from anywhere. Was this a coincidence? Maybe, but it was something to look into. David ran back to the mews as fast as he could manage and arrived there fifteen minutes later, steaming like one of Claudia's prize racehorses. He staggered into his studio, and was about to pick up the phone and dial the police, when it rang. It was his Arab client, enquiring about *his* racehorse, and the remote possibility of him ever clapping eyes on it again.

"Ah, good afternoon," grinned David. "I have some good news for you. The painting is now totally dried out and repaired, and it will be sent off tomorrow, first thing, so you'll receive it, hopefully, in a week's time, Allah willing!" (David threw this last bit in because he thought it would impress his client.)

The gentleman seemed pleased, and said that he couldn't wait to see it. David replaced the receiver, crossed himself theatrically like a Roman Catholic priest and whispered, 'Lord help me'. He rang the police station using the usual number – they had not yet had time to install his personal Bat Phone like the one Commissioner Gordon used – and spoke to the desk sergeant, who now called David by the abbreviated version of his Christian name. Ten minutes later, the Evesham desk sergeant had been informed by his Stourbridge opposite number that a reliable informer had imparted a red-hot tip-off. On Friday, at a time as yet unknown, an art forger by the name of Harry Millichip would try to peddle two multi-million pound paintings to Johnny O'Driscoll. It was crucial that the squad located and staked out the traveller's camp, so they could catch them all red-handed.

Exhausted but at the same time exhilarated and experiencing a very intense feeling of *déjà vu*, David trudged round to Trev's dreary office to check his mail and tend to his answering machine, before he made his way home for the evening. Outside, the wind was whipping up again, as another thunderstorm began to blow in over the estate. Poor old Trev was missing all the fun, and tomorrow was the big one, all being well. It was the day of reckoning for the scumbag whose gang had beaten Trev to a pulp, and hopefully, the day David returned Messrs Constable and Sargent to Edgecliff Hall.

CHAPTER 15

Harry in Heaven

David carefully packed the Stubbs copy away in a robust plywood box and left it by the door, awaiting the courier's arrival. He had done a first rate job, but he felt thoroughly ashamed of himself. Instead of owning up to destroying the original, like a man, he had chosen a route that went against everything his mother and father had instilled in him. It just showed that no-one was above immorality if the stakes were high enough, and boy, were they high. Coming clean would almost certainly have bankrupted him, and that, sadly, was where David was forced to draw the line. It was, therefore, with a heavy heart and jangling nerves that he finally handed the package over at two o'clock that afternoon. He knew full well that he would eventually have to be on the receiving end of a long-distance call with his heart in his mouth sometime the following week. The only thing he didn't yet know was whether the Arab gentleman would be ringing to warn that he was having him arrested or merely to congratulate him on a marvellous job.

David filled the Laser 'Maestro' and slumped down onto the chesterfield with one of his trademark heartfelt sighs. No sooner had he done so when the doorbell rang. It was Donald and Pongo, and they looked more serious that David had ever seen them look during their long association. They invited him to sit down again and joined him.

Harry Millichip, the ashen-faced officers sadly informed him, had been found dead on the edge of a lay-by just outside of Evesham. He had been shot in the back of the head. His car was found nearby and it was empty. Johnny O'Driscoll was indeed at an unofficial travellers' site a few miles away, where he'd been all day, according to undercover police officers. This didn't mean, of course, that he hadn't had a hand in it, but nothing could be proven.

David just stared at the wall, unable to speak. He was in such a state of shock that Pongo actually volunteered to make the tea for him.

Poor Harry. This was to be his last illegal job before he made amends. Now there would be no Bay of Islands, no little café and gallery, no new life. He was lying on a mortuary slab somewhere in Worcestershire with a label tied to his big toe and a nasty scorched black hole in the back of his head. Harry was one of the best painters that David had ever met, but the man didn't have a voice of his own. He was the Rory Bremner of the painting world – wonderful at being someone else, but in Harry's case, not great at being himself. Monet was arguably the most famous impressionist, but in a way, Harry was a better one; he had the bigger repertoire, in that he could impersonate just about anyone. Now he had paid the ultimate price for staying on the wrong side of the tracks - killed for the sake of a few square feet of old canvas with paint daubed onto it. And David knew who'd done this. He couldn't prove it, but he knew. He bit his trembling lip and swore a Sicilian oath of vengeance. La vendetta e una piatto che va mangiato freddo. Revenge is a dish best eaten cold. So far, O'Driscoll had stolen a caravan, wrecked a restaurant, ordered his heavies to beat Trev to a pulp and probably had poor Harry murdered. The crimes seemed to have become more and more heinous, and yet each time he was able to just walk away from them. This had to stop, and David made it his responsibility to see that it did. That very day, David had committed his first and last illegal act, (if one excluded breaking into Raymond's shop) and he was ashamed of himself. He was no better than Harry now. Perhaps catching and incarcerating O'Driscoll would act as a form of atonement for his sin.

Donald and Pongo were not renowned for their sensitivity, but even they realized that David was in a state. He was shaking visibly and deeply upset with himself for not trying to ring Harry in order to dissuade him from keeping his tryst with the travellers. If only the man had decided to sell the paintings to Herr Grunstrasse instead, he would almost certainly have still been alive. The fat man was obnoxious, but at least, once he'd deemed the goods to be kosher and had agreed a fee, he was as good as his word.

David suddenly sat bolt upright on the settee, which was always a sure sign that he'd had an idea. Unfortunately, it didn't necessarily signify that it was a good one.

"Donald, I know this is a hell of a long shot, but can you beat a phone number out of Raymond Bingham?" he asked.

"Whose number?" asked Donald, enthusiastically.

"It's a bloke by the name of Grunstrasse. He's that bent German art dealer that you arrested way back in 1972, do you remember? We caught him at Twopenny Green aerodrome, trying to buy the Monet."

"Bloody hell, yes. Is he still alive and kicking? He must be seventy-odd now if he's a day."

"Yes, he must be, and he's still every bit as bent by the sound of it. Our Ray was trying to sell the paintings to him, but you caught him before he could pull it off. I'm convinced that O'Driscoll was behind this murder. He must have sent his henchmen to meet Harry in a lay-by while he gave himself the perfect alibi. They took the originals from him in return for the promise of a wheelbarrow full of cash that they had no intention of parting with, and they gave him a little lump of lead to keep instead. The chap was barmy to trust them. So anyway, let's

140

assume, just for a second, that O'Driscoll has these paintings – just humour me here - what can he do with them? He needs a dodgy art dealer. Ray Bingham knew about Grunstrasse. Lord Hickman did too, all those years ago. They both knew who they could approach. The fat bugger has a big reputation, obviously. Maybe, just maybe, O'Driscoll knows him as well. His gang used to break into big stately homes to steal art and antiques, right? Where did they fence those then? Not on Evesham's Farmer's market of a Sunday, that's for sure. They needed an international dealer with lots of contacts and no scruples, and there can't be millions of such characters, surely? If I could get hold of Grunstrasse's number, I could find out if he knows O'Driscoll."

"How could you?" asked Donald. "Ring him up and ask him if he plans to meet a bloke called O'Driscoll soon to buy a Constable off him?"

"No, stupid. Credit me with *some* intelligence!"

"So how would you do it then?" asked Pongo.

"Well, erm, I'm not sure yet, but first things first. I need that number."

Donald rang the station and spoke to his senior officer. Apparently, Raymond 'Bingo' Bingham was being interviewed in Interview Room Two as they spoke. He said he would pop his head around the door and ask nicely for Grunstrasse's number, whilst nonchalantly swinging his truncheon around, and occasionally whacking it onto the table near to where Ray was being grilled. Meanwhile, Donald was asked to sit patiently and await his call.

David busied himself washing up the cups and making more tea, while Pongo read the newspaper. Donald wandered aimlessly around the studio, messing with things, being nosey and whistling 'Beautiful' by James Blunt, in his own haunting, atonal style. Beautiful it wasn't. After five minutes of this ghastly tape-loop of noise, David snapped and begged him emphatically to cease.

"I *like* that song," Donald informed him. "It's very catchy, but I've always wondered who Adam Shaw was."

David gave him one of his looks. "Adam Shaw?"

"Yeah. You know the bit. 'I saw an angel, of Adam Shaw'."

David closed his eyes and breathed in deeply through his nose. Donald's phone rang. It was his senior officer, reporting back. Ray Bingham had sung like a canary. They had Grunstrasse's number.

* * *

That evening, David sat in his kitchen at home, talking to Suzanne.

"Do you reckon I'm good at accents?" he asked her, out of the blue.

"Better than me," she conceded. "My Welsh always sounds like Pakistani according to you. Why?"

"What do you think of my Irish? Listen. Yay ken all come dyne tay my hyse nye for a wee drank, so yer can, there nye."

"Pretty good I suppose, compared to mine anyway. What, are you considering a new career as an impressionist? I doubt whether it would fool another Irishman."

"Yes, but would it fool a German, do you think?"

"You never know. Something tells me that this is leading somewhere. I'm almost scared to ask."

"Then don't," smiled David, "Now, if you'll kindly bugger off into the living room and shut the door behind you, I have a call to make, and please, don't let Jay or Lauren burst in while I'm on the phone, or I'm sunk."

Suzanne did what she was told for once. David drew a deep breath and rang the number. It rang six times, and then someone answered. He was breathing heavily, as if he'd run a marathon. If this was Herr Grunstrasse, it was probably just the exertion of getting across the room to answer the phone.

"Ja, wer ist da, bitte?"

"Ye'll have tay speak English, man. Ay cannae speak that German bollocks, so ay can't. Is everything okay still with our meeting, there nye?"

"Who is zis please?" repeated Herr Grunstrasse.

"Johnny O'Driscoll. I have a Constable and a Sargent to sell, remember?"

"I know no–one by zat name," Herr Grunstrasse assured David. "And why is it zat suddenly everyone is trying to sell me Constables and Sargents? Guten Abend!"

Herr Grunstrasse had put the phone down on him. Their conversation was brief, *aber sehr interessant*. The German didn't know O'Driscoll. This was disappointing, but then again, it was only ever a long shot. It would have been too good to be true if O'Driscoll had indeed been selling the goods to him. 'Everyone is trying to sell Constables and Sargents', Grunstrasse had said. Now that was the good bit. Was he just referring to the fact that Ray Bingham had previously tried to do so? Probably. Or was he admitting that another party had also been in touch, offering to sell the same pictures? Unlikely, unless of course, Harry's death was nothing to do with O'Driscoll, and now the new owners of the paintings were getting in touch with a view to selling. Very interesting indeed, but as usual, it just threw up far more questions than answers.

Perhaps David had even wronged Johnny O'Driscoll. Maybe he hadn't been responsible after all. As usual in David's life, things were getting more than a little complicated.

CHAPTER 16

An unexpected letter

"You look shagged out!" observed Laz, as he sat in David's kitchen stealing his biscuits as usual.

David was idly flicking through Suzanne's Daily Mail magazine. A full page advert caught his eye.

'A true gift of love - The Princess Diana commemorative toilette seat, hand-crafted from MDF, so that our precious rainforests can be preserved for future generations. Finished with real 24 carat Midasite® gold-effect fittings and studded with sparkling synthetic energizing crystals, which are proven* to heal most illnesses. When the seat is lifted, a hidden speaker plays Enya's breathtakingly beautiful instrumental version of George Michael's 'Careless Whisper', one of Diana's favourite songs, whilst a small battery-operated pump emits a subtle, single puff of a very similar perfume to Chanel Number 5, her favourite fragrance. This exquisite, limited edition collector's item comes in a regal, purple crushed velvet draw-string bag bearing Diana's signature embossed in gold, accompanied by a certificate of authenticity which has been printed using actual lithographic techniques onto high-quality paper. Pay no money unless you are absolutely delighted, enchanted and enthralled. Illustration shown at higher than actual quality. We regret that goods cannot be returned once used.'

"What?" mumbled David absently.

"Shagged out - you," repeated Laz. "Doesn't he, Suze?"

Suzanne nodded in agreement.

"Well, it's hardly surprising," moaned David. "This has been the most mental couple of months I've ever experienced. Even by our standards, it's been crazy. I'm getting on for fifty. I should be bloody slowing down, not trying to solve every crime in South Staffordshire on my own and painting the bloody Sistine Chapel ceiling in my spare time. No wonder I'm feeling jaded, I say!"

"Well, can't you take a week off?" suggested Laz. "You've done your design for the ceiling now and converted it to lines and numbers. You can't do anything else with it now till July the 18th, when the students turn up. Your Stubbs has been sent off to Saudi – what else do you have on?"

"Nothing pressing I suppose."

"Good, 'cause you're coming to Italy with me for a week."

"I am?"

"Yes. My treat. I've squared it with Suze. She's glad to get rid of you. I want to go on a fact-finding mission, starting with Florence. There's an agency based there that can supply good chefs who are willing to settle in other countries. I want to mooch round the restaurants, trying the food and seeing what sort of dishes we can serve in Michelangelo's, because it needs to be really authentic, like you said. You can go look at all those bloody galleries and museums that you like, and study the Botticellos."

"Botticellis actually."

"Whatever. I've sorted out a nice little hotel. I thought we'd stay a few days and catch the train down to Rome, so you can go and see the Sistine Chapel ceiling to give you a bit of inspiration. We'll have a few days there, eat and drink far too much as usual and then fly home, just in time to get cracking on my mammoth job. I'll pay; you can tip the waiters. Deal?"

David was thrilled. "You sure you don't mind, Suze?"

"No, I'm planning to get a nice black muscle-bound fireman in while you're away."

"Saves me a dirty job. It's a deal them, Laz, and thank you!"

"My pleasure, Dave. I was so chuffed with that painting you did for me, I came over all benevolent."

"Er, oh, right, er, thanks."

Suzanne disappeared and came back seconds later.

"I *thought* I heard the postman!" she said, handing him a white envelope. "Here, something for you."

David opened it and took out a letter. It was from Harry Millichip. It read:

Dear David,

Nice to see you the other day, and I hope you liked the painting. As you know, I'm off to New Zealand on Tuesday. I've sold my house just outside Worcester, but I didn't know what to do with all the stuff in my studio, which is a separate summer house-type building in the back garden. Where I'm going I can't take it with me, so I'll have to invest in new equipment when I get there, if I ever need to. The new owner said he'd leave it untouched until I decided what to do with it all, as he wasn't in a hurry to do anything with the old place. I was going to let him give away what he could to the students at the college and bin the rest, but then I thought about you. There's all sorts - paints, brushes, canvases, easels, palettes, frames, varnishes, art books, you name it. Stuff I've collected over a lifetime. If you want any of it, it's yours, and I know you'll put it to good use. It would make me feel better if you took it.

I can't wait for Tuesday now. I know you don't approve of how I earned my living, but as I said, Saturday is the day I finally say goodbye and good riddance to this dodgy career. I'm going straight, mate!

If you're interested, ring Richard Spratley on the number below, and he'll show you round the old studio. Take the lot if you want it, and as you squirt out a tube of my Burnt Sienna onto one of my old palettes one day, think of me, serving cappuccinos to the tourists in the Bay of Islands, with the Cobalt Blue ocean outside my front window, lined with Sap Green palm trees and a Yellow Ochre beach. Imagine the Payne's Grey tail of a sperm whale arcing majestically out of the water, or maybe the Cadmium Red of the hydrofoil boat that takes you on the dolphin- watching trip twice a day. Or you might like to sit and observe the Lamp Black penguins comically waddling up the beach like the seven dwarves after a hard day's fishing.

Goodbye, and wish me luck!

Harry

David stood transfixed. Suzanne asked him what was wrong, but he couldn't answer. His eyes had become blurred now, and he found himself weeping again. Laz took the letter from him and he and Suzanne began to read it. Laz threw a comforting arm around his friend.

"Did this chap do a painting for you?" he asked.

"Oh, erm, yes. He did a little job for me, nothing you saw I don't think," lied David, deeply ashamed and feeling utterly miserable. "I'm sorry folks, but to read that last bit, and to know that he's lying dead on a slab, it's all too much. It's so bloody cruel."

Laz rubbed David's back gently.

148

"I'll phone this chap, Spratley," said David, trying his best to pull himself together, "and I will collect Harry's stuff. I couldn't bear to see it wasted, especially now."

Laz finished off his coffee and said goodbye. The flight to Florence was on Monday at eleven a.m., so he arranged to pick David up at seven-thirty, even though it wasn't Laz's best hour. His hobby was buying alarm clocks and then smacking them heavily into the wall when they did what was expected of them. He'd got through eight in two years.

David waved him off, thanking him profusely for his generous gesture, and then slumped down into his soft leather settee. There was something in Harry's letter that he wanted to re-read. When he had visited the studio to deliver the ceiling painting, Harry said that he had two deliveries to make, and then he was a free man, or words to that effect. One on Friday, and one on Saturday, he'd said. Friday had been his ill-fated liaison with whoever had killed him, as he presumably tried to peddle his Constable and Sargent originals, so what was he supposed to be delivering today, and where had it been left? Could it be that whatever it was was still in the garden studio, waiting for its creator to come for it?

David rang Richard Spratley. His wife, Pat said he wasn't in, but asked if she could help. David told her who he was, and that he wished to empty the old studio in the garden of their new house. The lady explained that they hadn't yet moved in, and they were still living in East Sussex. They planned to move to Worcester the following week, and David was welcome to pop over then, which meant that he'd have to go once he'd returned from Italy. David thanked her, took her mobile number, and put the phone down.

Whoever was expecting Harry today, thought David, was going to be very disappointed.

149

Twopenny Green aerodrome was almost deserted, which was unusual for a Saturday. A cream and red Cessna four-seater plane stood on a distant corner of the field, looking bored. It had been there for two hours, becalmed, and the man who had chartered it at considerable expense was getting more than a little annoyed.

Herr Grunstrasse turned to Pierre van der Truck, his diminutive, swivel-eyed Dutch pilot.

"Three times in our lives, we haf been dragged to zis God-forsaken aerodrome, and three times it has ended in disaster for us. I haf had a nose-full of English criminals, Pierre. Zey are not reliable, *mein Freund*. Turn the plane around. Ve are going home."

CHAPTER 17

Anyone for Pene Arrabiata?

Santa Maria Novello train station hadn't changed at all since David was last there in the summer of 1972. It was still noisy, chaotic and bustling. Outside, it was still pouring with rain, and inside, a thousand Italians were still smoking, arguing, kissing cheeks, chatting and waving their arms around like crazy. It was wonderful to be back in the second-best country on earth again, and especially Florence, cradle of the renaissance.

"I hope you know where the hell you're going, because I don't," moaned Laz, trying in vain to guide his heavy suitcase across the uneven cobblestones outside the station with one hand, while shielding his head from the drizzle with a newspaper held by the other.

"God, this is sentimental," smiled David, also struggling with a case that made a Tesco shopping trolley handle like a formula one racing car by comparison. "When I was eighteen or nineteen, I stayed just over there in Lord Hickman's apartment."

"Was that the one you accidentally flooded when your towel blocked the shower plughole as you dashed to answer the phone?" asked Laz.

David grunted and changed the subject. "Just over in that direction is the actual perfume shop they used in that Hannibal Lecter film. What was that called now?"

"Hannibal?" suggested Laz.

"Yeah, that was it. And down there is the market with the bronze wild boar statue that everyone has to stroke for good luck. That's in the film as well, and you know the building where Hannibal slits that bloke's stomach open and his entrails fall out into the square, well that's…"

"Jeez, I've got the point," interrupted Laz. "Can you shut up about that or I'll be having nightmares tonight? Now find me this bloody hotel will you, if you know the place like the back of your hand. It's called Giovanni or something. Look at the leaflet; I don't want to get my hair wet or it goes all frizzy. I'm the sort who gets wet easily."

David took the soggy, crumpled leaflet from his coat pocket.

"It's Giaconda, cretin. I bet you don't know what that means."

"Haven't got a clue. Is it anything to do with Anaconda?"

"No, strangely enough. It's actually the real name of the painting we all call the Mona Lisa. The painting was stolen from the Louvre once, ages ago, and the thief hid it at this very hotel for a while, which is how it got its new name. Fascinating eh? It's in Via Panzani, which is just down here and turn right I think. Very convenient! According to this, your chef agency is just round the corner."

The two drowned rats eventually fetched up at the hotel, Laz with a wheel now missing from his suitcase and in his usual foul mood as a consequence. They grabbed their room keys, agreed to part company for a while to rest, freshen up and change out of their sodden clothes, and then hit the city to do some sight-seeing before dinner.

"Okay, where do you fancy?" asked a refreshed and slightly less ratty Laz, two hours later. "We haven't got very long today, but we've got all day tomorrow. It's your call."

"Let's go see Michelangelo's David then," said David, "being as we're here because of your restaurant. It's only a few minutes away. The rain's stopped now, so we can walk it."

Laz gave David one of his withering looks. He understood the concept of walking, obviously, but he'd never actually put it into practice. Here was a man who'd once asked the taxi to stop and wait for him outside the Spar supermarket in Kinver High Street so he could buy some fags, even though his eventual destination was the restaurant four doors away.

"I'll get the chap on reception to…" he began.

"No you won't," interrupted David. "You can walk. It'll do you good, and help get that stomach off you. I know a shortcut through an alleyway. I just hope Hannibal isn't lurking around, waiting for us."

Five minutes later, they were at the Galleria dell'Accademia queuing for tickets. Mercifully, the queue was smaller than usual due to the lateness of the hour, and half an hour later they were stood before the famous statue.

"It's massive!" enthused Laz, who'd only ever seen reproductions of it in magazines. "It must be nearly twenty feet tall. I had no idea."

"It is just that," confirmed David. "Michelangelo was given a huge, second-hand chunk of marble and told to do something good with it, so he did. Can you see how it looks a bit disproportionate in this room? The head is a bit too big, but that was done on purpose. Originally it stood outside on a plinth and you had to look right up at it, so to create the illusion of correct proportions from that acute angle, he made the top section bigger."

"Clever bastard," observed Laz, impressed. "None of these renaissance chaps had big knobs though did they?"

"Erm, it depends what you're used to," mumbled David. "Can you imagine him carving this out of a solid block of marble? I wouldn't have a clue where to begin. Just think about it for a second, Laz. It's mind-boggling."

"Beats me," agreed Laz. "And imagine having to carve that knob in perfect detail. If any civic dignitaries or maybe even the Pope dropped by to see how it was going and he was on the knob at the time – well, I suppose he'd get all self conscious."

"He was homosexual, so I bet he loved doing it," countered David. "Take a look at his carvings of women. Some of them are blatantly men with long hair and tits added on. I reckon staring at women didn't appeal to him, so if he got a commission for a woman statue, he got one of his gay mates to pose and he just adapted him a bit."

"What is it with these artist types?" asked Laz. David didn't dignify that with an answer.

"Just looking at that knob in detail, as we were," he continued, "have you noticed how he's done the old pubes? They're made up of shapes almost like curled leaves. I've just counted them as it happens. There are twenty-one of them, the same as the number of letters in the Italian alphabet in those days."

"Fuck me, Dave," frowned Laz. "You're the weirdest bloody chap I've ever met. What possessed you to count his bloody pubes, for God's sake?"

David flushed red. "I dunno, I just did. I have an analytical mind I suppose. And have you noticed that he's carved a deeper groove into some of those leaf shapes for some reason?"

"For Christ's sake mate, it's not something I'd notice, to be honest with you. Did Rube and Len drop you on your head when you were a baby or what? What a bloody thing to pick up on!"

"You are interest in his private parts, no?" asked the security guard.

"Er, no, no," stammered David, deeply embarrassed. "We were just admiring the skill, you know."

"Si, but you hava talk about his dick for a long time. Perhaps you move on now, eh? You maker theser old ladies behind you embarrass, eh?" The guard wandered off, glancing over his shoulder at them twice as he went.

"I'm intrigued by this you know," said David, taking out his Nikon digital and photographing the statue's penis.

"Dave, for *God's* sake!" hissed Laz, "he'll think we're a pair of lifters."

The guard wandered back. "Gentlemen, no photography inna here, *per favore*. Why did you take a peecture of his dick? I think you are obsessed by the dick, no?"

"I didn't!" protested David, lying through his teeth, "It's a wide angle lens, I was… "

"No photographs please," he repeated, and wandered away again, once more glancing over his shoulder.

"You're going to get us bloody chucked out, you nutter," whispered Laz loudly.

"Yeah, okay, let's go," said David distractedly. "Hell of a coincidence though."

* * *

David and Laz whiled away the next hour drinking cappuccini outside a café in the Piazza del Duomo.

"You are the weirdest straight bloke I've ever met," Laz concluded. David looked back at his friend, who had grown an impressive cappuccino moustache, and decided that no comment was necessary. "Who else but you counts pubes?"

"Look, as I pointed out, I have an enquiring mind, that's all. Listen to this, and then tell me if I'm mad. That carved willy had twenty-one individual leaf shapes, for the want of a better description. A few of them had extra deep grooves cut in them that you only really notice close up, rather than the standard fine curly ones, if you follow me."

"I can't believe this conversation. It's surreal."

"Listen will you? The fifth from the extreme top left had two deep grooves. The twelfth had one and the fourteenth had one. What do you make of that then?"

"Fuck all."

"Well don't you think it's a bit random?"

"Pubes aren't neat and tidy. Well mine aren't anyway."

"Fair enough, I accept that, but hear me out. I speak some Italian and you don't. The Italian word for penis is pene."

"Shit, no? I'll never order Penne Arrabiata again!"

"With one 'N', dick head - or *testa di cazzo*, as they'd say around here. Now imagine a simple number code, where one is A, two is B, three is C, etcetera, only remember that the old Italian alphabet doesn't have a J, K, W, X or Y. They only use those letters nowadays for imported foreign words. Michelangelo has carved deep grooves on the E twice, mark you, and on the P and N once. Those pubes spell out an anagram of PENE. If I'm correct, no-one has ever spotted this, in five hundred years."

"It's just a bloody coincidence," judged Laz.

"Not so," argued David. "What are the odds? I'm telling you, the old bugger had a sense of humour. We have discovered something of major importance here, I'm telling you."

"What, that Michelangelo wrote 'penis' in a pile of unruly pubes? I can't see it being a Trivial Pursuit question any time soon, can you? I can't imagine Jeremy Paxman asking it as a starter for ten."

"I agree," conceded David, "but it's not about one statue is it? It's surely about what *else* he might have done. We're off to Rome in a few days. I'm going to be seeing the Sistine Chapel ceiling in a whole new light now!"

* * *

That evening, David and Laz dined at a very smart restaurant overlooking the river, near the Ponte Vecchio. It was Laz's treat, and he asked David to photograph the menu and the food, in case the dishes could be recreated at Michelangelo's, once his chefs were found.

The waiter showed them to their seats and took their drinks order. He was a chatty fellow by the name of Tomaso, and clearly saw himself as a bit of a comedian, hampered only by his rather erratic English. He purposely made a bee-line for David and Laz in order to hone his language skills and pick up a few useful phrases, to the point where David feared he might have the man on his lap throughout the entire meal. Laz, on the other hand, being the more gregarious of the two, was lapping it up.

The food was without question the type of cuisine that Laz aspired to for his own establishment, and he and the waiter entered into in-depth discussions over a post-dinner grappa or two about the best way to progress this. Tomaso had many friends who might consider a move to England if it meant running their own place and being virtually given free rein to create quality menus. The way things were going, Laz might not even need to visit the agency. Tomaso had it all sorted out.

As the other two spoke, David remained on the periphery of things, sipping his grappa contentedly and soaking up the atmosphere. He gazed dreamily around the room, and his gaze was met by a pair of eyes he vaguely recognized. He slipped his reading glasses on and took another look, before whipping them off again and turning away. It was the security guard from the Galleria del'Accademia. He was dining with another young man,

157

and now this guard was pointing rudely towards David's table and whispering to his friend, who was sniggering.

"Of course, where we come from," he heard Laz saying to his new best mate, Tomaso, everyone eats Indian food. We're famous for Baltis in Brum. I love really hot curries, but this girly puff here can't stand 'em. Italian is his thing."

"I lover the hot curries too," agreed Tomaso. "The 'otter, the better for me. You wait 'ere – I show you something."

He shot off in the direction of the kitchen and returned with a small bowl of cashew nuts.

"You trya please," he asked Laz.

David reached into the bowl and grabbed a few nuts for himself. "I love cashews!" he declared.

"Not these you won't," warned Laz. "Don't put them in your mouth, Dave. They're infused with red hot chilli peppers I bet. This bugger's trying to play a trick on me."

Tomaso laughed. "You 'ear about these? You are right, my friend. It'sa the 'ottest chilli you can buy. Red Savina Habanero Chilli. You try a leetle taste, justa for me."

Laz made sure his lager was to hand, crossed himself and took the tiniest nibble possible.

At first, nothing happened, and then his face turned purple. His eyes bulged and steam appeared to be escaping from his ears in fine jets. He stood up. He sat down again. He placed his head on the tablecloth and groaned. Tomaso found this highly amusing. Laz grabbed his lager and downed it in one. He tried to communicate with David, but no words would come out of his bubbling lips, and all this from one miniscule nibble of an inoffensive looking cashew nut. If David had eaten a whole one, he would undoubtedly have died.

158

"Jesus Christ!" Laz eventually yelled, causing the other diners to glare at him angrily. This wasn't, as David well knew but Laz evidently didn't, the thing one said in pious Italy.

"JE-SUS!" growled Laz again, this time even louder. The security guard was glaring daggers now. David begged his friend to be quiet, hissing across the table that blasphemous remarks in front of devout Roman Catholics could end in fist fights. Finally, he seemed to get the message, and suffered in stoic silence from thereon in. David, who was very easily embarrassed, and usually at the hands of Laz, decided to visit the lavatory by way of a change of scenery. He strode past the security guard, who gave him a filthy look, and downstairs to the gents. He'd had a Peroni lager, half a bottle of Barolo, a glass of iced water from the jug and a grappa, and all of a sudden, he was desperate to pee. He slipped into the nearest cubicle, unzipped his fly and emptied his distended bladder, to his great relief.

Then, suddenly, he was aware of a burning sensation down below. It felt as if someone had poured sulphuric acid over his modest member. The pain was intense now, and his eyes started to water. It quickly became so bad that he was forced to yell out loud, and he began to panic. He burst out of the cubicle, his privates still hanging out of his trousers, and made for the sinks. Distressed and in severe pain, he punched the unfathomably trendy Italian tap, which responded by sending a ferocious jet of water into the sink, and then all over his chest. This was hopeless. He tried to climb into the sink in order to place his burning appendage under the stream of water, but it was impossible.

In the meantime, the pain, which, if measured on some form of scientific scale, had previously been, shall we say, a seven, now rocketed to a ten, causing David to squeal out loud like a pig being castrated. He catapulted out of the lavatory and back into the restaurant, his hands covering up his fiery little *'pene'*, and bashing into the security guard, sending his spaghetti flying across the table. Roaring with agony now, and ricocheting off every table in his path like a demented pinball, he headed for his and Laz's table and grabbed the jug of iced water. He ran out of the front doors and into the street, where he proceeded to drop his trousers and place his burning privates into the full jug, while howling at the full moon like a werewolf. Unfortunately, the Ristorante Bonini boasted an impressive pair of picture windows either side of the front door, so that diners could gaze out onto the Ponte Vecchio and the River Arno as they feasted. It was one of the world's most romantic views, but all they could see that evening was a mad Englishman with his penis immersed in a jug of iced water, screaming hysterically.

It was at this juncture that the security guard stepped in.

It was half past two the following afternoon before Laz managed to get David out of jail. The security guard had insisted that he was a sexual deviant, which didn't help, citing David's peculiar behaviour earlier at the Galleria del'Accademia.

"He hazza the penis fixation, probably because his own is very small," he had told the officers, as David was arrested for gross indecency, the previous evening. A small party of passing nuns, visiting the holy sites for the day, had to be sat down in the Ristorante Bonini and plied with strong espressos to calm them down. It was another hour or more before the burning sensation calmed down and David was able to be rational again. The sheer pain had taken him to the edge of sanity. All the way to the police station, he had been ranting about how Tomaso was going to die a horrible death by his hands, which also didn't help his case. It was only the following morning when reason had been restored to its throne, that he was able to quietly and rationally explain what had happened to him. The carabinieri had visited the restaurant to confirm his strange story, and given Tomaso a good telling off for playing his silly practical jokes. Worse still, for poor Tomaso at any rate, his boss had fired him instantly for almost destroying his restaurant's good reputation in one short evening. If this got back to the people at Michelin, he warned his trembling staff, they were *all* finished.

That afternoon David and Laz were keeping a low profile, eating a simple lunch in a small café, and hoping to God that the local newspaper didn't run an article on the Red Hot Sex Pest of Firenze. At least they'd be in Rome before it hit the streets, said Laz, trying his best to look on the bright side.

As they paid the bill and were about to leave, they encountered Tomaso, who told them of his misfortune. Laz, who somehow felt responsible for his sacking, took his number and promised to consider him for a job at Michelangelo's, with the proviso that he left his Habanero chilli pepper cashews behind in Italy. This seemed to raise the lad's spirits, and he wished them a pleasant train ride to the capital.

After lunch, which was, understandably, a subdued affair, Laz visited the agency, which promised to get in touch once he was back in England. The rest of the day was spent looking at Botticellis and mooching around markets, looking for presents to take home. Laz spent an hour or more in a record shop, digging out obscure Italian versions of his favourite Frank Zappa albums. For some strange reason, Italy also seemed to still be in thrall to Progressive Rock, a dinosaur that had become virtually extinct over in Britain some twenty years previously. Here they persisted in listening to Jethro Tull, Van der Graaf Generator and Genesis, which was interesting, culturally speaking. Either that, or it was Zuchero, a gravel-voiced home-grown 'talent' who seemed to infest every hotel lift and eatery, like some form of unchecked audio plague. After an hour's ecstatic rummaging, Laz made his final purchase, handed them his credit card and exited the tiny backstreet emporium, thrilled to bits.

"I've got loads of fantastic stuff you can't get back home," he enthused, "and I've even bought *you* something. Hopefully, it'll remind you of our week in Italy whenever you listen to it."

"Gee thanks," replied David, touched by his friend's generosity. "What is it then, flipping Zuchero's new album?"

"'Fraid not," said Laz, handing it over. "It's a cracking album called 'Californication', by the Red Hot Chilli Peppers."

* * *

Laz had drunk a few Peronis and a glass of wine or two with his first ever Roman pizza, and as a consequence, was singing loudly and out of tune on the open-topped city tour bus, much to David's embarrassment.

"Laz, be quiet, everybody's staring at us," he hissed, having moved three seats back from his friend to avoid guilt by association. "Besides, Arrivederci Roma is a stupid song to sing, being as we've only just got here."

"I'm enjoying myself," argued Laz. "When in Rome, do as the Romanians do, that's what I say. I'm gonna buy me a togo and get a nubile slave to feed me grapes while we watch Nero burn."

David closed his eyes - something he always did when he was truly, deeply embarrassed - and he mouthed the words 'give me strength'.

"It's a toga, moron. Togo is a small island near Saint Lucia, I think, wherever that is. Anyway, we have to get off here; we're at the Vatican City stop."

It had been, in spite of Laz's drunken singing, a wonderful morning. They had already been to the Trevi Fountain, the Coliseum, which was awe-inspiring, and the Spanish Steps, which were just some steps and clearly not Spanish, to boot, but this last stop, for them, was to be the highlight of the day. After suffering a queue that seemed to snake all the way back to Stourbridge, they eventually got to see Michelangelo's Sistine Chapel ceiling, and upon walking into the room, the hairs on the back of David's neck stood to attention out of sheer respect. It was an awesome spectacle that made him realize how insignificant his own talents were, in the scheme of things. Here was the result of Michelangelo spending four dreary, uncomfortable long years lying on his back, painting above his head in the most back-breaking of positions, with dollops of paint slopping into his eyes. Even the simple acts of eating or visiting the lavatory were a nightmare, thanks to the mountain of scaffolding he had to clamber down each time he returned to earth, or scale up again to resume work. It was common knowledge that he hated the commission he had been given; one he reckoned had made an old man of him before his time. Here was a person who had truly suffered for his art in a way that David couldn't even begin to imagine.

The two friends stood dumbstruck and stared upwards for what seemed an eternity. Even Laz, who wasn't overly interested in art, had to admit that this was a labour of love the like of which he'd never seen before, if love was indeed the right word to use.

"Will yours look anything like this?" he asked David after their long, thoughtful silence.

"Er, no," admitted David.

"Cheers!"

"Well, it's hardly fair to compare the two," argued David. "Your chapel is tiny compared to this bloody place for a start, and ours is a paint by numbers version, but for what it is, it'll still look fantastic, yes, absolutely. There won't be another restaurant in the world, probably, that has its own Michelangelo-style ceiling. It'll be unique, if you discount this one of course."

"True."

"I wonder if that great, complex masterpiece up there has any hidden messages in it," David pondered, "Or was the '*pene*' joke just a bit of fun; a one-off? When I get home, I think I'm going to present what I've discovered to the professors and art historians at Brum University. Maybe they'll begin to look at his work in a completely different way. It could make my name, I reckon."

163

"Or make you a laughing stock, one of the two," warned Laz, who was sobering up nicely now, just in time for dinner. "And talking of which, what was his actual name – Michelangelo I mean? Was that his first name or his surname? I've never understood it. Leonardo's surname was da Vinci, but people just say Michelangelo don't they?"

"I'm ashamed to say that I don't know the answer to that," admitted David. "It's one of the very few things in life that I don't know, but I can make amends. Look, here's a leaflet about him. I picked it up at the entrance, and – oh here we are, look, his name was Michelangelo di Ludovico di Liornardo di Buonarroti Simoni. What a mouthful!"

"Makes Larry Homer sound mundane."

"And David Day mundaner still, if there is such a word. Funny though, I've heard that name before - Buonarroti. It really rings a bell."

"Probably as common as Smith in Italian," reasoned Laz.

"Maybe," mused David. "Maybe - but I think not."

CHAPTER 18

Harry's Game

"Come on in!" smiled Richard Spratley. "You'll have to excuse the place, we haven't unpacked yet and everything's a mess. Sorry, I sound like my mother! Mind you don't fall over those. It's through here and out the back. Your friend Harry seemed like a nice enough chap, but the house will need some work doing to it. The central heating system is fifty years old if it's a day. I hear he's emigrated to New Zealand. Lucky sod!"

David wondered if he should break the news to them, but decided against it. There was no point, after all, and it might affect their feelings for the new house. Mr Spratley opened the back door and they walked out onto a pretty, if overgrown garden. They tripped down three steps and across the lawn to the studio, which was constructed of white shiplap and had a lovely covered front porch supported by wooden posts with ornate fretwork decoration at the top, just like a colonial building or an old cricket pavilion. Two steps led up to the white French windows, which Mr Spratley unlocked.

"I've been in here to nose around, but I haven't moved anything," he assured his visitor. "I'm glad you're taking everything, because we want to convert it into a proper summer house with blue Laura Ashley fabrics and wicker chairs and so on. It's gorgeous inside."

They walked in, and David would have known immediately that he was in an artist's studio, even if he were blindfolded. The wonderful smell of linseed oil, thinners and oil paint hit him instantly. To him, it was the best smell on earth, with lemons coming a close second. In the centre of the room were two easels, both empty, with a wooden stool. All three were liberally spattered with paint, as they should have been. There were a couple of large oak plan chests, a writing desk with an anglepoise lamp, and trolleys full of paints, palettes, pots of brushes and the paraphernalia of the artist. Along one wall was a simple, large bookshelf creaking under the weight of a thousand art books. Twenty or more swept frames leant against one wall, awaiting a painting that would fit. A huge glass-fronted cabinet housed hundreds of pieces of bric-a-brac that only an artist would collect, in the vain hope that they would one day be of use. The place was almost a mirror image of David's own studio. He felt like Howard Carter must have felt just after he'd broken into Tutankhamun's tomb. It was heaven.

"How on earth will you ever shift it all?" asked Mr Spratley. "You've turned up in a little Mercedes Coupe."

"I know a man with a van," David assured him. "I just wanted to see what I was up against today really. We'll pop back tomorrow, if that's okay, and then my mate Laz can help me with the heavy stuff. You'll have to dispose of the old cabinets and bookshelves I'm afraid, but at least I…"

David stopped halfway through his sentence. There were two paintings without frames propped against the wall, their old brown stretchers showing.

"Excuse me," said David. "Can I just look at these?"

He flipped the first painting over.

"Oh, that's a nice view," commented Mr Spratley. "Is that one of Mr Millichip's paintings?"

166

"Er, no, these two belonged to his dad, they're just old things, not really worth anything," replied David. "This one should be of an old bloke in a smoking jacket unless I'm very much mistaken. His, erm, great granddad, Harry said it was. He told me about these; said he especially wanted me to have them. Ah yes, here he is, the grumpy old bugger. Look how his eyes follow you round the room!"

"Shame," said Richard Spratley. "I wouldn't have minded that landscape one myself. Don't laugh, but it looks a bit like the sort of thing Constable used to do, to my untrained eye at any rate. Mind you, I am a chartered accountant, so what do I know?"

David laughed a tad too heartily – it was the first time he'd ever laughed at a chartered accountant's joke, as far as he could remember, but he was in a state of something approaching euphoria, after all. He said he'd take the paintings with him, and be back for the rest the following day, if that was okay.

* * *

Henry Tibbatts popped his head around the door and said hello.

"Goodness me," laughed David. "You back again?"

"Erm, yes. I have to declare the romantic interest, old chap. Claudia and I are what is commonly referred to as an item, though it's a phrase I can't abide. Love blossomed down at the stables whilst you were swanning around in Italy."

"Very pleased for both of you!" smiled David. "Now take a look at these drawings will you? Simon's had them forever, tucked away in an old box with various documents and this old letter. Any clues?"

Henry sat down at David's desk and studied them carefully.

"Very interesting indeed. Renaissance for a start. Fantastic quality, if a little creased, thanks to spending years in a bloody box. I couldn't possibly tell you who did them, but they are top class and probably five hundred years old, at an educated guess.

These alphabetic letters beneath the hands are strange - never seen that done before. I could get them looked at by the boffins and style experts if you'd like me to."

"Yes please," said David. "Now take a look at these." He produced the two paintings from Harry's studio.

Again, Henry fell silent for several minutes, looking at the pictures through his eyeglass.

"Well I never," he eventually mumbled. "I'm positive that these aren't the ones you showed me the other day for starters. Am I correct?"

"Yep!"

"And in my not so humble opinion, David, these are the originals, meaning that there are two fakes of each picture up at the hall, for reasons as yet unknown, making thee sets in total."

"Nope, by my reckoning - and maths admittedly isn't my strong point - there are *three* fakes of each plus the originals, making four in total."

"What? But why on earth would there be *three* copies in existence? I don't follow."

"Neither did I, but I think I do now, and it's bloody ingenious. Harry Millichip was an incredible forger, as you know, and well-known for being a hell of a quick painter. He must have had three lots of each painting going on a production line at once, and here's why. I reckon he painted one set for Ray Bingham, and another set for the hall, so he could abscond with the real ones. He did the initial set with purposely slightly altered details – the cows and peasants, and the pupils in subtly different positions, so that he could differentiate between the first two sets maybe, only no-one figured that Major Simon would actually spot the changes. Ray Bingham took what he *presumed* were the originals so that he could arrange his meeting with Grunstrasse, the German art dealer. Unknown to him, all he had was the second set of fakes – the ones with the correct peasants, cows and pupils. Meanwhile - and this is all guesswork you understand - old Harry must have had yet another set stashed away which he presumably tried to sell to the travellers, and that was where he came unstuck. Maybe they spotted that they were faked and got nasty, or far more likely, they never intended to pay for them anyway, took them believing them to be kosher and then killed him. I am willing to bet you a hundred quid that one day, that extra pair of fakes turn up somewhere – the Antiques Road Show or whatever. Harry told me that he was delivering two jobs on his final weekend, the first to Evesham, the second to Wolverhampton, and that's what set me thinking. I reckon he was intending to get money from the travellers for his third set of fakes, knowing they wouldn't have the expertise to know the difference, and he'd saved the originals for Grunstrasse, who definitely would know the difference. This way, he got paid twice – three times actually, if you count Ray Bingham's fee. Brilliant! The trouble was, by then, Harry was dead in a ditch, and Grunstrasse, who was maybe waiting for him at Twopenny Green aerodrome near Wolverhampton, presumably flew home empty-handed, which serves him right, the fat bastard."

"I need a sit down," complained Henry. "My brain hurts."

"Mine too," agreed David, "but I can't wait to surprise old Simon. He'll be absolutely thrilled. The hall isn't paying its way and he was considering selling the paintings, as you know. A couple of million quid will go a long way, that is of course, if you are now interested again."

"I am..." replied Henry, "...but your estimate is way off beam I'm afraid."

"Oh, really? I just presumed that…"

"A fairer price for the two would be around fifteen million, I'd have said. The Constable isn't a great one, in fairness, but it's a Constable nonetheless. The Sargent likewise. You're surprisingly out of touch on prices, me lad! I'd have liked both for the nation if we could afford it, but that might be more than difficult at the moment. We've overspent already this financial year on a nice but eye-wateringly expensive Van Gogh. If we can't stump up any cash, and it's doubtful that we can, I daresay we'll know someone who'd be able to. A wealthy Arab perhaps - they're the only ones with any dosh noawadays!"

This last comment saw David turn a whiter shade of pale. With all the excitement and the foreign travel, he'd completely forgotten about the Stubbs. The telephone rang without prior warning, as telephones are wont to do, causing him to leap like a rocketing pheasant from his seat, if indeed pheasants leap from seats. He made his excuses to Henry and answered it. It was, coincidentally, a wealthy Arab.

"Good morning, Mr Day," said Abdul Rashid, and he sounded a tad formal for David's personal taste. "I received the painting, but there is a problem with it. A very big problem with it, as it happens."

David had to sit down in a hurry. His breathing had become what is often referred to as laboured. In fact, he was actually snorting through his nose like a bull with sinus trouble.

"Oh, erm, right, er, what, exactly?"

"I picked the painting up from customs and then drove around to see my friend Mohamed for lunch. He works at the American Embassy. He is an art expert, so I wanted him to see your handiwork – give it his seal of approval, as it were."

David gulped and tried to say "yes, go on," but his voice had completely dried up. Abdul continued anyway.

"We are both art collectors. He collects Dutch seventeenth century works, and I am fond of English eighteenth and nineteenth century paintings, but that's by the by."

"Goomp!"

"I parked my Range Rover - I am fond of English vehicles too you see – and went to fetch him from his office, and as I waited for him in the reception area, suddenly there was the most almighty explosion. We felt the walls tremble and we were many yards away. When it was safe to do so, we dashed down to the street to see what had happened. It was carnage. Someone had planted a bomb in the car next to mine, and it had demolished half the street. Luckily, no-one was seriously injured, but that was more luck than judgement. So you see, my Stubbs has been totally destroyed, before I even had chance to admire you're restoration work. I am so, so sorry my friend, that all your hard work has come to nothing, and it goes without saying that I will pay you regardless."

"I s-s-see," stammered David. Henry glanced over at his with concern, no doubt wondering which of David's immediate family had died unexpectedly.

"You can imagine I am heart-broken," continued Abdul. "The Stubbs was the centrepiece of my collection. It cost me a lot of money!"

"I can imagine, and I'm very upset for you," said David, "but please don't concern yourself with my feelings. I was glad to help, and there's nothing either of us can do, other than you can maybe claim on your insurance. Listen, this isn't probably the best timing, but while I have you, would you be interested in a Constable?"

"A Constable? Well of course, if I could afford it."

"And how about a John Singer Sargent portrait?"

"Obviously. Not an English painter, but I'd consider such a quality piece, if the price was right. Why do you ask?"

"Oh, I have a friend who wants to sell them, but I fear the asking price might be too much for you."

This last comment was tantamount to accusing Abdul of being a homeless tramp, by Saudi standards. David perceived a marked stiffness in his response, which was of course, "How much?"

"Erm, sixteen million for the two. It's a lot, but we are after all talking…"

"The asking price does not frighten me Mr Day, if they are right, and have the provenance. After all, I paid nine million for the Stubbs."

"You did?" asked David, glancing over to his waste bin, with the mangled canvas protruding from it. "Well, I'll tell Major Winterfold - he's the owner of the pictures by the way - that you may be potentially interested, and then leave you to negotiate. Also, you may be interested to hear that I have Henry Tibbatts here with me, the curator of the National Gallery, who I believe you've spoken to before. He's just taken a look at the pictures and considers them absolutely genuine. How's that for provenance?"

"Excellent! I am mightily impressed with you and your contacts. Say hello to Henry for me, and thank you. I'll be in touch."

"And I'm extremely sorry to hear about your Stubbs," added David. "Goodbye!"

And with that, Abdul was gone.

David calmly rose from his chair, walked over to the middle of the room, and then screamed as loudly as he could, punching the air in delight. Once Henry had got over the initial shock of witnessing this strange spectacle, he naturally wished to know what had brought on this burst of raw emotion in his usually placid colleague.

"Oh, erm, just very pleased for Simon, that's all," David lied. "Now, would you care for a cup of tea and a chocolate HobNob, Henry?"

CHAPTER 19

The Michelangelo Code

David had just got back from visiting Trev at Russell's Hall Hospital, which explained why he was feeling a little subdued. Trev looked frail, and was still wearing the cage around his head which appeared to be holding it all together. He had more purple and yellow bruises on his body than a blind wicket keeper.

David filled the Laser 'Maestro' and studied Harry's ceiling artwork while he waited for it to boil. Everything was in order and ready to go when the students arrived at nine the following morning. In his absence, a courier had delivered the giant blow-ups of the numbered line-work, B&Q had delivered thirty large pots of specially mixed acrylic paint and the workmen had erected their scaffolding and left. Laz's building and refitting work was more-or-less completed now, so all that remained to be done was the front door signage, the ceiling painting, the menus, the wooden flooring, the kitchen's electrical equipment and, when everything else was completed, the installation of the furniture.

Once the tea was made, David turned his attention to his recently acquired library of art books which he and Laz had collected from Harry's studio. There was one huge, half-hundredweight slab dedicated to the works of Michelangelo that was particularly appealing, as it contained large blow-up details from the Sistine Chapel ceiling. While he sipped his tea, David flicked through the musty-smelling pages until he came to the famous panel, 'The Creation of Adam', where the two figures reach out to touch each other's hands. He stared at it silently for some five minutes, seemingly in a trance. Then he picked up the old renaissance drawings that Ray Bingham had stolen and dropped them alongside the heavy old book. Two of the hand studies were exactly the same as the two depicted in the book. This was a coincidence, but then again, these renaissance artists did rather go in for stock hand gestures. He flicked to another page and found several more hands shown in close up. After a brief search, once more he found exact copies amongst Simon's old drawings. This was very intriguing indeed. Impatiently now, he looked for more hands, and then for their counterparts in Simon's drawings. There was a match for every single one. Whatever page in the Michelangelo book he turned to, he could find an exact replica of whichever hand he chose. Indeed, he could not find a single one that *wasn't* represented in the old sketch sheets. From what he could see, the entire Sistine Chapel ceiling, with its four hundred-plus life-sized figures only consisted of twenty-one different types of hand gestures. Maybe, he reasoned, there *were* only twenty-one types of hand gesture, if one excluded the rude ones. After all, Roger Moore had carved a successful acting career out of only two facial expressions; quizzical and smug. In contrast, twenty-one was positively extravagant. And yet...... and yet, here was another coincidence, just like the Florentine pubes.

David studied a reproduction of the first of the nine ceiling panels, and began with the figure at the top left-hand side. He studied the man's two hands and located them on Simon's hand chart, as he now referred to it. According to the coded letters below the drawing, this spelt out R and A. He now focused on the figure to the immediate right of the first figure and located his hands on the chart. This gave him the letters F followed by another F.

Outside, dusk was slowly falling. David realized that he had lost all track of time, and Suzanne would be wondering where on earth he'd gone. An eerie rumble of distant thunder added to the drama of the scene, as if it were needed. It was a humid, atmospheric evening and the summer lightning was back. David switched on his angle-poise lamp and continued, beads of sweat trickling down his brow. He located the hands of the third figure along, and wrote down the two coded letters, A and E. The fourth figure only had one hand showing, which translated as L, and the next figure's hands spelt LO.

The first word he had managed to decipher was Raffaello. This was the Italian version of Raphael, and absolute proof, in David's mind at least, that his outrageous theory was actually correct. He was on the very brink of discovering something so important to the world of art that he could not stop his heart from pounding, so much so that he thought he might keel over from a stroke at any moment, caused by the enormity of it all. He stood up and took several deep breaths to compose himself before returning to his seat.

Then, one by one, he continued to painstakingly collect his letters, double-checking each one to be sure he hadn't made a mistake. Slowly, words appeared, or at least, they may have been words. They looked as if they could well be some form of Italian, but David couldn't tell where one word began and another ended, and this was seriously hindering his progress. After Raffaello, everything else was, to him, just gobbledegook. What he really needed was someone who could translate it, if indeed it was translatable. Whoever volunteered could also try to translate Simon's old letter while they were at it. David switched off his lamp, and was about to phone home when Suzanne beat him to it.

"Where the bloody hell are you?" she asked, a tad predictably.

"Just coming," he replied. "I got held up as usual. Look, let's go to Giovanni's tonight. Tell Jay and Lauren they can have a pizza, they'll love that, instead of having to eat your cooking. If you can quickly get ready, I'll pull up outside and peep the horn.

* * *

It was a quiet night at Giovanni's, so the proprietor was able to sit with David and translate his letter for him. This should have been a simple task, but it wasn't. The writing was extremely difficult to read and the style was not like modern Italian at all. There were all sorts of dialectic words and phrases. It was, according to Giovanni, like a German trying to read a letter written by a Dutchman. Nevertheless, he persevered over a grappa or two, the very aroma of which was bringing back unpleasant memories of Bonini's Restaurant for David.

"*Allora!*" said Giovanni eventually, after he had studied the document carefully for several minutes in silence, his reading glasses perched on the end of his nose. "Okay, here goes. This letter is addressed to a man named Umberto."

David pulled his chair closer in anticipation.

"There's a hairdressers in Stourbridge called Umberto Giannini," chipped in Lauren, as she busied herself sending texts to her friends, her thumbs zipping about at incredible speed. David flashed her a critical look. For reasons he couldn't quite explain, whenever she was composing her texts, she reminded him of a very industrious little crab. He begged Giovanni to continue.

"Yes, Umberto. His full name is Umberto di Buonarroti Simoni."

"Hang on," interrupted David. "That's Michelangelo's surname."

"I didn't know that," replied Giovanni. "Anyway, it says, '*Caro cugino Umberto, probablimente non vedrai mai il mio soffitto a Roma*', which translates as Cousin Umberto, you will probably never get to see my ceiling in Rome. It continues, '*Dopo quattro*

176

anni di tortura, avevo bisogno di questo momento per ristabilirmi.' But believe me, after four years of torture, I needed the quiet time with you to recover my health.'"

"Stop there!" shouted David. The elderly couple in the far corner of the restaurant glared daggers at him. David was so excited; he was wriggling around on his chair like a child who needed the lavatory, his eyes as wide as saucers.

"But this is incredible! Did none of you get that? This is a letter written by Michelangelo himself. Didn't you hear? My ceiling in Rome, four years of torture. It *has* to have been written by him. My God, so the priest who ran the old chapel on the Tutton estate was his cousin. Hang on, let me get my head around this. That actually makes sense you know! Major Simon told me that there was a Roman Catholic priest called Umberto Buonarroti, but at the time I didn't know what Michelangelo's surname was. Read some more please Giovanni!"

Giovanni looked at David the way a headmaster looks at a child who has just accidentally broken wind halfway through his sermon in assembly.

"I was trying to," he explained patiently, "but you keep interrupting me. "The next bit says, 'I hope you liked my little… I think that word is present or gift, to thank you for your extended hospitality.' It's something like that anyway. That's near enough what it says. I think it mentions that he has been there, in England I suppose, six months. Then the next bit says something like, 'Please study the drawings that I gave you and keep them safe. You will see that each hand has a letter of the alphabet beneath it. *'Ci sono quattrocento immagini sul mio soffitto a Roma'*. There are more than four hundred full-sized figures in my Rome ceiling, each gesturing with their hands, but the Pope doesn't realize that they are speaking a type of sign language which can only be understood by… I think that means 'referring to' or observing your lettered hand drawings, and you

177

have the only copy, good cousin. '*Sarà il nostro segreto che teniamo fino alla tomba*'. It will be our secret that we take to the tomb or grave.' I think that's the gist of it," frowned Giovanni, removing his specs for a while to rub his tired eyes. "Forgive me if every word isn't correct, but our language has evolved a good deal in five hundred years you know. There is a bit more here, but I just can't understand it, about his ceiling again I think, and then the last bit is cut off, as you know. That's probably just where he signed and sealed it."

David had remained dumbstruck throughout Giovanni's translation. Suzanne had disappeared to the ladies, and typically, James and Lauren remained unimpressed and preoccupied with their own affairs. Only Giovanni and David knew what they had in the palms of their hands. It was possibly one of the most important documents in the history of art. Proof that one of the greatest artists of all time had hidden messages to the world within his masterpiece - his vision of creation. What had he deemed so important that it had caused him to hide it in this way? Would it, once unravelled, change the world? The ceiling was a major religious work, depicting scenes from the Old Testament. Were his hidden footnotes meant to augment the messages of his paintings, or maybe even contradict them? Were they perhaps clues that might lead to hidden treasure? Would the secrets of the cosmos be deciphered by a humble restaurant manager and a scatterbrained middle-aged artist?

David showed Giovanni the photographs of the hands and his photocopied blow-ups of the nine ceiling panels. Giovanni had his waitress clear the table, whilst David relegated his family to the one nearby. Churchill no doubt did the same when he and his generals had finished dinner and wanted to study maps of Berlin.

"I began translating this," explained David, "but I couldn't tell where one world ended and another one began."

He showed Giovanni his notes.

"Ah, okay," he mumbled, marking the paper with his biro. *"Allora...si, perfetto.* This one ends here, see, and this one ends here, like so."

Then Giovanni began to laugh loudly and bang the table. The elderly couple paid the waitress and left in a huff. They had chosen Giovanni's hoping for a quiet evening. Now even the proprietor was becoming boorish. David begged him to elucidate.

"This is very funny!" giggled Giovanni. "It says, *'Raffaello non è degno di pulire il mio culo. Il mio cavallo sa dipingere meglio di lui.'* Raphael isn't fit to wipe my arse - that's an approximate translation by the way - and then he brags that his - Michelangelo's - horse can paint better than him."

David stared at him incredulously. "So that's the earth-shattering observation that the great Michelangelo saw fit to hide from the world? I don't flipping believe it!"

Giovanni was laughing again, wiping his eyes with a napkin.

"This one says, *'Il Papa Giulio secondo è un grosso porco tirchio'*, or Pope Julius is a fat, tight-fisted pig! Do you have any more for me, David? This is incredible!"

"Not yet, I only had time to translate two of them."

David studied the photocopies again, while his friend Giovanni tried his hardest to control a giggling fit.

"Bloody hell, I've just realized something else. You won't believe this, Giovanni. I have to ring Laz NOW!"

He pulled out his mobile and tapped in Laz's number. Laz answered.

"Laz, it's David here. Sorry about the late hour, but this is very important. You remember in Florence, when I discovered the pubic writing? Right, and I said he might have hidden something within the Sistine Chapel paintings. Well he bloody well did, and I've discovered it. This will make history, old pal. He's created hidden messages all over the ceiling with a form of sign language. He's used the hands to spell out words, and wait for this. The '*pene*' has finally dropped. I reckon he's used the knobs as punctuation!"

* * *

It was ten a.m., Monday morning, and David, having just heard his doorbell ring, strode over to answer it. He was greeted by seven art students in varying stages of decomposition. He resisted the temptation to sing 'Hi Ho, Hi Ho' and asked them in. Having quickly established that Tim Beasley wasn't amongst them, his mood lightened considerably. So much so that he was almost prepared to forgive them for being an hour late.

The Seven Dwarves were what could be accurately described as a motley crew. There was:

Gareth, a tall, stick-thin, gauche specimen with Gothic-style badly-dyed black hair that flopped over his eyes, causing him to brush it out of the way every ten seconds with long, bony hands that were decorated with nibbled black nail varnish. David was curious as to why a person who wished to be an art student would favour a hairstyle that effectively prevented him from seeing, a prerequisite for any artist, in his humble opinion.

Megan, a small, dumpy girl with extremely long hair, made to appear even longer by the shortness of her body. She was wearing a very long skirt too, which might well have only been a mid-length skirt on anyone else, and a sloppy jumper with a picture of a puppy on the front of it.

Dingbang Wang, a Chinese lad who seemed pleasant enough, but was somewhat handicapped by the fact that he didn't appear to be able to speak more than eight words in English. His name, for those expressing a general interest or just doubtful of its authenticity, apparently means Protector of the Country, Hope, Wish.

Barry, a young man whose hairdo and general fashion sense indicated that he may well have been better equipped for the Chartered Accountancy course.

Craig, a ginger, long-haired hippy type with white skin and freckles that suggested he had accidentally fallen asleep on a scorching hot Spanish beach with a colander over his face to prevent sunburn. David made a mental note to frisk this exotic creature as soon as possible, in order to locate the inevitable Celtic armband tattoo and pack of Rizla cigarette papers.

Rose, a beautiful woodland nymph who probably weighed less than a bag of no-added-sugar muesli. The girl appeared to be so ethereal that she seemed unable or unwilling to communicate with mere earthlings.

Errol, a stocky West Indian lad who was listening to hip-hop through headphones and facing the wrong way.

If these were the best John Auberton could muster, David surmised, the worst must be crawling around in Petri dishes. He gave them all a cup of tea or coffee – except of course for Rose who was too unworldly to have need of drinks, and Gareth who probably only drank bats blood – and explained to all of them - except Dingbang who couldn't understand a word, what had to be done.

Gareth nervously raised a black-nailed bony hand. David invited him to take the floor.

"Erm, that might be a problem for me," he began, with his self-conscious, barely audible voice. David resisted the temptation to try and increase his volume with the nearby TV remote.

"Sorry, you'll have to speak up. Only bats can hear you."

"I'm scared of heights," mumbled Gothic Gareth.

"Oh," frowned David. "Did John Auberton not explain what this job entailed?"

"Yes," mumbled Gareth.

"Right. I see. Look, the scaffold is virtually like another floor. All you have to do is climb the steps and then…"

"I can't do it," mumbled Gareth.

"Okay, fair enough, here's your bus fair back to Wolverhampton."

"My friend can come instead if you like," mumbled Gareth.

"Is his name Tim Beasley?" asked David wearily.

"Yes, but how did you…"

"It's fate, that's what it is. I know at this juncture I could say that six dwarves, erm, I mean students will suffice, but I saw this in the stars. It would be hopeless to fight it. Tell him to report for duty tomorrow morning at nine sharp, or ten as you students know it as, and warn him that if he sets fire to the hall, or destroys the chapel, or accidentally poisons all of the racehorses, I will personally disembowel him and fling him out of the bell tower, like Hannibal Lecter does to that chap in Florence, in the film that is apparently called Hannibal. Is that understood?"

"Yes," mumbled Gareth, sloping off towards the door. "He's okay nowadays though. All those years in industry have improved him."

David had never heard of a few years building sheds described so eloquently before, but he let it pass. Gareth flitted off to his cave, and then there were six. David led them in a line to the chapel, where they met Laz, decked out in his Hi-Vis jacket and yellow hard hat.

"Hi-Ho!" David grinned. "It's off to work we go. Follow me, folks, and remember, while you're working with me, we say blokes, chaps, boys and girls, people, fellows even, but woe

182

betide anyone referring to anyone else as 'guys'. Do so and I hand you your P45. Understood? Jeez, I hate that expression, especially when they're referring to women as well. I also do not want to hear that bloody awful Australian implied question thing. You know - that you students *do*?"

The dwarves glanced nervously at each other with quizzical expressions, stepped inside the chapel and looked heavenwards.

"Wow!" they chorused in unison.

"Wow indeed," smiled David. "Are we enthused? Well follow me. Take your time up these steps, for God's sake. We don't want accidents. Up there it's railed off for your safety and there's a solidish floor, not loose planks, so it's just like being on the ground really, apart from the edges. Careful though. It's a very low ceiling, for reasons that will become apparent. Don't bump your heads. First, we have to position these huge plans on the ceiling with masking tape. I'll take charge of that, so don't worry. They all have to be exactly aligned. Then, you take a sheet each. You neatly and accurately go over the lines and numbers with these 9H sharpened pencils. The backs of the plans are coated with graphite, so you'll end up with a perfect fine line on the white acrylic undercoat. Make sure you've done every single line before you tear the sheet off. It's a bugger to re-align them. All understood?"

Five dwarves nodded. One Chinese one grinned.

"Barry, show Dingdong or whatever his bloody name is would you?"

Barry nodded. The Chinese one grinned some more.

"Okay, when the sheets come down, you should be left with a great big octagonal line drawing with numbers all over it. The numbers correspond to these pots of paint, over here. There are thirty of them. Ah, good, that's perfect! You've got five each. Barry, take one to five, Rose, six to ten, and so on - they're your allocated colours. The brushes are over there. There are big ones

183

for large areas, and smaller ones for smaller areas. I can't explain it more simply than that. Barry, show Dingaling, will you? Now, painting overhead is hard work, and that's why we've got a low ceiling and these old hospital trolleys and cushions, courtesy of Russell's Hall. The best way to tackle this is to lie on them, side by side, like you're going to have a nap, with your tub of paint maybe by your side or even on your chest - up to you. Make sure you are wearing tatty old clothes please, because the paint will drip, and always wear these safety goggles. Then begin with a number, and carefully colour in all the segments with that number, before cleaning your brushes and moving onto the next number. Got that?"

Five dwarves nodded. One grinned inanely.

"Final thing, and then we can start. We'll operate a rotation system. Three trolleys painting and gliding about. Three students stirring paint, handing them brushes, making the tea, being generally helpful, resting a while even. On the hour, you swap. It's tedious work and I don't want you knackered, and calling in Elf and Safety. There's a portaloo just outside. Any questions?"

"What will Tim do then?" asked Megan.

"Something in a far distant paddock, with a bit of luck. I'll worry about him tomorrow. Let's get started!"

* * *

David asked Major Simon to open his eyes.

"Oh, what are these doing here then?" he asked, puzzled. These were up at the hall last night."

"No they weren't," David assured him. "Those four at the house are fakes, as you know, whereas these two are the real thing."

184

"You're joking!"

"I never joke about....well that's a lie for a start, I joke about virtually everything, but these are the originals, yes. It's a long story, and I'll explain it more fully over one of Horace's half-cups of tea, but suffice it to say, Inspector Day strikes again. Sherlock Holmes must be quaking in his boots nowadays, I reckon. And now the really good news. Do you still want to sell 'em?"

"Want is the wrong word," replied the major. "Need is the word. Why do you ask?"

"I've found a rich Arab chap who wants them, but he's not willing to pay a couple of million."

"Ah!"

"He's willing to pay sixteen million, or thereabouts."

Had the major's HobNob not gone the wrong way, David felt sure he would have sounded much more appreciative. David slapped him on the back several times until a chunk of soggy biscuit flew out and adhered to the studio wall for several seconds, before slithering down to the floor.

"*How* bloody much?" asked the major.

"Sixteen was what I asked, and it didn't faze him. He paid eight for that thing in the waste bin over there."

"But that would sort out all my money worries in one fell swoop. David, you are a one-off. I'm so pleased you moved into the mews."

"Me too," grinned David. "It was getting too noisy and disruptive to concentrate back at home. And now, if you'll excuse me, I'm very busy!"

CHAPTER 20

Aaaarrrgh, it's Tim!

The six dwarves, being art students and therefore never having previously completed a full day's work in their lives, were in shock. They lolled around on the hospital trolleys, groaning. Usually, after an hour or so, they would have gravitated to the canteen for a two hour break and a Kit Kat. Some days, if they were feeling a trifle fragile after a hard evening at the students' bar, they'd jack it in there and then and head home to their grotty bed-sits. This day, however, they had received their harsh indoctrination into the world of real work. David had given them a generous hour for lunch, and a few brief rest periods here and there, but the remainder had been a hard slog, just like he was used to, day after day, year after year, decade after decade. David could paint for eight solid hours if he really had to, without once stopping. He was match fit. A quick peek around the scaffold suggested that this was not the case with the six dwarves. It was half- past five now and Megan was asleep, snoring her head off on a trolley. Craig was too tired to strum the acoustic guitar he'd brought with him. Errol had a glazed look and there was hip-hop spillage leaking out of his ears. Rose had tried to brush her hair but was too weak; her hand slumping to the ground as if she'd gently died. Even Dingbat had stopped grinning.

David climbed the scaffold and said hello. Those that still could offered a feeble reply.

"So have we enjoyed ourselves?" he asked, smiling broadly.

And strangely, they had. There is a very satisfying type of exhaustion that comes with a job well done, along with a wonderful sense of camaraderie, if it was a joint effort. They were professionals now, working on a big project. They wore their exhaustion with pride. They were a team. David asked them to open their tired little eyes for a while and take a good look at what they'd achieved. The first half of ceiling had been drawn out, and on Tuesday, they would finish the remaining half. By Wednesday, they would be ready to commence the really interesting part - the colouring in. Two weeks later, they could climb back down those ladders, and once the scaffolders had taken their equipment away, the ceiling would be revealed in all its glory. Okay, it wasn't four years of torture, but by student standards, it was a close-run thing.

David bade them good night and wandered back to his studio. He sat down with the photocopies once more, and continued where he'd left off. It was a painstaking job, and complex. He had to be extremely careful to get the figures in the right order, or else the letters would make no sense to Giovanni whatsoever. The rule seemed to be that, like writing, he must begin top left and work his way across to the end of the panel, before dropping to a lower layer of figures, if indeed there was one. The difficulty was, some figures overlapped in places, and a misplaced pair of letters could render a sentence illegible. Then there were the figures showing no hands, or one hand, and the figures that were reaching down to another figure below. It was the stuff that migraines were made of, and, as if all this were not difficult enough, there were nine massive, complex panels of the stuff. It was like trying to separate hundreds of intertwined snakes. David estimated that there could well be ten or twelve vitriolic comments – maybe even more, hidden amongst those four hundred scantily-clad characters floating around in the firmament. This was by far the most mind-boggling, exciting thing he'd ever been part of, and there were, in fairness, quite a

187

few contenders to choose from. Not bad for a working class Black Country boy from Brierley Bank, he mused. His name would surely go into the history books as the man who cracked the Michelangelo Code. Maybe a writer might even buy the rights and pen a best-selling novel or movie script about it. Yes, the Michelangelo Code did have a ring to it. It was a good title, but who would believe it? It sounded so far-fetched and ridiculous, but it was true, as the best stories often are. And to think that if he and Laz hadn't gone to Florence, this might have remained undiscovered for all time. The chances of someone finding and deciphering a document in Tutton on Stour were slim enough, but for that person to also be engaged in painting a copy of the Sistine Chapel roof - well, the odds must have been a million to one. That said, coincidences did follow David around like lost puppies, and had done all of his life. He seemed to act as a magnet for them.

He toiled under his angle poise for another hour, until Suzanne rang him and demanded that he return home before his children forgot who he was. Feeling ashamed by this fair rebuke, he gathered together his photocopies and his jottings and locked up for the night. He was prone to obsessive behaviour, and this was dangerous. He did need to spend more time with his kids, after all. Suzanne was right about that. He decided to go home, relax, have a good dinner and a few glasses of wine, and then maybe Lauren would help him decipher a few more sentences after their pudding.

* * *

Tuesday meant Tim Beasley, and David was experiencing an understandable heaviness of heart. A nameless fear hung over him like a personal black cloud. If he'd had any sense, he'd have told this Jonah not to come, but for some completely inexplicable reason, he'd almost invited it. Tempting fate, it is commonly called. That strange, impulsive trait inside us all - some more than others it has to be said – to have a go at stroking the big barking dog, even though we know it may well bite us. To touch the electric fence to see if it's switched on, even though we know that there's a fifty-fifty chance of it giving us a nasty jolt. It is the same basic flaw in our psyche that sees women attracted to bad men, or otherwise cautious walkers inexplicably drawn to the cliff edge. Whatever the reason, David had virtually invited the chap to join his team with open arms, knowing full well that his track record was appalling.

The doorbell rang, and David answered it. It was Tim, looking a little older since their last encounter; a little stockier too, and with shorter hair.

"Dave, mate, how's fings?" he asked cheerily, offering his hand to be shaked.

"Nice to see you again, Tim," lied David. "Can you believe it's been eight years since you burnt down our cricket pavilion?"

"Er, fanks for reminding me. Time flies."

"Been keeping out of trouble?"

"Yeah. I left the college as you know, but the call of art was too strong. I've been back a while now and I'm determined to finish my degree vis time."

"Glad to hear it. Any accidents?"

"Not to speak of."

"Any you can't speak of?"

"Nah! Nothing serious anyhow. I'm a changed man, Dave."

"You needed to be. Let's go and meet up with your mates then. I'll show you what you have to do. I hope you've speeded up a bit in these eight years. I remember a drawing you did of Gary Glitter that took you about three terms. There's a bloody deadline for this restaurant you know."

"Understood. I suppose I was guilty of being a bit of a perfectionist back then."

"You're not now?"

"No."

"Marvellous. Follow me."

The Six Dwarves were already on site with their Bob the Builder lunchboxes and flasks. Barry informed David that Gothic Gareth had had an accident back at the college. Apparently, he had been walking across a narrow workman's plank en-route to his class when he slipped and fell heavily, breaking his ankle. Ironic, thought David with a wry smile, that a chap who confessed to being afraid of heights should fall off a narrow plank, inches above the floor and do himself damage. Maybe now he would not only be afraid of heights, but also of widths.

The Seven Dwarves, as they now were, followed David up the ladders, ready for another hard day.

"Right, Tim," said David, once they had reached the summit. "Everyone has a task, and a new nickname. You know most of these people already, I'm sure. This is Megan, who is known to all as Sleepy, Barry, who is now Anorak, Craig is Col - that's short for Colander, this one here is Bing Bong, Dingaling or whatever - we change his name every hour; Errol - or Ear 'Ole, say hello to Tim, and that's Titania, Queen of the Fairy Folk over there, plaiting the daisies into her hair. For those who don't know him already, this is Jonah, who used to have his own full page feature in the Beano and the Dandy. Anorak, show Jonah what to do, and may the Lord have mercy upon your soul. I'm popping out for a while, so behave yourselves."

* * *

Giovanni was having another quiet lunchtime, which was a worry. David ordered Penne alla Bolognese, and while he waited for it to arrive, he spread his notes across the table for Giovanni to see.

The restaurateur donned his reading glasses and scanned the pages with interest, again striking a line in ball point pen where he imagined the spaces between words should be. For a while, he sat in silence, amending lines here and there, and gradually, a broad smile appeared on his face, followed by more roaring laughter.

"This man is raging against the world," he observed, "and in a comically modern kind of way. Here was I, expecting great wisdom and profound insights, and we get this. *'Leonardo da Vinci non sa tagliare nemmeno un arrosto di manzo.'* Leonardo da Vinci couldn't even carve a joint of beef. Or how about this one, from panel number nine? *'Quattro anni della mia vita passati, solo per creare questa merda.'* Four years of my life gone, just to create this shit."

More hysterical laughter followed. Giovanni had to remove his glasses yet again to wipe his eyes. "David my friend, can you imagine some po-faced Pope commissioning this masterpiece of art for a prime religious building in Vatican City, and all the time, Michelangelo is writing rude graffiti all over it. Priceless!"

David's lunch arrived, so he ate it while his friend continued to translate, all the time convulsed with laughter. Occasionally, a sentence would make no sense whatsoever, until wrongly placed letters were rearranged, and then Giovanni would be laughing again, begging David to listen to the latest outrageous statement.

"David, stop eating for a second or you may choke. How about this one? *'Che la famiglia Medici prenda la malattia venerea!'* May the Medici family all catch venereal disease. And this written on a ceiling in the Holy City!"

191

There was a buzz of excitement in the chapel on Wednesday morning as the first colours hit the ceiling. David had been shopping and managed to find some decent quality gold paint which would look just like gold leaf from down below - ideal for adding finishing touches such as halos and the detail on robes. Even the shock discovery that Ping Pong was colour blind couldn't dampen his spirits. The paint by numbers system was perfect and almost foolproof. If the lad saw the number 13 written on the ceiling, that was the pot he used. The fact that he saw red as green didn't matter a jot.

Tim Beasley, it had to be said, was a changed man. Maybe, thought David, his few years with the shed company had actually done him good. He was still slower than the sloth that had come last in the annual sloth marathon, but at least his work was reasonably neat; he hadn't killed anyone yet or set fire to the ceiling, and that was a blessing.

Downstairs, Laz was getting excited. He had been in communication with the Italian agency, and they were sending him three experienced men to run the kitchen; Goffredo, Maurizio and Luca. They had all worked in top restaurants in Florence, and could create the type of authentic cuisine that Laz was after. The three men would be arriving soon in order to familiarize themselves with the kitchens and begin work on a menu. They would then work at a 'friends and invited guests only' evening to road-test their food and, if need be, iron out any little niggles prior to the grand opening. Laz had negotiated a good deal with Major Winterfold on a tied cottage that was currently unoccupied, just a stone's throw away from the chapel, so their accommodation was also taken care of. Meanwhile, Tomaso, the waiter sacked from Bonini's in Florence had been invited to work front of house, with the proviso that he didn't ask the punters to nibble on his nuts. The remainder of the staff would be English, head-hunted from the local eateries and trained by the Italians to be the first waitresses in the entire West

Midlands area to actually pronounce the names of the various wines and dishes correctly. Giovanni, in particular, was driven to distraction by Britain's ineptitude when it came to speaking foreign languages.

"You *cannot* advertise ham and cheese paninis," he would rant, to anyone who would indulge him. "Panino is singular, panini is plural, but oh no, not here in bloody England. Over here, for some crazy reason, panini has become singular and paninis is plural. Do none of you understand anything about basic grammar?"

It was also not advisable to get him started on the pronunciation of *Pinot Grigio, proscuitto, lasagne, gnocchi, Bolognese* and *tagliatelle*; all words that were regularly mispronounced on a regular basis at his restaurant. Not that he was belligerent. His criticisms were all delivered with good humour, and he was the perfect front man with a lot of charm; well liked by his customers. It was just a pity he hadn't got a few more of them. He knew all about the opening of Michelangelo's and wished them well, but he had seen a lot of new, swanky restaurants come and go. One minute they were the hot new place, and then customers would hear about some other new, exciting venue and move on. Michelangelo's would almost certainly dent his takings for a while; he accepted that. It was the thrill of the new, but there was also something to be said for the old, well-worn and cosy places, so he wasn't overly worried. After all, he mused, all that glisters is not gold leaf. Sometimes it's just gold acrylic paint from B&Q.

CHAPTER 21

Two Weeks Later

Downstairs, Laz was showing Tomaso, Maurizio, Luca and head Chef Goffredo around for the first time. Meanwhile, upstairs, a celebration was about to begin. The ceiling was finished except for one last little segment of colour, and it looked spectacular. The Seven Dwarves had worked as they had never worked before. John Auberton, who had taken the afternoon off to view the masterpiece, was forced to sit on the edge of a hospital trolley to regain his composure; such was the magnificence of the spectacle. He would never have believed it possible that these seven individuals could ever bond as a team and produce something of such beauty. David had asked for the cream of his flock, but in truth, the best of the bunch had returned home for the break, leaving him a ragbag of humanity to choose from. Why else would he have been forced to offer Tim Beasley as first reserve?

And now, here they were, as tightly knit as a military unit. One preparing areas for painting, one making tea while one washed brushes, three on their backs painting and one stirring paint. It was enough to make a hardened old lecturer shed a tear of joy.

"Right, attention everyone!" shouted David. "There is one small, final segment to paint, and then we're done. Horace has kindly staggered over from the hall with three bottles of Champagne, courtesy of the major, so can we each raise a glass

194

and join me in a toast to Michelangelo's restaurant – okay, don't fret Titania, you can have the elderflower cordial instead. To Michelangelo's! And the honour of colouring in the last segment goes to Tim Beasley, a changed man. Come on Jonah, lie on the trolley and dip your tired and wilting little brush into number 26, muffin beige, for the last time."

The six remaining dwarves, their slave driver and their Head of Department cheered and applauded as Tim Beasley picked out his number 4 brush and climbed onto the trolley, adjusting his pillow theatrically before he began. There was a breathless hush as he dipped it into the large tub of paint perched on his stomach, wiped off the surplus on the rim and began to colour the segment. Slowly, methodically, he filled in the six inch by four inch area, his tongue poking out at a jaunty angle. Eight pairs of critical eyes followed his every stroke, just in case his edges were not up to scratch. Had one amongst them accidentally dropped a pin, the others would have heard it land. Below the scaffold, the Italian chefs, Laz, Horace and every workman present was similarly silent, having been forewarned by David that a moment of great symbolic significance was about to take place. Finally, after a few seconds respite to wipe a dollop of beige from his right eye, the segment was completed, and a huge cheer echoed through the chapel. Tim sat up and acknowledged his fans with a regal flourish of his arms, before jumping down from his trolley.

Ideally, Tim would have preferred his size ten feet to land on terra firma, but they didn't. Instead they planted themselves squarely into two large, open tubs of paint, one Cobalt Blue, the other Cadmium Red. The paint, dramatically displaced by the forceful downward thrust of the shoes, blasted skywards out of the tubs like a two-tone Trevi fountain, splattering the semi-circular arrangement of onlookers from head to toe. The central section of the ceiling painting, depicting Adam and Eve in the Garden of Eden, received most of the rest, causing the two naked lovers and their snake to look as if they had succumbed to a highly contagious rash. Tim, who was understandably disorientated by this violent volcanic explosion of colour, tried to escape its epicentre by running from it, an enterprise doomed to fail when one has two five litre tubs of B&Q paint attached to one's legs. He fell heavily, rather like a mafia victim about to be thrown into the Chicago River, making a last minute bid for freedom with his feet set in concrete. Seeing the wooden floor coming up to meet his face at a rate of knots, Tim, totally out of character, did what any right-minded person would do. He flung his arms out to break his fall. Unfortunately, most right-minded people aren't surrounded by thirty large tubs of paint, and Tim was having difficulty trying to locate a clear area to land in. Seeing several tubs blocking his progress, he frantically tried to shove them out of his flight path as he descended, but was only partially successful. His left hand managed to roll over a full tub of Cadmium Yellow which thankfully still had its lid intact, while his right elbow landed in an open tub of Deep Purple. Tim's face took the worst of the fall, landing squarely into a tub of Midnight Blue.

The deservedly lengthy description of these events would perhaps fool the reader into thinking that they unravelled over a period of some minutes, but this was not the case. From Tim's initial leap from the trolley to his present prostrate and multi-coloured state took no more than a couple of frenetic seconds, meaning that those present had little time to do more than gawp, or perhaps bite their knuckles. It was, therefore, perfectly excusable that not one of them was able to rescue the large, unopened tub of Cadmium Yellow before it rolled off the edge of the scaffolding floor into the abyss below.

Downstairs, the assembled dignitaries had been hanging on in silence, awaiting David's instruction to cheer, and to better judge this moment, they had gathered around the perimeter wall, where they could get a glimpse of what was happening upstairs. This, in hindsight, was a mistake, for had Goffredo the head chef not been where he was, the large upended tub of Cadmium Yellow would not have hit him squarely on the brow.

The scene within the chapel was now nothing short of carnage. People ran hither and thither like headless chickens. The Six Dwarves fell over each other to try and rescue their precious handiwork with the aid of wet rags, before the many dollops of red and blue paint dried. John Auberton and David examined their ruined clothing with utter dismay, whilst downstairs, Horace, unsteady at the best of times, had dropped his tray of best cut glass flutes and broken the lot, losing three bottles of decent Champagne in the process. Goffredo, surrounded by the other Italians, lay flat out on the floor, dead to the world, and Laz just stood motionless, staring at the underside of the scaffolding in a daze.

Meanwhile, the instigator of this mayhem rose unsteadily to his polka-dotted knees, his right arm a fetching purple colour, and his bespectacled face completely obliterated by a thick, oozing layer of Midnight Blue paint. As he opened his mouth, presumably in order to whimper or groan, a fly on the wall would have noted that Tim's two front teeth were missing.

An hour later, things looked slightly brighter, and not just because Tim had covered every available surface in paint. The dwarves had managed to wipe the wet paint off the ceiling areas before it set into a hard skin, which was the main thing. They had purposely worn old clothes anyway, which had at least saved David a sizable bill for new garments. Unfortunately, neither he nor John had done likewise, not seeing the need for it. The downstairs team had fared worse, with ten Royal Brierley Crystal Champagne flutes in ten thousand pieces and three bottles of Dom Perignon lubricating the floor tiles. All this paled into insignificance, however, when compared to what had happened to poor old Goffredo. Only now was he returning to the land of the living, and it was patently obvious that all was not right.

197

"How many fingers am I holding up?" asked his friend Maurizio, deeply concerned.

"Fifty-seven," replied the chef shakily.

Maurizio gently slapped his boss's face, though there is little medical evidence to suggest that this does anything other than distress the victim even more.

"What is your name? Goffredo, what is your name?"

"Marilyn."

Maurizio looked up at the people gathered round the body. "This is serious! Goffredo, my friend, listen to me. Concentrate. How do you make *Risotto con funghi e asparagi*, per favore?"

Goffredo's brow was furrowed with thought. He gave the question due consideration and replied, "Pig shit," before taking another nap. It was at this sorry juncture that it was deemed best to order an ambulance, pronto.

A few yards away, a Midnight Blue and Purple creature sat, forlorn, on a decorative old millstone, his two false front teeth still missing.

"I *am* a bloody Jonah," he sobbed to himself pitifully. "I might as well just jump off a cliff right now, like a lemon, and end it all. I'm useless."

Meanwhile, back in the chapel, Horace was making tea for the troops. He handed David and Laz half a cup each, to steady their nerves. He would have been well advised to drink a cup himself.

"I actually invited this!" sighed David moodily. "You were there when he burnt down our cricket pavilion, so you know what he's capable of. He's a walking disaster movie. And tell me, Laz, is it just me, or have we just accidentally walked into an episode of Fawlty Towers?"

CHAPTER 22

One week later

" 'Put the bloody kettle on, Laz' is your answer to everything!" Laz moaned, as he put the kettle on. "Incidentally, this here article in the Daily Mail says that we Britons drink one hundred and sixty-five million cups of tea every day, based on us having just three cups each. In our lifetimes, we each drink seventy-eight thousand, six hundred and eighty-one cups, and with teabags at only a penny each, it adds, that's a modest seven hundred and eighty-seven pounds total expenditure per person. Well that's bollocks for a start. I reckon you drink at least seventy-eight thousand, six hundred and eighty-one cups per *day*."

"Give or take," admitted David nonchalantly. "And your point is?"

"My point is, sitting here drinking tea isn't getting the baby washed, as they say around here. I'm a head chef down and my preparation for the big opening night is in shreds. The other two are just communist chefs, or shoe chefs, or whatever they bloody call them, and they need the head chef there to organize them. They are just lolling around becalmed and flipping rudderless at the moment. Old Goffredo's flown home with memory loss and severe concussion, so I've had to ask the agency to send over another head chef that I won't have even have had time to talk to before the restaurant opens. They've had to trawl the country to find this chap. They say he's brilliant, if a teeny weeny bit temperamental, to use their exact words."

"Jeez, just what we need."

"Exactly. I don't want some bloody prima donna refusing to cook because the colour of the kitchen wall upsets his feng shui."

"Oh, he's probably okay," said David, secretly curious as to why Laz was talking about oriental food when his restaurant was an Italian one. "They're just being professional and a bit over-cautious, that's all. I've worked for Henry at the National Gallery for yonks, and we get on great, in spite of some arsehole I used to work for giving me a reference I could have done without; accusing me of being 'difficult'. The cheeky sod only said that because he was a bloody useless art director who couldn't direct traffic down a one-way street. If you're professional, you can't work with idiots who aren't. The second you open your mouth to complain at their incompetence, suddenly *you're* the one who's 'difficult'. See what I mean? Henry and I have never had a cross word and he thinks I'm dead easy-going, which I am. And the reason for this mutual admiration society? Because he's professional and I respect him, and vice-versa. I'm sure this chap…"

"Andrea," said Laz.

"That's a girl's name," said David. Nothing got past him.

"Not in Italy it isn't, apparently, only in fairness, it's actually pronounced An-dray-a I think. They really struggled to find someone at such short notice, but Goffredo wants to come back when he's better, so it's only temporary. The problem is, this Andrea chap can only get here on the day before the press and friends bash on the Friday, and we open proper on the Saturday, so talk about in at the deep end."

David sympathized. He was also a control freak who didn't like surprises. He understood what poor old Laz was going through.

"Should be a great day though, on Saturday," he continued, trying to raise Laz's flagging spirits. "It's the Tutton Country Fair on the afternoon, in the big field over there by the lake. They've got a motorcycle display team, dogs doing tricks, cake stalls, throw the wet sponge at Tim Beasley in the stocks – I thought of that one – bucking bronco, paintballing, a coconut shy and the territorial army brass band; Major Simon got them cheap because of his connections. Then it's a quick change into the old suit for the grand opening, and you've got a full house for your first night. It'll be fab!"

"Almost full," corrected Laz, ever the pessimist. "We've got one half-empty eight-seater table. What if it gets progressively worse? I'll be bankrupt, and then…"

"For God's sake!" interrupted David. "The table's always half-empty with you isn't it? He's bankrupted already and he hasn't opened yet! Have faith. Andrea will be great; they said he was brilliant didn't they? The restaurant looks spectacular, the ceiling is sensational, the waitresses are fully *au fait* and raring to go. I actually heard one say *tagliatelle* with the correct silent 'G' and a nicely rolled 'L' today, like she was born in Milan. Not bad for a Netherton wench I thought. So relax, take a deep breath. *La vita e dolce, no?*"

"I'll let you know after Saturday," replied Laz grumpily.

David couldn't help thinking that his old friend would have fitted in perfectly with his team of dwarves. He'd already thought of a perfect nickname for him too.

* * *

Andrea arrived late on Thursday but was so exhausted that he treated himself to an early night. First thing Friday, Laz introduced him to his colleagues, and straight away they got down to work. The dishes were discussed in depth, waitresses and waiters were briefed in military fashion and no stone was left unturned in ensuring that the place would look stunning when the

201

first guests arrived. Andrea was a perfectionist who ran a tight ship, but he wasn't a bully, like some super-chefs can be, which pleased his nervous wreck of a boss no end. The staff liked him, and he appeared to be getting on famously with them; especially the Italian ones. The chapel though, was the star of the show. Its simple, whitewashed walls and oak flooring were lit by huge white church candles on mediaeval-style wrought iron stands, and the incredible faux-renaissance ceiling was illuminated by hidden spotlights, giving the illusion that the diners were eating outdoors in an enchanted place as angels looked down upon them. The sounds of Italian opera floated ethereally around the building, so that every sense would be satisfied. At David's insistence, Zuchero was banned, apart from in the kitchens, where it served to prevent the Italians from becoming home-sick.

At seven in the evening, the first of the diners began to arrive. They parked their cars and followed the floor lights to the chapel, which was illuminated in dramatic fashion. All the local papers had sent a party, headed by their respective food critics, giving Laz slight cause for concern that, after a few drinks, the evening might degenerate into a food fight. Major Winterfold, Claudia and Henry, now a permanent fixture, walked over from the hall in elegant evening dress. The Seven Dwarves pulled up in the college minibus, driven by John Auberton, who gave Tim Beasley strict instructions not to touch anything except food, and even then to be careful. The mews tenants, or what was left of them, were next to arrive, followed by Suzanne, the children and Laz's wife Annie. Trev had been sent an invite, but was still far too frail to attend, so David had promised to send him one of Andrea's dinners to eat at the hospital, when he was up to it, even though his nurse reckoned it might have to be pureed in the Magimix first. Donald and Pongo, both off duty and attracted to a free dinner like moths to a flame, arrived with their wives by taxi.

Laz, in his best Hugo Boss dinner suit, welcomed everyone personally as they crossed the threshold. They were directed to a trestle table manned by a waiter who offered them champagne, and then shown to their tables. In the kitchens, to keep things simple on the dress rehearsal evening, Andrea and his team were preparing the following:

Antipasti:

Bruschette 'Andrea'

Funghi al forno ripieni di ricotta

Sushi del chianti

Crostini

Primi:

Fazzoletti di seta pesto

Spaghetti con gamberetti e rucola

Risotto ai carciofi

Secondi:

Pesce spada alla griglia con la 'Salsa di Goffredo'

Contorni

Zucchini in padella

Zucca al forno

Dolci:

Sorbetto di pere

Torta di riso

Fichi secchi con formaggio

David had suggested that the set menu should not be translated into English. Had he been aware, the first time that he had been asked to try pasta with a black sauce, that it was squid ink, he would not have tried it, and consequently missed out. No matter that his tongue looked as if it had been dipped in a bottle of Quink, it tasted wonderful, and that was the point. His grandmother, Bertha, would not have entertained the thought of trying something called *Pollo Milanese*, because it was 'foreign muck', but if she'd been told that she had chicken in breadcrumbs for tea, all would have been well.

Course after course arrived at the tables, to the almost universal delight of the customers. Food writers busied themselves scribbling superlative-filled notes for their Saturday reviews, and diners chatted and stuffed their faces, sound in the knowledge that someone else was paying for it all.

Tim Beasley, his inner ears still a fetching shade of Midnight Blue, picked at his food carefully, conscious that he was holding two potentially lethal weapons in his hands. He resolved to be on his guard until the bitter end, to avoid over-relaxing and then having someone's eye out over the desserts. The other dwarves, who had never experienced such fine food before, and were used to existing on beans on toast washed down with either Banks's Mild or Kenco Decaffeinated depending on the hour, eyed each new course with deep suspicion. Colander, after prodding his main course several times with a fork, eventually left it untouched in favour of several Embassy King-sized, which he seemed to regard as food, and several pints of Pino Grigio. Titania, Queen of the Fairy Folk, who had no need of food, merely sipped the minute droplets of water from the lilies on her table like a butterfly, and appeared to be engrossed in her battered copy of The Hobbit.

At eleven o'clock, once the plates had been cleared away, the guests flopped back in their leather chairs, opened the top buttons of their trousers, sipped grappas and espressos and chatted contentedly. Major Winterfold chose this time to stand and clank his wine bottle with a fork, as he always used to do in the officer's mess, until eventually the room became quiet enough for him to speak.

"Ladies and gentlemen," he began, "I'd just like to say a few brief words. I was very upset about having to sell off the old chapel, because it had been in the Winterfold family for five hundred years. I was worried that the new owner would turn it into something ghastly, like a lap-dancing cocktail bar, if indeed there is such a thing, but let me say that I was worrying about nothing. Mr Homer has created something wonderful with Michelangelo's restaurant. The refurbishment has been very sympathetic and tasteful, and the food is even more tasteful – my congratulations to Andrea and the rest of the staff for a superb meal. Grazie mille! Perfetto! Bravo! I would add even more Italian superlatives but I only know three. Now let's all hope tomorrow is as good as tonight, and not just tomorrow, but every night. This place can only be a force for the good, and I welcome the latest attraction to the Edgecliff Estate."

The assembled diners raised their glasses and applauded enthusiastically. The major begged their indulgence for a few moments more.

"Now, I've had a quick word with Tomaso and the wine waiter, and I've got you all a little present to take home. I've managed to do a deal on the remaining sixty-five bottles of the special Montepulciano D'Abruzzo that was served tonight with the limited edition Michelangelo's labels, which I'm sure you'll all agree was splendid, and I'd like to present you with one each as a thank you from Claudia and myself. I'm not usually so generous, but I found out today that I've closed the deal on the sale of two rather important paintings. Lastly, I would like to thank David Day for so many things, I really don't know where to begin. Can I just simply say thank you David for everything you've done? You know what I'm talking about. I'd point him out and ask him to take a bow, but thanks to a very peculiar condition of mine called prosopagnosia, I can never remember what his face looks like without a prompt!"

David stood and waved, and was heartily applauded by all, even though most of them didn't have a clue why they were clapping.

As the diners slowly made their way home, David slipped over to the major's table and congratulated him on the sale. It was all good news, of course, but he couldn't help thinking that the Winterfolds had lost a lot of their heritage in order to steady the financial ship. The chapel was gone, and the two most famous paintings, but at least Simon had his Harry Millichip replicas to hang in their stead, and a spare pair for when they were in the wash. The chapel may not have been his property any more, but at least it was still there to enjoy, in the same spot it had always been, and now he had a deluxe eatery that he could walk to if he fancied a drink or two. All in all, he couldn't complain. And now it was time for David to spring the big surprise of the evening, with Henry's help.

"Simon," he began, "thanks to selling your Sargent and Constable, you are now bloody rich, and it couldn't have happened to a nicer chap. I was thrilled that I could help out, and there's absolutely no need to offer me a substantial private cheque, I insist. Relax, only joking! But I have a bit of extra good news for you. You know those drawings of hands from your old box? Well, my friend Henry here has something to say about them, don't you Henry?"

"I do," said Henry. "I came back this weekend for two reasons, so I'll start with the second one first. Simon, maybe you should sit down I think. Take the weight off that leg of yours. Claudia and I wanted to use tonight's dinner as the perfect time to announce our engagement. If you really don't mind, I'd like to ask you if you'd allow me to marry your sister!"

Simon seemed genuinely delighted by his sister's choice of soul mate, especially after the disastrous Raymond de Winter debacle. He regarded Henry as a sound and likeable fellow, and the comparison to his odious predecessor just seemed to accentuate his many good points in the major's eyes. There followed much back-slapping and handshaking, which was curtailed by Henry, who was keen to unveil his second surprise as soon as possible, before it burst out of him of its own accord.

"Oh yes, and those old drawings," he continued, as nonchalantly as he could manage. "I don't suppose, before we talk about those, you still have the stuff you took to your prep school for the show and tell table, do you?"

The major eyed him with jovial suspicion. "Why do you ask?"

"Just wondered."

"Well I do, as it happens. When father went mental at me for butchering the old letter, I retrieved the scrap book I'd glued it in and I still have it in my drawer somewhere. We never got round to sticking the bottom bit back in place on the letter, but yes, I still have them as a painful reminder of that episode. Why?"

"We'd like to take a look at it, if it's not too inconvenient," said Henry. "Once I've had a look, it will confirm something I'm ninety-nine percent sure of anyway. Just let's say that in my position, one has to be cautious. Show me the scrap book, and *then* I'll tell you the news. How's that?"

"Fine," agreed Simon. "Tomorrow a.m. okay for you?"

"How about now?" suggested David.

Ten minutes later, Simon, David, Claudia, Henry and Laz were stood in Simon's office with a brandy and dry ginger each, by way of winding down after a hectic evening. Suzanne, Annie and the children having long gone home by taxi.

Simon reached down into his bottom drawer and pulled out a tattered old book with a charming fifties-style picture of two puppies driving a pedal car down a country lane on the front. The spine had been sellotaped together crudely many years previously, and the tape was now brown and flaking. The many items that had been inserted into the scrap book had given it a lumpy, uneven appearance, giving David cause to wonder if Simon had glued his old, deceased hamster into there. The major handed it to Henry, still nonplussed as to what the fuss was about. Henry leafed through it carefully, his heart in his mouth. He flicked quickly past faded old school certificates, faded black and white photographs, plastic medals that came free with the cornflakes and theatre tickets for pantomimes. Then he found it. The bottom of the letter was held in place by more rotting sellotape, but remarkably, the red wax seal was still intact. The ornate signature next to it read:

Michelangelo di Ludovico di Liornado di Buonarroti Simoni. 1513.

Henry and David took synchronized gulps of their brandy and dry gingers and gawped at each other, prompting Simon to ask what on earth was going on.

"What is going on," explained David, "is that you are now ten million quid richer than you were five seconds ago. The National gallery had sworn to curb their spending until they clapped eyes on your hand drawings. Henry old chap, get your cheque book out!"

CHAPTER 23

Life is a drag sometimes

It was early Saturday afternoon, and David had just returned from the Tutton Country Fair with Suzanne, Lauren and James. He thought he would look in on Laz to see how things were shaping up for the opening night, but Laz was noticeable only by his absence. Tomaso was there, however, still enthusing wildly about his new job and life in England. He apologized to David for being the only person at the restaurant, explaining that he still had a few things to prepare for the opening. The other Italian lads, he added, had gone for lunch in Tutton as part of their team-building exercise, and afterwards they planned to do a little sight-seeing, beginning with the Museum of Egyptian Life, where David had worked immediately after leaving college. Laz, meanwhile, had gone to the wine merchants a few miles out of Stourbridge. Major Winterfold had purchased every single bottle of the specially labelled Pinot Grigio, which was good for business, of course, but it now meant he'd had to replenish stocks for the coming evening. David left a note to say he'd called by, and would pop back mid-afternoon to offer a hand if anything needed doing.

Laz was standing in the wine warehouse, explaining to the proprietor why he needed so many bottles of Pinot Grigio after only one night's trading. Unfortunately, the company was not able to supply another batch with the bespoke Michelangelo's labels at such short notice, so Laz was about to load up his little white van with the regular, off-the-shelf bottles instead, when, through the wine merchant's window, he spotted Jean Jacques, his old restaurant manager from the Aeroplane Food days. The Frenchman appeared to be luring him outside by means of elaborate, beckoning hand gestures, which Michelangelo would no doubt have appreciated and even perhaps labelled alphabetically, given the opportunity.

Laz duly made his excuses to the proprietor and sidled outside to see what all the fuss was about. If the truth were known, he was pleasantly surprised to find that Jean Jacques was still willing to communicate at all, albeit with hand gestures, after the demise of the aeroplane restaurant. A week or so before Johnny O'Driscoll had seen fit to strip the place to the bone, words had been exchanged between these two equally hot-headed individuals. Accusations were levelled, followed by spirited counter accusations, resulting in the two protagonists not being on speaking terms. In a nutshell, Laz had suspected that Jean Jacques had had his chubby little Gallic fingers in the till, and the Frenchman had hotly denied the allegation and begun to scream four letter words at his employer. This soon gave way to bread rolls being thrown, which in turn developed into cutlery, but when Jean Jacques' weapon of choice became the rolling pin, Laz called a halt to the proceedings by beaning the Frenchman with a Le Creuset saucepan and handing the man his P45 when he came round.

However, time is a great healer, as is Germolene, and a lot of water had gone under the bridge since this unfortunate episode in the cramped galley kitchen of a Boeing aircraft. Both men, presumably, had had time to reflect on their actions in the interim. Laz had mellowed to the point where he'd decided to give the man the benefit of the doubt, and Jean Jacques had realized that, if he would persist in borrowing the odd twenty pound note from the till, he couldn't blame his employer for getting tetchy.

"Bonjour, Monsieur Larry," said Jean Jacques somewhat nervously. "Long time no see, eh?"

"How do you do, Froggy," asked Laz, eyeing him as a mongoose would a snake.

"We need to kiss and make up, I think," smiled the Frenchman, offering his chubby mitt. Laz shook it and asked why the come hither look and mad beckoning.

"Monsieur Larry, I was just trying to save you from being ripped off, that's all. Do you buy all your wines and spirits from him?"

"Yes, why?" asked Laz.

"Everyone knows he is a rob-dog, that's why! You'll never make a profit if you use this place. What were you buying?"

"Pinot Grigio, Barolo, Montepulciano d'Abruzzo..." Laz consulted the shopping list that Tomaso had written for him. "...Chianti, allsorts."

"You have an Italian place now?" asked Jean Jacques. He was nothing if not observant.

"Yeah," said Laz. "I thought I'd dip my toe in the water again, now that the pain of the last place is but a distant memory. So where *should* I be buying my wine?"

"Well, I can give you a few names, but I might be able to help out myself, on a one-off basis," said Jean Jacques. "I've just closed down my restaurant in Brum, because I'm going back to Paris to work. I have hundreds of bottles of fine wines in my friend's lock-up that I need to sell quickly before I go home, and I'm desperate to shift it."

"Is it all French shit?" asked Laz, the connoisseur.

"How dare you!" grinned Jean Jacques. "No, it's not actually. My restaurant wasn't specifically a French cuisine place, so we had wines from all over the world. I have a hundred or so bottles

211

of pretty much everything you've mentioned, plus some Frascati, Soave and Lambrusco if you're interested. And there's some Australian Shiraz and Merlot. I'll let you have it for a ridiculous price, just to shift it, so I can get back to France. How much is he charging you for the Pinot?"

"Trade price?" asked Laz. "Four quid a bottle. We sell it for fourteen."

"You can have everything I've got for two-fifty," said Jean Jacques," and that's like giving it away. "Apart from the Barolo of course – Six quid a bottle for that. Interested?

"And this isn't cheap piss?" asked Laz.

"Check the labels," advised the Frenchman, with a Gallic shrug.

"Okay," said Laz, "lead me to it."

* * *

"Shouldn't those Italian buddies of yours be back by now?" asked Laz, sweating profusely after he and Tomaso had carried forty boxes of wine into the restaurant.

"Si," said Tomaso, wiping his fevered brow with a napkin. "Maybe we go looka for them in the car. They coulda be lost!"

"No need," chipped in Claudia, who had just popped her head around the door. "My friend Jane who runs the Cat just told me that there are two Italians in the bar with a woman. She wondered if they belonged to us. Two Italians is a bit exotic for Tutton, she reckoned, so she figured they'd come from the new restaurant."

"Well that accounts for two out of three," frowned Laz. "But I don't like the sound of this. I'm going to fetch 'em back before they end up pissed. That Tutton Ale is like dynamite."

He dashed out to his van and bumped into David, returning to lend a hand if needed. They drove the short distance to the pub, screeched to a halt and dashed across the car park towards the rear entrance.

David was first to arrive at the lounge bar. He attracted the barmaid's attention and asked if she'd seen any wayward Italians. The girl's look said it all, so she added nothing to it, other than a finger pointing towards the tiny bar room at the front of the pub. David and Laz strode purposefully past her and into the adjoining room, and it was immediately obvious that all was not well. As the two men entered the room, the two Italians and the lady began to sing a Zuchero song at the top of their voices, in a range of key signatures, much to the annoyance of the regulars. Then, just before the first chorus, Maurizio vomited into the fireplace and sank to his knees groaning. Luca, who was made of stronger stuff, poured the remainder of his Tutton Ale over his fallen comrade. David turned his gaze to the woman in their midst, and wondered why she was so fluent in Italian, albeit in a slurred way. It was then that he realized who she was.

It was Andrea. And he was not only in drag, but also severely plastered.

David gave Laz a look that a thousand words could not begin to explain, and yet Laz understood it completely. It was as if, on Friday night, he had been the proud captain of the Titanic as it set sail on its maiden voyage, and now, he felt like the captain of the Titanic all over again, but this time as she assumed a jaunty angle, the ice-cold water already lapping around his toes.

He tried to articulate his sentiments, which were many and varied, but all he could manage was a simple, "OUT.....NOW!" Which nevertheless did the trick. As the three filed past him, he added brokenly, "Why are you dressed as a woman, you twat?" to which Andrea replied:

"I told you I was gonna buy myself a special outfeet for the opening night, thass why!"

213

"It isn't a fucking fancy dress event," snarled Laz. "When you mentioned getting some new clothes for the opening yesterday, I presumed you meant a shirt and some bloody trousers."

Andrea glared at him. "I am a cross-dresser, and I am not ashamed of eet. I demand the right to wear what I want, and you have no power to stop me. It is against my human rights, and I can close your restaurant down, you sheet. Every time, with every boss, it's alwaysa the same. You can fucka your restaurant."

Luca placed an arm around his cross-dressing comrade and begged him to be quiet.

"Signor Laz has been good to us, Andrea," he slurred. "Donna offend heem, or he will sack us all."

Maurizio vomited into a nearby plant pot and then nodded, by way of backing up his colleague's comment.

"This is a bloody nightmare!" wailed Laz. "They're completely wrecked. I may consider suing the pub, or, or, or Tutton Ales. Yes, that's it. I'll sue the brewery, the bastards. They've only gone and ruined me, that's what they've done. I'm ruined before I've even opened. Temperamental, hah! - They said he was temperamental, but I couldn't have bloody foreseen this. Jesus Christ! I've hired Eddie Izzard."

"How dare you blaspheme!" shouted Andrea, grabbing Laz's collar.

"Fuck off!" replied Laz, punching Andrea square in the lipstick. He fell heavily to the ground and began to sob.

"Donna you hit my friend," warned Luca, "or…"

"Or what?" asked Laz, punching Luca in the eye without awaiting his response in full. "And if you want some as well," he screamed at Maurizio, but Maurizio was pre-occupied with his projectile vomiting and didn't wish to contribute to the discussion.

214

Feeling he'd made his point, Laz turned on his heels and made his way across the car park, hotly pursued by David.

"What the bloody hell am I going to do now?" Laz yelled, kicking chunks out of his little white van.

"Calm down for starters," advised David, "or you'll have a stroke. It's obvious we can't use those three idiots tonight. Can Tomaso and the English lads muddle through between them?"

"Are you having a laugh?" asked Laz, with a deranged look in his eye. "We have three chefs. That's it. Two are pissed as farts and their leader is not only as pissed as a fart but also dressed as Marilyn Monroe. I'm bloody ruined. I never want to go near a bloody restaurant ever again, not even to eat in one. What the hell can we do?"

"Well I'm going for a walk, I don't know about you," said David.

"WHAT? Are you serious? I'm about to implode and you're going for a bastard walk?"

"Yes. It gets the endorphins going. The little grey cells, as Poirot used to say. I'll be back in half an hour, hopefully with a solution. Meanwhile, don't go anywhere near the kitchen knives. Have a strong coffee and a fag, and sit down."

David powered across the estate with a determined stride, heading for the Sheep Walks, all the time breathing in deeply through his nose and exhaling through his mouth. Shortly, he came across a gaggle of geriatric hikers who were taking up much of the path and proceeding at approximately a mile a week.

David had always been a considerate child, brought up properly by his doting parents, and in his youth he was something of a sensitive young flower. If he came across an elderly lady walking slowly and with some difficulty, he would always overtake her at a pace that was just marginally faster than hers, rather than zoom past at a rate of knots. He did this because

215

he was conscious of the fact that his burst of speed might well have drawn the old lady's attention to her own tardiness, causing her to reflect on her failing health and stamina, thereby making her miserable and even depressed.

In spite of his impatience, David's principles were still firmly in place, and consequently, he slowed down to a snail's pace as he came alongside them. It transpired that they were the Brierley Bank Senior Citizens Rambling Club (Est 1987), which interested David, as he had been born there.

Brierley Bank, or Brierley Bonk as they pronounced it, is in most experts' opinions, the very epicentre of the Black Country. The local accent is unique, and reckoned to be the truest, most authentic Anglo Saxon dialect still being spoken in England. Tomaso, who was from Pisa, was coming on nicely with his English, but were he to meet anyone with a proper Brierley Bank accent, his many hours of diligent study would have been to no avail. It is for this reason that, just as the Italian sections of this tale were translated to aid the reader, so must the Brierley Bonk ones be, for, if anything, they are harder to understand.

"How bist thay? (How are you?)" asked one elderly gent as David drew alongside. "Thist looken lyek one ayten en throwed up. Bist thay or-right, ode pal? (You look like you've been sick. Are you okay?)"

David explained that he was having a stressful day and was taking a walk to sort things out in his mind.

"Yome a bit la-di-da fer Brierley Bonk ay thay, chap? (To say you emanated from the same neck of the woods, your accent is not as strong as ours, my friend)" observed a rather obese lady with huge, batwing arms and a triple chin.

"Oh, yes, sorry," said David. "It's because I went away to college."

"Weer's thee bin? (Where did you study?)" asked a tall, gangly rambler with a moustache.

216

"Erm, it was only Wolverhampton actually," explained David, embarrassed, "but the students were from all over the place, so we had to speak proper English so that we could all understand each other."

"An yo ever 'erd annythen ser saft, Basil? (Have you ever heard anything so silly, Basil?) He lost his accent in Wolverhampton. Ess onnay eight mile away! Mind yo, they dun talk funny theer, doe thay Bernard? (Wolverhampton may only be eight miles away from Brierley Bank, but, surprisingly, they do have a markedly different lilt there, don't they, Bernard?)."

"Why did you just call him Basil, and then Bernard?" asked David, edging slowly ahead of the pack as he spoke, in accordance with his game plan.

The obese lady, who was walking even slower than her colleagues, explained that Bernard looked, to their minds at least, "Just like that saft chap off the tellay, him ez runs that yampy hotel (Bernard, in their opinion, bore a passing resemblance to Basil Fawlty)."

His query answered satisfactorily, David bade them a good day, moved up a gear and slowly disappeared around the next bend. Once out of sight, he steamed off like a greyhound again, but still the endorphins lay sleeping. The truth of it was, his oldest friend, Laz, was truly in the shit. He would have to abandon the opening night, make some excuse about a kitchen fire or whatever, and reschedule for the following Saturday, once he'd had time to sober up his chefs or find abstemious replacements. The trouble was, how on earth could he let people know at such short notice that they shouldn't bother to turn up? The whole thing was a debacle, but in fairness, David had warned him back at Pizza Express. Laz should have known not to dabble again, after the disaster that was Aeroplane Food.

David was jogging now, hoping that the increased pace might finally shake his lethargic little endorphins into action, but still nothing came to mind, and then, just as he was about to give up

217

and return to base, pop! An idea fizzed into his head, thanks to his brief encounter with the Brierley Bonk Walkers. David's motto, 'Out of Desperation Cometh Inspiration' had proved itself correct once more. He turned around, took a deep breath, and rocketed back towards the chapel. Meanwhile, the Brierley Bonk Walkers were crawling along in the opposite direction, and chatting about David.

"He was a poor ode soul wor ee, Baz? (he was a poor old soul, wasn't he, Basil?),'' observed Fat Mavis breathlessly.

"Ar, ee could hardlay walk fer such a young chap. Weem eighty-odd, half on wey, and he couldn't even overtek wey! (Some of us are eighty-somethings and he struggled to overtake us).''

No sooner had the words left their lips, when David charged around the corner approaching fifty miles per hour, scattering pensioners to the four winds. As he rocketed by, he attempted to wave, thank them profusely for their input and apologize, all in one hurried gesture. Now was no time to stand and chat. His previously comatose endorphins were wide-awake and raging. Minutes later, he arrived at Michelangelo's, and when Laz dashed outside to see what the fuss was all about, David was bent double, trying to suck air into his heaving lungs and unable to speak. It was two more minutes before he was capable of communication, but when he did eventually succeed, Laz was all ears.

"Do you remember, after Tim bloody Beasley had knocked Goffredo unconscious,'' gasped David, "that I said it was like being in an episode of Fawlty Towers?''

Laz nodded sulkily.

"Well, there was an episode where they were having a gourmet evening, and everything went wrong. Wasn't the chef pissed or something?''

218

Laz said that he knew the episode well, and added that, had he been in the mood, he might have laughed heartily at the comparison with his own situation, but he wasn't, so he wouldn't be.

"Hear me out," begged David, still panting. "Can you remember what Basil did, when his chef became inebriated and fell in love with Manuel?"

"No, not really, offhand. My memory doesn't work so well whenever I'm feeling suicidal."

"Well I'll tell you. He called on his old mate who ran the local restaurant in Torquay, and he cooked the food and sent it over in the car."

"Oh yes, I remember now; there's a mix up with the food, the car breaks down, Basil goes mental and whacks it with a stick, the diners end up with blancmange instead of duck, and the evening ends in disaster. Bloody marvellous!"

"Listen, will you?" hissed David. "We could ring Giovanni right away, and see if he and his boys could work at your place tonight. If they got here early, they could study the menu, and hopefully they'd know how to cook most of it. They're experienced people and proper Italians."

"And have you seen the bloody flaw in your master plan, Sherlock?" asked Laz, uncharitably. "Like, who's going to run *their* restaurant for them on a busy Saturday evening? Maybe Andrea, Maurizio and bloody Luca could do it!"

"Good point," admitted David, crestfallen, "but the last time I spoke to Giovanni, he was dead."

"What, so now you're a clairvoyant?"

"Ha bloody ha! His restaurant, I meant. Why not phone him and ask how many bookings he's got tonight. If it's quiet, maybe you could offer him enough dosh to close up and zoom over here. Look, it's the best I could come up with after a half mile walk. Why not try it?"

Laz took his mobile from his pocket and rang the number. Giovanni answered. There followed ten minutes of frantic negotiation, before Laz ended the call and returned the phone to his pocket.

"He'll do it," sighed Laz. "He only had one booking tonight, for four, and we have a spare half-table that would take four here. I told him I'd bring his customers over here and feed them for free. He was a bit concerned that they might then switch their loyalties to Michelangelo's after that, so I had to offer him a lot of money to sweeten him."

"I heard that bit," admitted David, wincing. "Two grand? That's wiped out your profits, I'd say."

"At this precise juncture," replied Laz, "the money isn't important. We need to rescue the evening or I'll be a laughing stock. Giovanni's chefs are on their way."

"Right then! We still have a good few hours before the first punters arrive. We can pull this off. What's happened to the Three Stooges?"

Laz explained that Tomaso had hauled them off to the tied cottage and put them under house arrest. He told them to stay put, and he would sort things out on Sunday. Apparently, they were keen to stay holed up in case Laz started punching them again.

David staggered back to his studio to make a cup of tea and to steady his nerves before the next whirlwind hit Tutton on Stour.

He had a sneaking feeling that his night out was going to one to remember.

CHAPTER 24

It'll be Alright on the Night

Giovanni's chefs arrived at five and got down to business straight away, with a little help from Tomaso. After many years spent in England, they had become resigned to creating massive portions of Anglicized Italian fodder, and it was therefore exciting for them to be given a chance to cook the old way. The only problem was, they'd forgotten how. Thankfully, Tomaso had been watching Andrea and the lads in the kitchens, and was now passing on tips to the new boys. He would have preferred a week, rather than two hours, for his knowledge to sink in, but life is seldom perfect. The situation was not ideal, by a very long chalk, but with the judicious axing of certain tricky dishes and the introduction of several easier ones, plus a lot of swearing and several hand gestures that Michelangelo had never got round to recording, by seven o'clock, they were sort-of ready. Giovanni arrived by car with his four customers, who didn't quite grasp what was going on but seemed to be excited by it all anyway, leaving Laz free to mope, smoke, swear and fret in the order named.

Shortly afterwards, the first diners arrived, parked up and walked the short distance to the restaurant, which was looking every bit as grand as it had looked the previous evening. They were offered a glass of champagne and seated in the cosy pre-dining area to study their menus whilst listening to Tomaso explaining to them about the many changes he'd had to make.

Laz had intended to greet customers at the door, but decided at the last minute to ask Giovanni to take over, so that he could disappear to the kitchens and irritate the chefs instead. It also gave him the opportunity to sneak off to the lavatory every five minutes to smoke a cigarette, in the hope that it would calm his frayed nerves.

By eight, everyone who was coming had arrived, and the place was buzzing. Tomaso gestured to David that the champagne table was almost empty, with several guests still waiting for a glass, so he trotted over to the wine store to grab a couple of bottles which he duly handed to Tomaso. Tomaso opened them and poured out the fizzing champagne into eight more glasses and handed them to the gaggle of guests with their tongues hanging out, gathered around his table. Elsewhere, the waitresses were sidling in and out of the various clusters of diners, offering smoked salmon and cream cheese blinis, mini pizza slices and grilled asparagus spears wrapped in proscuitto di Parma. Then, as David was about to return to his seat in order to study the menu, he overheard a rather pompous gentleman complain loudly to Tomaso that there was something wrong with the champagne. He reckoned that there was no taste to it. David made his way over to the table and grabbed a glass for himself. He took a long swig. The man was right. It was carbonated water, and not even San Pellegrino at that.

With some urgency, he returned to the wine store, and grabbed a selection. Back at the table, he and Tomaso opened a champagne, a Barolo, a Montepulciano d'Abruzzo and a Pinot Grigio. They all contained water. Suddenly feeling very sticky around the collar, he made his excuses and tracked down Laz, who was still sitting on the lavatory sucking on a cigarette.

"How's it all going?" he called from within the sanctuary of his cubicle.

"Er, well okay, as it happens," replied David, but there's a but, I'm afraid."

"A but?" asked Laz, his voice quaking with nerves.

"Yes. That booze you got from Jean Jacques. It's all water."

"WHAT?"

"All water. He's done you. Perhaps he hadn't forgiven you after all."

"The bloody frog bastard!"

"Quite! So tell me where your other wine is. Tomaso is panicking."

"We don't have any more bloody wine. That's it!"

"Well praise the Lord! Old Jean Jacques Jesus has performed a miracle. He's turned the wine into water. You didn't perchance buy and bread or fish from him as well, did you? Look, I strongly suggest that you get off the crapper and pop to Wine Rack in Wollaston, and I mean now."

"But I'll have to pay the retail price there," moaned Laz. "The trade place has closed for the night now, so I won't be making any money."

"Laz," barked David, "that is the last of your worries. You'll have a bloody riot on your hands soon. Get moving!"

Back in the restaurant, things were getting awkward. Table after table were sending their wine orders back, citing a distinct lack of alcohol content, and, for that matter, taste. Thankfully, the beers and spirits were still okay, but many of the ladies didn't want beer or spirits and were beginning to whine about not having wine. Giovanni, ever the statesman, begged the diners to be patient, and promised that replacement bottles were on their way.

However, unknown to Giovanni, Laz and his van, loaded up with six hundred and fifty pounds worth of wine, were sitting at the Stewponey traffic lights two miles down the road, while several police cars, an ambulance and a fire engine dealt with a road traffic accident. Cursing and spitting, he yanked the gear stick into reverse, screeched the van around, Starsky and Hutch-style, and blasted down the A449. He careered down a country lane in search of a back way to Tutton and was making reasonable headway when he hit a huge mound of horse manure, which sent his van skidding out of control and into a hedge. Unfortunately, the van did not wedge itself into the hedge, but blasted clean through it, eventually coming to land in a duck pond, instantly curing one elderly, dozing mallard of its constipation problem.

Back at the restaurant, just when it looked like things couldn't get much worse, things did. Tomaso, experienced waiter, comic, raconteur and diplomat was trying his best to calm a particularly offensive table of four people who were complaining about the wine in the most obnoxious and unpleasant manner. He was promising them free drinks, offering to reduce their bill, and all but volunteering to pick up their remaining mortgage payments, when suddenly the tallest, ugliest member of the group stood up and began to rant at the top of his voice.

"Listen, wop, you get me a bottle of fekking wine right nye, or I'll give you a good hiding, you got me?"

David, who had been busy hiding his head in his hands for the last ten minutes in the hope that everyone would just go away, suddenly jerked upright. He knew that voice all too well. Johnny O'Driscoll and three of his cronies were inside Michelangelo's. Who on earth was responsible for letting them in, he wondered. If Laz had been on the door, he would have recognized them, but he wasn't. Poor old Giovanni didn't have a clue. He'd probably welcomed them in with open arms. And where on earth *was* Laz? He should have been back ages ago. David looked around for back-up. The major would have been good, but he wasn't there.

He'd elected to come the night before instead, the lucky sod. This was shaping up to be a blood bath.

Tomaso tried to pacify the Irishman by promising to return with a bottle of real wine, on the house. He dashed to the wine store and rummaged around, eventually finding one of the original specially labelled bottles of Pinot Grigio up a corner. Snatching it up, he ran back to O'Driscoll's table with his corkscrew at the ready.

"What kept yer, yer little greasy fekking wop?" snarled O'Driscoll. "Busy running away from the war were yeh? Give me that bottle nye, and fekk off, you oily little shite."

"No needa to be aggressive, gentlemen," begged Tomaso. "Here, on the house, just to keep you going till the food arrives, a bowl of cashew nuts!"

Four huge, tattooed hands grabbed for the bowl at the same time and shovelled the cashews into four hungry, gold-toothed mouths. Tomaso walked away from the table, waiting in eager anticipation for the results of his handiwork, like a terrorist briskly striding away from a car bomb. He didn't have to wait long. Behind him, agonizing screams rent the air. The bottle of water, previously the object of their anger, was now a prized commodity – a life-saver. There have been many theories about spontaneous self-combustion over the years, and photographs bandied about on the internet showing bodies reduced to ash, with just the feet still visible. No rational explanation has ever been given for the cause, but that was because no-one thought to ask Tomaso Caleffi.

Then, just in the nick of time, the police arrived. Not that anyone had called them. It was just Donald and Pongo, who had happened to be passing by and felt a little peckish. They waltzed through the front doors fully expecting to see eighty satisfied diners tucking into their pasta, and instead saw what resembled the start of a Wild West bar room brawl. Johnny O'Driscoll had kicked his table over and was raging and ranting incoherently,

225

lashing out like an animal in deep distress, which of course he was. His cohorts were in agony too, snatching iced water from the other tables and pouring it down their throats in desperation.

Donald and Pongo called for back-up, and got it quicker than they bargained for, thanks to a passing police car that had just arrived at the estate from a road traffic accident, with a muddy and distraught specimen of humanity flopped across their rear seat.

The four coppers immediately set to work on the four travellers with relish, whacking them with truncheons and dragging them outside. Inside, diners screamed, while others gathered their overcoats and headed for the door without paying.

Laz, plastered in mud from head to foot, with a black eye and a varied assortment of tears in his clothing, tottered into his beloved restaurant and surveyed the carnage, aghast. If this was what happened when people were denied alcohol for an hour, he mused bitterly, he was better off drinking far too much, like he always did. Everywhere he looked was devastation and chaos. Poor Giovanni was staggering round shell-shocked and telling everyone that he had only come in the first place to help a friend. Tomaso was being cautioned for throwing a wine bottle at the travellers by a flushed-looking Donald, now that all but one of the O'Driscoll gang had succeeded in escaping and disappeared into the night. It was not so much that Donald objected to Tomaso's strategy, which he felt was basically sound, but he did take issue with the Italian's awful throwing technique, which had resulted in the missile beaning him, rather than its intended victim.

An hour later, once everyone had gone home, Tomaso poured everyone a strong espresso and a large grappa each. David, Laz, Giovanni and his staff sat around a table and just stared into the middle distance in shock, no-one uttering a word. As opening nights went, or closing nights, for that matter, it was interesting. No-one would forget it in a hurry. If one looked on the bright side, it was undoubtedly memorable, and life was all about memories. One day - maybe not soon - David and Laz would sit in Pizza Express Stourbridge again and laugh about all this. Not for maybe thirty years or so maybe, but one day.

* * *

That same night, or more accurately, very early the following morning, Major Winterfold was walking his Labrador dogs. It was two-thirty a.m., and most people were fast asleep by then, but not the major. Life in Iraq had made him an occasional insomniac – another long Latin-sounding medical word to add to his considerable list of complaints.

He was passing Michelangelo's restaurant, which was now in darkness, when he heard a noise from within which gave him cause for concern. It sounded as if burglars had broken in and were trashing the place. He ran as quickly as a man could with only one real leg, in the direction of the field which previously had played host to the Tutton Country Fair. Now, all that remained of the event was a large marquee and several smaller tents in a huddle around it. He arrived at the first of the tents, shone his torch at it, bent down and called out to whoever was within. The man that was within soon came out, looking bedraggled, and was just about to give someone a sizable piece of his mind when he realized who it was that had unceremoniously roused him in the middle of the night, and wisely decided to defer, deeming his original course of action to be a poor career move.

"Very sorry to wake you, sergeant," whispered the major, "but I think we have a situation down at the old chapel. Burglars, unless I'm very much mistaken. If you want to see some real action, howsabout rounding up the men, pronto and we'll go on a night manoeuvre. You'll have to be quick, mind."

227

It was a real credit to the Territorial Army Brass Band that they were assembled and almost awake less than three and a half minutes later. One and a half minutes after that, they presented at the front door of the chapel, ready for action and buzzing with adrenalin. The front door was slightly ajar and the inside of the little chapel was lit by a full moon, so Major Winterfold took a sneaky look inside, and didn't like what he was seeing. Around eight men were busy trashing the interior of the restaurant with hammers and shovels. One tall, wiry-haired man was blasting a paint-balling gun at David's ceiling, splattering it with vivid red paint bombs, and laughing in a deranged, maniacal way as he did so. Another was throwing wine bottles full of water at the walls, because, like singer Nick Lowe, he loved the sound of breaking glass. It was time to act.

"Okay, men," whispered the major, thrilled to be back in charge of some soldiers, albeit part-time musical ones, "I know who these people are, I think, and if I'm right, they are hard cases, and they have makeshift weapons, but we are militarily trained, and there are twice as many of us too. Now, just remember what I was teaching you about the SAS hand to hand combat techniques. You'll be fine. Unfortunately, we can't shoot the buggers, but you all have your rifles, nevertheless. I'll go in first. With a bit of luck, just seeing us pile in will scare the shit out of them and they'll come quietly. If not, stick to the plan, and look out for each other. Good luck!"

And with that, they burst in, screaming their blood-curdling battle cry, which made a nice change from playing trumpets, euphoniums and tubas.

* * *

Laz and David were first on the scene the following morning to survey the damage. There was a lot of it to survey. The place was trashed, and tragically, David's magnificent ceiling was ruined. Unknown to the major, the travellers had arrived drunk at the

Country Fair late in the afternoon after he'd left, caused a bit of trouble and stolen a paint-balling gun. They had found a suitably destructive use for it quicker than they had imagined. There were red and yellow splashes covering every square yard of the ceiling, and nothing could be done to remove it. Part of the ceiling was also structurally damaged, caused by a shotgun, the major had informed them. He shuddered to think what would have happened had they fired the thing at the soldiers, as they charged through the front doors. Luckily, the two shots that wrecked a section of ceiling emptied the gun, and before it could be reloaded, the owner was incapacitated.

"The bloke with the shotgun," said David dully, "was it O'Driscoll?"

"You know me with faces," smiled Simon. "Might have been. Was he really big, with curly grey hair and no front teeth?"

"Sounds like him," replied David, "but he had a full set of teeth, I thought."

"Not any more he hasn't," Simon assured him. "I took them out with my rifle butt. I tell you what; it was a hell of a scrap though. My boys gave them a frightful hammering."

"Good," said Laz, who looked grey.

"The police arrived in droves and carted them all off. Most of them were unconscious to be honest, so they offered little resistance. We went a bit OTT, if I'm truthful. It was our way of saying thank you for what they did to Trevor and poor old Harry Millichip. The cops phoned really early this morning to say that the three who beat Trevor to a pulp had been identified from his photos, and will be charged with attempted murder. It's probably the same ones who did for Harry as well. O'Driscoll fully intended to shoot me too, only I was too quick for him and rearranged his dental work while he tried to reload. That means he'll cop a long stretch, all being well. Now the cops will ransack his squalid camp site and hopefully retrieve a lot of stolen property. It's a great result in one sense, but at a terrible price."

"You're telling me," sighed Laz. "I'm ruined."

CHAPTER 25

One week later

Workmen were once more swarming around Michelangelo's, but it was no longer a joyous sight to behold. A scaffolding team was erecting a small tower in order to inspect the shotgun damage to the ceiling. Down below, trashed tables and torn leather seats were being carried off to removal vans. A man busied himself sweeping up piles of broken wine bottles, vicious shards of glass from shattered mirrors and big, ugly chunks of porcelain that once belonged to lavatory seats and elegant wash basins. Laz and David stood in the middle of this scene of devastation, unable to think of anything to say to each other. David glanced over at his old friend and saw that his bottom lip was quivering. Laz, suddenly aware that his friend was watching, pretended that he had a piece of grit in his eye, caused by the man on the scaffold yanking at the shattered ceiling panel. David knew better. Laz was broken-hearted because his dream was over before it had begun. He had already instructed David to shoot him if he ever so much as uttered the word restaurant again. He should have listened to David in the first place, back at Pizza Express, when he reminded him of the Aeroplane Food debacle, but no, this time it was going to be different. Well, it wasn't. It was exactly the bloody same, even down to the cause of its demise.

Major Simon arrived, and called over to the two forlorn characters stood in the middle of what was once an elegant dining area. He asked Laz, once he'd worked out which one of the two he was, if he was free for a second, and the two men stepped outside into the glorious sunshine, the only redeeming feature of an otherwise catastrophic and depressing scene.

"I know it's not the best time to have a chat," the major began, "but I wanted to put a proposition to you. As you're probably aware, I felt pretty awful about having to sell the old chapel in the first place, after it had been in the family for five hundred years, but to be frank, I needed the money. Anyway, thanks to your mate David, who arranged the sale of my two paintings and the Michelangelo drawings, I'm considerably better off, so unless you plan to start again, and I don't think you do, I'd like to buy the old chapel back, and to make up for all your losses, I'm willing to offer fifty grand more than you paid me. In spite of the damage, it's still in a much better state than it was, what with the refit, the rewiring, flooring, lighting and so on, so it's worth it to me. What do you say?"

"Seriously?" asked Laz, smiling for the first time in a week.

"Seriously. I've lost the works of art; I accept that, but I'd like my chapel back please."

"It's a deal," said Laz, shaking the major's hand. "But what will you do with it?"

Simon scratched his chin and pondered. "Well, I was chatting to Claudia, and we reckon it would make a lovely tea room and gift shop. We get loads of ramblers over here, plus the cricket teams, the footballers, the anglers who use the lakes, and people who just like to pop somewhere for a piece of cake and a pot of tea of a weekend. I'm sure it would do well. At least fifty percent of the furniture is still intact, and there's still a bar and a till. We just need to repair the ceiling and the loos and we're in business. I'd like to call it Michelangelo's Tea Rooms, if that's okay by you, unless of course you need the name for another venture…"

Laz flashed him a look that spoke volumes.

"Okay, well that's fabulous – we'll steal it then," smiled the major.

At this juncture, David called over to them from the front door of the chapel, Apparently, the workman on the scaffold was desirous of a word to the proprietor about the scale of the shotgun damage. One panel, near the edge of the ceiling, had been shredded quite badly by two separate blasts from the gun, and would need to be replaced. To this end, he began to prise it free of the battens it had been nailed to, warning those below that it might well be falling to earth imminently. As the panel came away, it revealed an ornate border of blue and gold, painted onto the original old ceiling beneath.

"Looks as if someone put a false ceiling in at some time," he observed.

"That was done in the early eighteen hundreds, when the Methodists briefly ran the place," shouted Simon. "They didn't like all the fancy Italianate mouldings and so on. They preferred their churches on the plain side I think. Crying shame, but there you are. They got rid of a lot of the interior too. Maddening, but I wasn't around then so I couldn't do much about it!"

"Shall I cut you a new panel and replace it, boss?" asked the workman.

"No, let's rip the false ceiling out while you're up there," replied Simon. "I bet the ornate one is nicer. I can get it restored to its original condition."

"Er, isn't that for you to decide?" whispered David to Laz. Laz explained that, as of two minutes ago, Simon was once more the proud owner of Michelangelo's, and he sincerely hoped the chap had more success with it that he had.

Henry and Claudia arrived, wearing hard hats, which did nothing for Henry's Savile Row suit whatsoever.

"What's going on?" he asked. David made some wisecrack about the National Gallery filing a missing person report, and then explained about the original ceiling. Meanwhile, the workman was going about his duties with gusto, as two more panels fell in quick succession.

"David," said Henry, tugging at his sleeve with some urgency, "take a look up there, would you?"

A semi-naked, well-built man, his modesty preserved by the strategic use of a white sheet of material intertwined between his legs, reached out to a well-padded, solid-looking woman reclining on a fluffy cloud that, in reality, probably wouldn't have borne her weight. All around them, winged angels appeared to be dancing with glee at the prospect of their union.

"Does that, David, to your trained eye," he continued, "remind you of anyone?"

"B-Bloody hell, yes!" blurted David.

The workman tore down another two panels, revealing more figures. The painting was quite small, compared to David's paint by numbers creation, and circular, framed by a raised gilded moulding.

"Erm, now be VERY careful removing those panels, please!" begged Henry. "I think we might have something VERY special here. Something VERY VERY special indeed. And may I add another VERY, for good measure?"

"What's the matter with you two?" asked Simon, puzzled. "That old bloody painting's been there for yonks. "My father knew about its existence, but he said it was too much effort to rip the false ceiling out so he left it covered up."

"Tell him, David," said Henry, his voice all of a quiver.

"Simon, that old letter talks about Michelangelo coming here to visit his cousin. What with everything that's been going on around here lately, we haven't had chance to talk about that yet, but believe me, when you announce it to the press, it will be a huge story. But that's not the half of it. I've discovered something that will hit the art world like an atom bomb, all thanks to your old hand drawings. I'm not exaggerating here – what I've discovered is mind-blowing. Currently, only me, Laz and Giovanni know about the Michelangelo Code. And now this! I saw that look in Henry's eye when the panels came down, and I knew exactly what it meant, because I recognized it right away myself. That painting, up there on your ceiling, Laz…"

"My ceiling, David," corrected Simon.

"Sorry, *your* ceiling then, is by Michelangelo himself, or I'm a Dutchman - like Van Gogh was, as it happens. Sorry if I'm rambling; I'm in shock. Old Michelangelo must have painted it for his cousin's chapel as a thank you present for six month's worth of hospitality, when he disappeared from Rome after painting the Sistine Chapel ceiling. It's only small – heaven knows, he'd done enough painting to last him a lifetime by then, but he obviously felt the need to repay his cousin in some way, and this was his way. Look at the hands. They're exactly as Michelangelo painted hands. I must study them closely later, just in case they're saying something! And look at the female figure; a bloke with tits as usual. The letter refers to a gift to his cousin. I'll bet you a million quid this was that gift. Simon, you don't realize what this means. You will have art lovers flocking to see this – the only British Michelangelo ceiling in existence."

"And they'll buy cakes and pots of tea while they're here!" Simon added gleefully.

"And reproductions of the painting on postcards, and tea towels, and jigsaws, and desk diaries," added David, who had an eye for the commercial angle himself.

"And tasteful fine art prints, miniature statuettes of David, and books about the Sistine Chapel ceiling, and calendars, and bone china mugs," chipped in Henry.

"Erm, Simon," said Laz thoughtfully.

"Yes, Laz?" said Simon, like David, still in deep shock.

"Any chance of me hanging on the place after all, do you think?"

CHAPTER 26

All's well that ends well

Laz Homer burst through the front door of Pizza Express Stourbridge with such gusto that nearby diners looked to be in fear of their lives. A mobile phone glued to his right ear, he was concluding a somewhat terse conversation with a man from Amsterdam who apparently manufactured cast iron pub tables, albeit at ridiculous prices. He barged past little boys' birthday parties, romantic dinners for two and after-hours business liaisons en route to the top, right-hand corner of the room where sat a tall, scatterbrained, forty-eight year-old artist with receding hair and a dreamy look, nursing a large glass of Montepulciano d'Abruzzo and a dish of olives.

"Dave!" called Laz, slipping his mobile back into his trouser pocket, "Sorry I'm late, old pal. God, I need a drink; where's that bloody waitress gone? It's impossible to get served in here. Lord knows why you come every flipping week."

He pulled out a screeching chair and flopped into it.

"Good evening to you, too, Laz," said David. "Listen, I've been thinking about this Michelangelo Code thing. I don't know whether I should tell the world about it after all."

"Why not, for God's sake?" asked Laz, incredulously. "You'll probably make a fortune out of it, end up on every chat show that's going – it'll make you a celebrity. It wouldn't surprise me

237

if they invited you onto 'I'm a celebrity, get me out of here!' and made you eat kangaroo testicles. Why wouldn't you want to tell all?"

"For precisely the reasons you just stated, for starters," replied David, screwing his nose up in disgust, "but the main reason is that the Sistine Chapel ceiling is a major tourist attraction, and a religious one at that. What we discovered would make the thing into a laughing stock. You've have millions of Japanese tourists with their specially printed code-breaker books complete with the twenty-one hand illustrations, flashing their poxy little cameras at it, and no-one would bother to look at the art any more. It would just end up as one big joke, and it would be all my fault. I've spoken to Giovanni and Simon, and Henry too, and we all agree. We just need your vote, as the fifth conspirator, to maintain a vow of silence. Let it be our little secret that we take to the grave, just like Michelangelo asked his cousin Umberto to do in his letter. Besides, I'm getting too old for all this adventure stuff. I'm forty-eight and a half and I just want the quiet life. You and I have had some mad scrapes in our time, but this last one takes the biscuit. I'm exhausted, and I don't need the limelight any more. So what do you say?"

"Fine by me. I'll keep it under my hat if you lot will. Now hand me that menu – I'm starving."

"Are you ready to order, gents?" asked the waiter.

"Not yet," growled Laz, without even looking up. "I've only just arrived. Give us a minute, will you?"

"Evening, Dave!" said the waiter. David glanced up from his menu.

"TREV!"

"Lads!"

"God, it's great to see you!" smiled David. "You're looking fit and well. What on earth are you doing here?"

"I'm the manager, I'll have you know. I've cleaned up my act since the accident as well. No more booze. I'm teetotal, believe it or not. When I got sober, I realized what a bloody mess I'd become, so I turned over a new leaf. Smartened myself up, got some new clothes – you can't keep me out of the shower nowadays. I was down here one night, havin' me dinner with a sparkly water and lime cordial, and I got talkin' to the Polish waitress."

"Oh, Gabria," said David. "Nice girl. How is she? Come to think of it, where is she?"

"Gone home now," replied Trev.

"What, to Poland? That's a shame, she was alright."

"Nah! Wordsley. She's just finished her shift."

"Ah, right. You were saying…."

"Yeah, I was talking to Gabby, and she reckoned the manager's job was going, so I applied for it. I'd just about had enough of the lonely, late nights spent sat in freezin' cold cars with a camera, the seedy hotels, and having me head stoved in by scumbags. I'm getting too old for all of that, and I needed to settle down. Before the P.I. business, I used to run a pub in Tipton, which was where I learnt how to drink away the profits. It did teach me about this kind of trade though, which was useful in my interview. Anyway, to cut a long story short, I was offered the job, and I've been here a couple of weeks now, and lovin' it. Oh yeah, and me and Gab are what's known nowadays as an item, so life is good. How's things been with you two, while I've been away?"

"Oh, quiet!" smiled David.

"Boring, really," added Laz, flashing his friend a look. "So anyway, Trev, can I get a bottle of this red stuff he's drinking?"

"Sure thing, Laz, and are you ready to order?"

"Sorry mate, I've been talking and…"

"One 'la Reine' with Parma ham instead of your normal ham, and extra oregano, and a 'Sloppy Giuseppe' for him please, Trev."

"Coming up, boys," grinned Trev.

David poured half of his wine into Laz's empty glass and raised his.

"Okay, Laz, a toast, to the quiet life, To old friends, to Major Winterfold - thank you for your fifty grand cheque, to my new farmhouse in Tenbury Wells, to Henry Tibbatts and Claudia, his bride to be, to poor old Harry Millichip, God rest his soul, to Giovanni, to Tomaso, hoping he gets another job soon, to Annie, and Suzanne, Lauren, James, and my mom, Ruby - God, I'm getting maudlin here! To Michelangelo di Ludovico di Liornardo di Buonarroti Simoni, to Tim 'Jonah' Beasley, to Donald and Pongo even – I'm scraping the barrel now. To all of you! Here's to the quiet life. Cheers! Salute!"

And from somewhere deep inside the Pizza Express kitchens came a little tiny, faraway utterance that sounded a little bit like 'KUT!'

The End

Finito

With grateful thanks to the following:

My lovely Mom, Ruby and my much missed Dad, Len,

Susan, Laura and Jamie Tristram and Rosie the Spaniel

- thanks for the encouragement. When can I have it?

My genius brother David (and family) for inspiring me to write comedy

Larry and Anne Homer, friends of some thirty years

Eleanor Andrews, for my Italian translations, grazie!

Pizza Express, for your sponsorship (and your pizzas!)

4edge Limited, for printing all my books

Steve Jolliffe, for the book covers and the paradiddles. Get well soon!

My wonderful, if deranged readers and your lovely emails

Books Unlimited, for selling lots of my books

Dudley Library Services for buying lots of them

The Quarry Bonk Society

Tarmac and Carillion, past sponsors

Dr David Edwards and Operc, likewise

Aileen Fraser, for proof reading most of them

My long suffering neighbours in Wollaston

Enville Cricket Club, my *raison d'etre*

Loyal friends, The Tit Club – You know who you are

The Whittington Inn, for my mad book launches

Stourbridge Music Centre, but I can't think why, offhand

Sally Oldaker (Limited Edition Magazine) and Rob Williams (Penguin and BBC)

Groucutt and Haynes, George James and all the book launch musicians and magicians,

and especially Phil James, the musical prodigy and his family

Stepalong Shoes, because there's no bookshop in Wollaston

Wolverhampton College of Art

Quarry Bank Primary School and Tipton Grammar School wot educated me!

243

Those of you who have read a David Day book will know how addictive they can become. At first, you think you can take them or leave them – you are an adult with a modicum of willpower, after all, and no mere book is going to rule your life. Quite soon though, you realize that you've started reading a quick chapter while you're in the bath or the lavatory. From there it is but a short step to the torch under the bed sheets at midnight and the paperback hidden inside your desk at the office. You'll find yourself reading the final chapter extra slowly to make it last longer, savouring every word and even reading good bits twice. Then, when you can stall no further and the book is finished, you will go through an awful mourning process, whereupon an intense craving will kick in. You'll need more and you'll need it NOW. Bad-tempered due to the crippling withdrawal symptoms, you'll probably complain that the author isn't nearly prolific enough for your voracious appetite, and begin to call him rude names. Extreme cases have even been known to try and climb the walls in anguish. Friends will turn against you because you will insist on regurgitating the plots *ad nauseam* while they're trying to watch the X Factor on television. It will get so bad that you might seriously consider a spell in a rehab clinic, electric shock therapy or maybe a course of hypnotism.

Well, help is at hand. Why not join the David Day Fan Club? It's a bit like Alcoholics Anonymous. You sit around in a circle and confess, "My name is Deirdre Sponge and I'm a David Day fanatic." (Obviously, you don't say this if your name i*sn't* Deirdre Sponge. That was just an example.) Then the others get up and hug you, with a bit of luck.

If you email me at gt@geofftristram.co.uk I'll keep your name on file and let you know when a new book is due to be released into the wild. Unlike other authors who are now too important –

people such as J.K. Rowling and William Shakespeare for example, I promise to be approachable, grateful, humble etc., and always write back. That's with the proviso that you tell me my books are great, of course. I don't want any sour-faced old scrooges writing in to tell me I'm rubbish and that I deserve to be horse-whipped on the steps of my club. Maybe I could cope if you've spotted a glaring error, or a bit you didn't think made perfect sense, but obviously, I'd prefer it if you to told me how a paragraph had made you wet yourself on the train, or prevented you from leaping off a high building to certain death. You can suggest things that David can get up to in future stories, if you wish. I might even write *you* into a book. After all, most of my characters are based on real people, believe it or not! Oops! Shouldn't have admitted that – now no-one will believe that legal disclaimer in the small print at the beginning.

Anyway, I'll leave it with you. The offer's there. You can lead a horse to water but you can't make it drink, as my Granny Bertha often tried to say after a couple of sherries. I hope you've enjoyed 'David's Michelangelo'. If that didn't make you laugh, I'll refund your money – I'm that confident.

That was a joke by the way. You have to be so careful in this litigious age. I need the money for a new bathroom - I can't afford to give it back. The bookshops keep forty percent anyway. And another thing - will you stop lending my books to everyone when you've finished them? Let them buy their own. I'm never going to be another J.K. Rowling at this rate.

Geoff Tristram.

Other books in the David Day Series

A NASTY BUMP ON THE HEAD

Eleven-year-old David Day finds the curmudgeonly toy shop owner, Miss Kettle, murdered in her shop. He duly informs Scotland Yard, only to bump into her in Tenbury-Wells the following week.

MONET TROUBLE

First year art student David Day is persuaded to forge a Monet painting by the mysterious Lord Hickman, but unknown to either of them, several other artists have the same idea.

VINCENT GOUGH'S VAN

An art college murder mystery of Shakespearian proportions, littered with psychic sewing teachers, entrail-painting students and Sapphic assassins.

THE CURSE OF TUTTON COMMON

David sets about trying to improve Britain's worst museum, and ably assisted by a cat named Hitlerina, he discovers an ancient Egyptian tomb in South Staffordshire.

PAINTING BY NUMBERS

Thirty-year-old David is having a mid-life crisis, made worse by the fact that his art studio has exploded, and the ninety-year-old 'paint by numbers' enthusiast he has befriended is not what he seems.

STEALING THE ASHES

Forty–year-old David Day overhears two Australian cricketers plotting to steal the Ashes, and, ably hampered by Laz, he tries his best to thwart their plans.

THE HUNT FOR GRANDDAD'S HEAD

The prequel to Nasty Bump! Daleks have invaded Brierley Bank, but David harnesses their power to see off the neighbourhood bully.

...and two new novels featuring a new hero!

THE CURIOUS TALE OF THE MISSING HOOF

Writer Adam Eve hires a pantomime horse costume, but forfeits his deposit when he loses one of the hooves. His obsessive efforts to locate it create mayhem!

MR. MAORI GOES HOME

Adam Eve's hell-raising uncle has died and left him a substantial amount of money – on condition that he returns a rare Maori carving to New Zealand.

For more information, email gt@geofftristram.co.uk